USA Today, and *Wall Street Journal* bestselling author, Nina Levine, lives in Brisbane, Australia, and is the author of more than thirty romantic suspense and contemporary romance novels, including the international bestselling Escape With a Billionaire and Storm MC series.

CONNECT ONLINE

ninalevineromance.com

authorninalevine

AuthorNinaLevine

YOURS ACTUALLY

USA TODAY BESTSELLING AUTHOR
NINA LEVINE

DEDICATION

This book was a joy to write and it's dedicated to all the readers who love reading a fun couple. Callan & Olivia were a breath of fresh air for me and I hope you feel that too. I hope you smile while you read their story as much as I did while writing it.

N xx

1

CALLAN

IF THERE'S one thing I should never be in charge of, it's holding the wedding rings for any of my brothers on their wedding day. I was put in charge of my eldest brother's rings precisely half an hour ago and I've already misplaced them.

"You've lost the rings?" Olivia asks when she realizes I'm searching for them.

"No, I've momentarily hidden them." I reach into my suit jacket and check the pocket inside. The rings aren't there, and Olivia's expression conveys her lack of surprise over this. My best friend knows me better than I know myself, so she's more than aware that when I say I've momentarily hidden them, I actually mean I've put them somewhere really fucking safe and may never find them again.

"Jesus, Callan. Bradford should have known better than to ask you to safeguard those rings." She's got that look in her eyes that says she's taking charge of the situation now. It's a look I know well. Olivia's been taking charge of my situations since we were eight.

"In my defense, it's been a hectic half hour."

"Where were you when he gave them to you?"

"In his bedroom."

"Do you think you might have put them down somewhere in there?"

"I would have thought I'd put them in my jacket, but clearly not." My attention drifts away as I spot Olivia's plus-one weaving his way through the wedding guests who are gathered in Bradford's grand salon for pre-ceremony cocktails.

Slade fucking Sullivan.

I wasn't aware she was working with him again or that she intended on bringing him today. I might be a fan of the New York Power hockey team, but their goalie is another story. He's nothing but trouble and I don't like that Olivia has to work with him, because he cuts in on her personal time with all his fucking antics.

His smile is broad when he reaches us. "Callan. Good to see you again."

"Slade. I didn't realize you were back working with Olivia."

He grimaces. "The team gave me an ultimatum. Fix my shit or I'm out. Our girl here is the best and is going to help me do that."

Our girl?

I manage to hold my tongue, but only just. Olivia's a crisis management expert and she *is* the best at what she does, but she's not *his* fucking girl. I want to point that out; however, if I learned one thing while she managed Slade's last crisis, it's that Olivia doesn't appreciate me stepping into the middle of her professional life.

Slade and I got into it one night when I mentioned how handsy he is with her. Olivia had to break us apart before it turned physical, and she and I ended up in the middle of an argument the likes of none we've ever had. I don't want a repeat of that because I endured a day of radio silence from her afterward. Olivia is like air to me; I need her to function. So, Slade gets to have a free pass from me now, and that's stealing every ounce of focus I have because it's the absolute last thing I want to give him.

Olivia eyes him. "I just need a few minutes to help Callan with something and then we'll go over the interviews I've got lined up for you next week."

"Thanks, babe."

I don't miss the way his eyes soften when he calls her babe.

Fuck it, I can't hold my tongue any longer while watching him saunter away from us. "Babe?"

"Callan." Olivia's voice contains a warning.

"I'm just saying, babe isn't keeping it professional."

She shrugs. A little too casually in my opinion. And completely out of character for her. Olivia is a stickler for rules and professionalism, and in all the clients she's worked with over the years, I've never known her to allow any of the guys to call her that. "You know what he's like. He doesn't mean anything by it."

I arch a brow. "Really?" Slade has a reputation for sleeping with every woman he ever meets. He's smooth, and he doesn't give a fuck about any of them from what I can tell. I don't know if Olivia is interested in him, but I saw the way he won her over five months ago when they first worked together and I could imagine her developing feelings for him. The last thing I want is for him to hurt her.

"Give him a break. The guy gets a bad rap in the press. If you knew him better, you'd know he's nothing like the media presents him. He calls every woman babe."

"Why's he your plus-one? I thought you were bringing Wade."

"Hayden called this morning and asked me to work with Slade again, and since Wade came down with a stomach bug this morning, I figured I'd kill two birds with one stone. While we're waiting for the ceremony, I can get some work done." Her features turn serious. "Now, we need to find these rings. What did Bradford do after he gave them to you?"

"There were people everywhere, Liv. I was jostled from wall to wall. I don't know what Bradford did after he left me."

Her lips quirk. "You were *jostled*? Since when do you use that word? And really? His entire bedroom was filled with a crowd? And why are you so snappy today?"

"Do you prefer pushed? Or maybe shoved? And yes, his fucking entourage of advisors were all over him. I will never understand how he copes with all those people in his space all the time." I've never been more pleased that I wasn't the brother our parents encouraged into politics.

What I *do* recall is coming downstairs after I left Bradford and finding Slade in the grand salon with Olivia and Hayden, one of my other brothers. They were laughing over something Slade said, which was right before he put his hand to the small of Olivia's back and leaned in close to whisper something in her ear.

More unprofessional conduct.

That's what's stuck in a loop in my memory.

"Okay, we need to go up to his bedroom." Olivia's already on her way before my feet even begin moving. I'm too busy formulating ways to rid Olivia's life of the goalie.

"Callan." Hayden meets us at the top of the spiral staircase on the second floor. "I need the rings." Yes, he does. He's the best man and looking after the rings is his job.

"Give us a minute," Olivia says.

"Jesus." Hayden looks at me. "You lost them?"

"No," Olivia says. "He hid them." Her eyes sparkle with silent laughter as they come to mine. "But just for a moment. We'll have them for you soon."

Gage, another of my brothers, joins us. "Why would anyone think it a good idea to trust you with those rings?"

"Fuck you both," I mutter.

"Bradford should have invited Abigail as your plus-one if he wanted to put you in charge of shit," Gage carries on.

"In case you weren't aware, I manage many things in my personal life without my assistant's help."

"Yes, because you have a wife managing all those things." Gage eyes Olivia. "Fuck knows what your life would look like without Olivia by your side."

This is a running joke with Gage, referencing Olivia as my wife. I love my brother but he's been giving me shit for one thing or another since the minute I was born.

"How about you do something useful and help us find the rings?" I suggest.

Olivia takes charge of the three of us. "Callan and I will check Bradford's bedroom. You guys check the bottom floor. I'd pay particular attention to the kitchen."

Hayden grins at the in-joke about me and Ethan, our youngest brother. "Yes, those rings are probably in the fridge."

His mention of the time I put Ethan's cufflinks in the fridge when I was distracted by a cheesecake in there jogs my memory. "Fuck, I know where the rings are."

"Where?" Olivia asks.

"In Bradford's bathroom."

"Why are they in there?" Gage asks.

"Because Ethan texted me right after Bradford gave me the rings. I needed a minute away from the crowd in his bedroom and the only place I could find was the bathroom."

Olivia's eyes soften. "What did he say?" She knows more than anyone how much I've been waiting for that text from our absent brother.

"Not much. Just that he's definitely not coming today."

"Oh, wow," she says. "I really thought he'd show up."

"Yeah, you and Bradford both."

"He knows Ethan's not coming?" Gage asks.

"Yeah, Ethan texted him too." I suspect Bradford was more disappointed than he let on. But he and Hayden are the experts at making allowances for Ethan's choices in life, so he just carried on like it was a reasonable decision.

Hayden frowns. "Why isn't he coming?"

"He's off on some fucking pilgrimage or something. Walking the Camino de Santiago, which is obviously more important than coming home for his brother's wedding."

Olivia places her hand on my arm. "Callan," she murmurs.

I cut her off before she can stick up for Ethan. "No, Liv, he's being a selfish asshole and even you can't find a way to make a decent excuse for this choice of his."

Olivia finds compassion for everyone, even when I'm not convinced they deserve it. She's able to compartmentalize aspects of people, letting go of whatever she doesn't think matters in certain moments. Me? I can't separate shit like that. It all matters.

Ethan left New York eleven months ago after we argued over the woman he was dating. The woman who broke his heart and stole a chunk of cash from him. I'd always been suspicious of her, and he never liked hearing any of my thoughts. It didn't surprise me when she betrayed him. What did surprise me was his willingness to overlook it and go after her. I said things I regret during our argument. It was all true, but saying it cost me my brother. He hasn't been home since.

Out of all my brothers, I'm closest to Ethan. I never imagined he'd cut and run. I'm angry that he won't take my calls or reply to my texts, but more than that, I'm fucking disappointed in him, especially today. Our brother is getting married. Ethan should be here for this. That's what you do for family: you put shit aside for the big moments.

"You're right," Olivia says, "I can't make an excuse, but we don't know what's happening in his life right now. Ethan wouldn't blow off Bradford's wedding unless he had a good reason."

I love her way of caring for those who are important to her. However, it's the bane of my existence at times because I can also be a selfish asshole, and there are times I only want to think of myself. Olivia often helps me shift perspective when I need to, but on this, not even she can make me change my mind.

Hayden reads the room like he always does. "Okay, let's get these rings. We can discuss Ethan later."

That's code for: let's get into this at a scheduled time later, which is always Hayden's preference. He doesn't shy away from discussing hard things, but he always has a timeline for when those discussions will take place. I'm the brother who challenges him on his schedules, but today I'll go along with it because I don't want to ruin Bradford's big day.

With one last glance at Olivia, who's watching me like she knows this could go either way, I nod and follow Hayden into Bradford's bedroom to locate the rings.

Ten minutes later, the rings are where they should be and I'm seated next to Penny, my date for the wedding. Olivia is on my other side deep in conversation with Slade while we wait for the ceremony to begin.

I'm deep in conversation with myself over both Ethan and Slade.

I'm only just managing to hold myself back from texting Ethan and telling him exactly what I think of his decision. I'm also working overtime on not leaning across Olivia and telling Slade that he'll have me to answer to if he hurts her.

Penny provides the intrusion into my thoughts I need when she places her hand on my thigh and brings her mouth to my ear. "FYI, this suit you're wearing today would look so much better on my bedroom floor."

I meet her gaze. "And ruin the good thing we've got going? Not a fucking chance."

She rolls her eyes while keeping her hand on my leg. "You're so boring, Callan. There is such a thing as friends with benefits. I'm sure you of all men have heard of that."

"Me of all men? Should I be offended by that?"

"You've never met offended. Don't pretend you have now. You're happy to sleep with every other woman you meet. Why won't you fuck me?"

"I don't sleep with every woman I meet."

"Okay, so maybe I exaggerated, but only just. The least you could do in return for me being your plus-one is give me some orgasms."

I've known Penny for five years and she's been my plus-one at many social events for the last two years. It's easy with her and neither of us have any strings attached, which is how I prefer it. Sex has never been on the table as far as I've been concerned. I don't fuck women who are friends. Not after I did that once years ago. It's the fastest way to ruin a friendship in my opinion. Penny doesn't share my belief and has brought it up the last few times I've seen her.

"I'll introduce you to Slade. I have no doubt he'll provide what you need."

With one last eye roll, she removes her hand from my thigh and sits back in her seat. "For a guy who doesn't follow rules, you're good at following that rule of no sex. I can totally see why you and Olivia are still friends after all these years." She gives me a questioning look. "Have you two seriously never had sex?"

Penny knows the answer to this. She's asked me this before. "Why is it so hard to believe a man and a woman can be friends who've never contemplated having sex?"

"Because it never happens."

"It does. Olivia and I are proof."

"You've really never thought about it?"

I'm about to tell her no when the piano player at the side of the ballroom starts playing. The rich tones of a cello match the warmth of the piano notes a moment later. Bradford chose an instrumental version of "All of Me" by John Legend for his bride, Kristen, to walk down the aisle to and when I turn to the back of the ballroom, I see Kristen's bridesmaid, Jenna, coming our way.

There's a collective sigh when Kristen starts on her way to Bradford. As she walks past us, Olivia turns and looks at me. Leaning in close, she whispers, "I'm so glad Bradford found her. She's just perfect for him."

She's not wrong but instead of thinking about what she said, I'm struck by thoughts about *her*.

The soft look in her eyes.

The genuine and stunningly beautiful smile on her face.

Her mouth against my skin as she whispers to me.

Why have I never imagined sex with her? Her legs wrapped around me? Her lips on mine? Her hair falling onto my chest?

Christ.

Penny has fucked me up with that conversation we just had.

Olivia leans even closer to me when Kristen reaches Bradford. Her fingers grip my suit jacket at the waist as she whispers, "Look at how he's looking at her. It's so beautiful. I need to find a guy who looks at me like that."

Her dress on my bedroom floor. That's what I'm suddenly fucking thinking about and I want to strangle my wedding date for putting that image in my head.

I'm deep down the rabbit hole of those thoughts when Bradford and Kristen exchange vows. It's a fucking miracle I can even focus on the wedding now that my best friend is the star of my dirty fantasies.

By the time my brother kisses his bride, I'm reciting baseball stats in my mind. Batting averages and home runs fill my head like they never have. And that's saying something because baseball stats are something I think about a lot.

When Penny's hand lands on my thigh during the wedding reception and she casually mentions how much she'd love to see me naked, I take hold of her wrist and say, "Good because that's exactly what you're going to see later tonight."

Her eyes flare. "You're going to break your rule?"

"Yes."

It turns out that baseball stats can only preoccupy a man for so long. I need something to take my mind off my best friend and tonight that something is going to be Penny. And with any luck, I can chalk these confusing thoughts up to a temporary blip.

2

OLIVIA

MAY in New York is a firm favorite of mine. Spring is thinking about taking a nap while summer is getting ready to come out and play. My anticipation for all things summer is high in May and my planning game is strong. I'm looking forward to weekends at the beach, late afternoon swims during the week, long lazy days in the sun. And ice cream. So much ice cream.

The other thing I love about this time of year is the weddings. I could live and breathe only romance for the rest of my life and I'd be a happy girl. And honestly, with the way weddings are taking on a new life with so many fun new trends, I'm giddy about it all.

There's only one small problem this year: I don't have a date for any of the weddings I've been invited to. I'm not opposed to attending parties or galas or any social event on my own, but weddings are a different beast. Especially so when you've just broken up with your boyfriend who everyone adored. If I attend alone, I see nothing but looks of sympathy and questions over the breakup. Not to mention the drunk guys who think any single girl at a wedding is desperate for attention and sex. No, thank you.

I've got four weeks until my first wedding of the season and I'm making it my mission to find the perfect plus-one. I'm in the elevator up to Callan's condo early Monday morning scrolling through my friends lists on social media looking for candidates when the doors open and I'm presented with something I never thought I'd see.

Penelope Rush. Callan's constant plus-one. In his condo at 7:12 a.m. on a Monday morning in a state of disarray that can only mean one thing: she slept over last night. And unless you're me, a sleepover with Callan means a long night of sex.

I blink.

I blink again.

I'm stuck in the middle of my brain catching up with real time events when Penelope glances up from her phone and sees me. The same look that's always in her eyes when she catches sight of me appears. Displeasure. It never lasts longer than a moment and if I wasn't a particularly observant person, I'd miss it, but I never do.

My existence annoys Penelope. Or to be more precise, my existence in Callan's life annoys her.

Callan believes she doesn't want anything from him except a date for various events. He's wrong. Penelope wants him as a partner. And while she's got Callan fooled, I see her for what she is. A woman who's playing the long game, making very calculated moves to embed herself in my best friend's life. I'd be okay with that if I thought she'd love and cherish him for who he is rather than for what he can give her, namely his billions, but I don't have any doubt that cherishing him isn't high on her agenda.

"Olivia," she greets me, her fake smile now plastered across her face.

"Penelope." I'm trying to find more words for her when Callan rounds the corner and joins us in the foyer.

His mouth lifts up into the smile he reserves for me when our eyes meet. "Ace."

Penelope's lips press together. She hates it when Callan uses the nickname he's had for me since we were sixteen. As fast as those lips of hers smoosh together, she has stepped into his space, nestled into his side, and placed her hand on his stomach possessively.

When I woke up this morning, everything was in place in my life. My overnight oats were made for the week. My lunches were lined up next to them in the fridge. I went to my 5 a.m. Monday morning yoga class to start my week calmly. I confirmed my meditation class for tonight. I did a little life admin and ensured nothing was missing from my to-do list for this week. *Now*, everything is not in place. That hand on Callan's stomach is all the evidence I need to know this.

The smile slips from his face, replaced by a frown as he looks down at that hand.

Penelope interprets his expression expertly. I mean, anyone who knows Callan knows he doesn't sleep with friends and that once he has sex with a woman, she rarely makes another appearance in his life. I almost feel sorry for her because that look on his face is all she needs to know this might not go down how she hopes. However, she's not a woman who gives up on anything without a fight, and I don't imagine she'll let his body language deter her.

"I'm gonna go," she says, giving his white dress shirt a quick scrunch before removing herself from his personal space. "Thanks for the weekend. It was fun."

The weekend?

She's been here since Bradford's wedding on Saturday?

I did notice how close they appeared at the reception, but I was a little distracted by Slade, who is in the middle of an existential crisis, his words, not mine.

Callan nods. "Yeah, it was."

With a casual flick of her long blonde hair and a flirty grin, she tosses out, "For the record, your suit does look better on a bedroom floor and there are still no strings attached to that suit. I'll call you in a couple of weeks so we can figure out the plans for the wedding you mentioned." She then grants me a smile. "I'll see you at the wedding. Let's text so we ensure we don't wear the same shoes again." She's referencing a party we both attended three months ago wearing the same Jimmy Choos.

I use my manners and agree even though texting with Penelope is one of the last things I want to do. But I do many things for Callan that I wouldn't do for anyone else, and causing tension with one of his friends is something I actively avoid.

I follow him into his kitchen after the elevator doors close with Penelope safely tucked away inside. I desperately want to ask him what's happening with her. I mean, that's our thing. We talk about *everything*. We have since we were kids. But I think I may have found something I don't want to know.

Callan and I have never come close to taking our friendship further but it's something I've thought about a lot. He was the guy I crushed on in my teens. He was the most popular guy in school. The football player every girl wanted. He had a new girlfriend so often that I would have lost track if I wasn't actually keeping track of every little thing about him. I attribute the weight I carried in high school to all the ice cream I consumed on Friday and Saturday nights when I sat at home studying while he was out with his latest girlfriend or finding a new one at a party.

My crush on him remained firm until I was twenty-two when I met a guy who became my first serious boyfriend. After I broke up with that guy, I settled into a happy dating rhythm and let go of my crush on Callan. I'd be lying, though, if I said I didn't still imagine what it would be like to be his partner in life rather than his best friend.

I feel so free with Callan like I could say or do anything and he'd never walk away from me. That's what I imagine a partner brings into your life and I've never met another guy who just gets me and accepts me like he does.

Blair, my other bestie, never stops telling me to explore my feelings more, but there's no point. I'm the complete opposite to every girl he's ever been with. Where I'm curvy with dark hair, Callan's type is generally blondes with no curves. And where I'm the nerdy girl who enjoys slow weekends at farmer's markets; creating spreadsheets for all manner of things; obsessing over my stationery collection; and doing everything I can to avoid nights out at clubs, Callan's type seems to live in clubs; obsesses over the latest gossip; and might never have opened a spreadsheet in her life. I literally shudder at the thought of not using spreadsheets. How does one calculate important things without them?

Also, there's the sex rule he has about friends.

Except, maybe that rule no longer exists.

Blair can never know about this. She'll step up her demands for me to explore my feelings.

And what is it with those feelings right now? Why the heck am I avoiding asking Callan about Penelope? I can't recall anything I've not wanted to ask him. Not even when we were teenagers, and I was heartsick over all the girls on his arm. I always want to know what's happening in his life and how he's feeling about it.

I zero in on the mail he's left on his kitchen countertop and quickly reach for the large pile of letters in an attempt to shift my thoughts. Managing Callan's personal mail has been my task since college. He wasn't born with organizational skills and often paid bills late and missed social events, so I took pity on him and helped him out. Now, he simply leaves it out for me to take care of. "Do you have any dry cleaning you need dropped off?"

"Yeah, but only if you're going that way. I can have Jane take it tomorrow when she's in." His housekeeper comes three times a week. She's one of my favorite people in Callan's life because she truly cares for him and doesn't want anything from him.

I start different piles for his mail, sorting it into categories. "I'm collecting some dresses today. I'll take it." I note the two letters that appear to be wedding invites.

Holding them up, I say, "Is everyone you know getting married this summer? This brings your total weddings to seven this season."

He grimaces as he opens the fridge. "Make it nine. There are two more invites at the office."

When he bends to inspect the contents of the fridge, I try not to let my eyes wander down his body.

I fail.

Good god, Callan needs to stop all the exercise and sports he does. Between the rowing, the running, the weights, the core work, and all the casual sports he plays randomly when friends ask him, he's got thighs, and arms, and abs, and an ass that stop women in the street. I know because I've seen them do it. And his muscles make it so those women don't even bother trying to hide their appreciation. They just stop, stare, and swoon. Kinda like I am right now.

I mentally try to slap some sense into myself.

Where are all these thoughts coming from?

The last time I checked Callan out like this was five months ago when we went skiing with his family. I fell and he came to my rescue, and let's just say that even with at least three layers of clothing between me and his muscles, I was still taking a good look.

I go back to the mail. "Nine weddings is insane. I hope Penelope can spare that many weekends." And there it is. I really *do* want to know what's happening between them.

He places the ingredients to make scrambled eggs on the island between us. Callan's super serious about his macros and rarely deviates from the spreadsheet I created for him to calculate and track his food. "I'm not certain Penny will be my plus-one anymore."

The way my stomach just settled says a lot.

I finish with his mail and meet his gaze. "Because you slept with her?"

"No, because of what she thinks the sex means."

As he reaches for a knife to cut the vegetables for his scrambled eggs, I move around the island and take the knife from him. He steps to the side and passes me the onion. Callan can cook but he prefers my cooking.

"Were you drunk when you decided to break your no-sex-with-friends rule?"

"No."

I'm pretty sure I almost chopped my thumb off at that. "So, you've ditched that rule now?"

He sighs and appears pained about all this, which is just odd. Not only does Callan easily move on from the women he dates or sleeps with, but he'll also talk to anyone about sex for as long as they want. There are days I wonder how he managed to build a company the size of his because sometimes it seems like all he thinks about is sex. "No."

I stop chopping so I can dedicate my full attention to our conversation. "I don't understand then. I didn't think you were into Penelope."

"I had my reasons."

When I don't respond, because he's being very vague and it's not in our nature to be vague like this with each other, he takes the knife from me and attempts to take over the vegetable chopping.

I nudge his hip and reach for the knife. "Let me cook. And stop being weirdly vague. Why did you fuck her?"

"Fuck, Liv," he mutters, sounding as pained as he still looks.

"What?" I frown. "What's going on? Why do you seem so confused about this?" My eyes widen. "Wait, are you into Penelope but don't want to be? That would make so much sense."

"No, I'm not into Penny, but why would that make so much sense?"

"Because you appear conflicted over this, and I've never seen you conflicted over sex. I imagine the only reason you would feel that way now is if your feelings are messing with you."

He shakes his head. "Jesus, is this how all women think?"

"What do you mean?"

"Do you all overthink shit like you just have?"

"I don't overthink. You underthink."

"Is that even a word?"

"Don't change the subject."

He scrubs a hand down his face like he does when he's mildly stressed about something. "I fucked Penny because I wanted sex. It was as simple as that. And now she's got her hands on me in ways I don't want them on me, so it's time to end our arrangement."

I narrow my eyes at him. "I don't think I buy that."

"There's nothing to buy, Ace."

"Well, there's *something* going on here."

"There isn't."

He's saved from this conversation when his cell phone rings, and by the way he answers the call faster than I've ever seen him answer one, I'm guessing it's something important.

I finish cooking his breakfast while he takes the call in his office, and I think about how out of character he's being this morning. Telling me he had his reasons for sleeping with Penelope but not being forthcoming with those reasons is not like him at all. My mind runs wild with possible scenarios.

Does he actually have feelings for her?

Is he feeling pressure at work?

Has he developed a sex addiction?

Is he depressed?

I conjure up way more ideas than that, and when I start wondering if he's depressed, I know I need to stop. Callan is far from depressed. And while I pride myself on being a good friend, I am really overstepping boundaries by assuming this is any of my business. If Callan has something going on, he'll eventually talk to me about it. He always does.

"You got a minute?"

I glance up from my computer just after 10:30 a.m. and find Hayden in the doorway of my office. I lean back in my seat and nod. "What's up?"

He comes and sits in the chair across the desk from me. "How are you coping with having Slade added to your schedule?"

My brows pull together. I've worked for Hayden for two years and while he's always cared about my workload, he's never stopped by my office to check how I'm coping with it. "I've got it handled. Why the concern?"

"Because we just got a call from Mace Hawkins's team."

"Jesus, how do these hockey players get themselves

into so much trouble?" Mace is the third New York Power player we've had a call from in the last two weeks.

"He's got a wife who's about to be an ex-wife intent on causing problems for him, the latest problem being she's stolen half a million worth of jewelry from Penelope Rush and the news has been splashed across every gossip account this morning."

I sit forward at the mention of Callan's Penelope. Immediately, I wish I could scrub those two words from my brain. I hate that I put them together. "This just happened today?"

"Yeah. Penelope's on a rampage about it now."

"I saw her this morning and she was fine." I've no idea why I'm even saying this. It's not relevant and obviously something has happened since I saw her, but my mind seems to be in slow motion right now. Not a place I'm familiar with generally, which is only adding to my perplexed state.

It's Hayden's turn to furrow his brows. "I wasn't aware you and Penelope were friends."

I adore Callan's older brother. In so many ways, he and I are alike. I mean, we both went into law for one. But besides that, we're fastidious about our attention to detail and I value that trait in another person.

When Hayden asked me to come and work in his law firm, I jumped at the chance. Not only is it one of the most successful firms in the country, but I also like the culture of genuine care for clients he's created and the vision he has for his company. I had no idea my job would turn into crisis management, or that I would love doing this work so much, and I'm so grateful to him for giving me the freedom to build this arm of the firm.

I shake my head. "We are definitely not friends. I just ran into her this morning." I push past all the weird thoughts and feelings swirling through me and bring the conversation back to work. "Mace is coming in today?"

"He'll be here in an hour. Can you fit him in?"

Hayden knows I will but I like that he never assumes anything. "Yes."

"Thanks, Liv. I owe you for taking these guys on."

"You don't. It's my job, Hayden."

"Yeah, but lumping you with Slade at the last minute on Saturday was a lot on top of everything else you're working on, and now this. I appreciate you adding extra to your plate."

After he leaves, I finish up what I was working on and am about to start researching Mace Hawkins when I receive a text from Blair.

BLAIR

Where the hell has Callan's brain disappeared to?

She links me to an Instagram post which was posted earlier today by the hottest gossip account at the moment.

@thetea_gasp

Besties! @therealpeneloperush appears to be having a little menty b over some missing bling she's ISO. Word on the street is that @macehawkins soon to be ex @maceskatie helped herself to it during a party a week or so ago. Sheesh. We wish we had that much bling that we only noticed it missing a week later #goals. If anyone can help her through this latest crisis, it looks like it might be @callanblack. And I oop. These two were spotted being all cozy at lunch yesterday and IYKYK that's not Callan's usual play. He's often seen with Penelope but this spotting looked like much more than just FWB. TBH we don't ship them, but this might be a whole new era for Callan. We'll keep you updated! And on the bling too, but for real, we're more interested in whether another Black brother is ready to start searching for his forever bae. Send the carriage if so #pickme

That settled feeling I felt when Callan told me he didn't think Penelope would be his plus-one anymore is all but gone once I've read this post, which is just dumb because I know never to trust gossip. However, while I like to believe I'm a rational thinker, I'm not immune to feelings that can be irrational at times.

The photo that accompanies this post shows Penelope practically sitting on Callan's lap at lunch. I've seen Callan dance with women, flirt with women, take women home. What I've never seen is him engage in public displays of affection like this after he's slept with them.

My phone sounds with another text.

BLAIR

Are you ignoring me?

OLIVIA

No. I just read the post.

BLAIR

And? Did you know about this?

OLIVIA

She was at his place this morning.

BLAIR

We need to stage an intervention. Sage his condo. Cast a protection spell.

OLIVIA

Stop pretending to be a witch.

BLAIR

Wicca will be my new religion.

OLIVIA

I'm rolling my eyes so hard right now.

BLAIR

Just tell me that he's not really seeing her. I won't cope if Penelope fucking Rush becomes a constant in my life.

OLIVIA

As far as I know, he's not seeing her.

BLAIR

Why do I sense doubt here?

I'm about to reply to her text when my phone rings and Callan's name flashes across the screen. He might have been acting strangely this morning, but he hasn't forgotten our eleven-a.m. call.

This daily call has been a fixed part of our life for seven years. Ever since we both started working after college. The first time was on his third day in his first job. He called to grumble about a work colleague. I then called him at the same time two days later when I needed to vent about something. It became part of our routine after that.

These days, even when he's being smashed by the demands of his company, he blocks off fifteen minutes each day for the call. The only day we've missed in all these years is when I refused to answer because I was angry with him over a bullshit fight he got into with Slade and tried to tell me how to conduct my professional life. I'm not proud of shutting him out that day, but I was angry with him in a way I never have been.

I answer his call. "I see you're still alive. Did Abigail forget to bring her poison to work today or have you been on your best behavior?"

"Smartass."

I grin. His assistant has a love/hate relationship with him. Mostly, she loves working for him, but when he becomes moody because his days are long and he's traveling a lot, which he has been, she threatens to poison his coffee. Abigail is firmly on my list of people I adore. She handles Callan perfectly and is skilled at letting him know when he's being an asshole without overstepping boundaries.

"Question: are you busy Wednesday night at seven?" I ask.

"I might be. Not sure yet. Why?"

"I've got a contractor coming to give me an estimate for the remodel I want to do in my bedroom but I forgot I've got a hair appointment that afternoon. I'm hoping you're free to come and talk with him until I get home. I should only be about fifteen minutes late. If you can't make it, I'll just cancel my hair because this guy is super busy and I'll have to wait a couple of months to reschedule."

"I'll make myself free. Don't cancel your hair. And who's this guy you've booked?"

I know what he's saying without saying it. He would have sent his guy, Brett, who has never found something he can't fix, build, or demolish.

"He's a guy that one of the girls at work recommended. I didn't want to bug you about this while you're so busy."

"I'm never too busy, Liv. I'll get Brett to come over too and give you a quote. Fuck knows there are enough shady assholes out there who'll take you for a ride."

I frown at the shift in his tone. "You sound like you're dealing with one today."

He exhales a long breath. "Because I am."

"You wanna talk about it?"

"No. I want you to tell me one of your highs from this morning to take my mind off it."

"That bad, huh?"

"You've no idea."

I don't push him to talk about it. He'll open up later, once he's moved through whatever it is. Instead, I file through the possibilities of what I could tell him, smiling when I hit on the one I know will work best. "Okay, prepare yourself for the most amazing news of life!" I pause for dramatic effect before gushing, "My favorite planner is being released in orange. Orange! Can you believe it?"

He chuckles and I take that as the sign my mission was accomplished. "How many emails have you sent her requesting orange?"

"One on the first of every month for the last year."

He's silent for a moment, like he's distracted. "Okay, so orange is popular. They've already sold out of the smaller planners. It's a good thing you prefer the larger ones."

"Stop right now, Callan Black! Get off their website and do not pre-order one for me. I've already placed my order." If he thought I wouldn't have, that's just another sign there's something off with him today. I mean, I feel like my love for Edith Corin planners should surely place me as her number one fan, but there must be at least a million other women around the world who feel the same way. Probably more. There could be no chances taken this morning when I received my Monday morning email from her announcing the orange planner.

Halle, my assistant pops her head in my door. "Have you got a minute? Slade's on the line for you." She rolls her eyes. "He's being quite dramatic about needing to speak with you right now."

I nod. "Gimme a minute."

She eyes my cell and calls out, "Hi, Callan. Such a shame your team fucked up on the weekend." She grins. "You owe me."

Callan groans. "Put me on speaker." When I've done that, he says, "You'll owe me after this weekend, Halle."

With more of that grin, she says, "We'll see. Now, hurry up and get off the phone so Olivia can get back to work."

"She's been hanging for this phone call so she could say that to you," I say after Halle leaves. These two bet with each other on the baseball and love ribbing the other over losses.

"She won't be hanging for next Monday's call after her team loses. Shit...I've gotta go."

"I hope today gets better. And I repeat, do not buy me that planner or anything else you might find on that website."

"My day has already improved. And I'm not making any promises."

Five minutes later, I'm deep in Slade's world of problems and wondering why I enjoy crisis management work so much when I often have to help guys who have impulse control issues and seem to have no idea how to help themselves.

Slade might be my biggest challenge to date. He's in love with a woman who has made it clear she wants nothing to do with his wild behavior. They got engaged last year after a whirlwind one-month fling. She knew nothing about him or his career before meeting him and soon decided they might not actually be a great fit. They broke up just before Christmas but he managed to woo her back in January. Now, however, she's ended the engagement again and from what I can ascertain, she means it this time. Slade is refusing to accept that and I can see I've got my work cut out for me. Not only am I tasked with improving his reputation, but it also seems he's relying on me to help him win the love of his life back.

"How much do you want this?" I ask, cutting him off after listening to him carry on about his problems for a good five minutes.

"You know how much I want this, Olivia." He sounds pissed off at my question.

"I know you've said a lot and made many declarations

about what you'll do to clean up your act. What I haven't seen are any actions, Slade, and let me tell you that when a woman has reached the point Christa has reached, she's looking for actions not words. So, tell me again how much you want this and then tell me what actions you're willing to take to make it happen because I'm telling you now that we won't still be working together in a week if you don't start cleaning up your act. Nothing I do can really help you if you're still carrying on with your bullshit."

He turns silent for a moment. "Damn, this is why you're my girl."

"I'm waiting to hear what you've got to say and"—I check the time—"I've only got five minutes before my next client will be here, so I suggest you hurry up and lay it all out for me."

As he rattles off his list, I receive a text from Sasha.

SASHA

SOS, I need you tonight! And I don't care that you have your Monday meditation class. This is a wedding crisis!

OLIVIA

What kind of crisis?

SASHA

The kind that involves you and Blair coming to my place and telling me that my wedding dress is the actual right dress. I'm not sure anymore.

OLIVIA

I'll be there. And honey, your dress is absolutely the actual right dress. It's the most beautiful wedding dress I've ever seen.

SASHA

I'm going to need to see you in person to hear that so I can see it on your face too.

OLIVIA

I'll see you tonight.

"Olivia," Slade says abruptly, "Are you listening to me? It feels like I'm talking to myself here."

I look at the notes I've been making while he's been talking. "I'm listening. So far, you've said you're going to cut out the clubs, the booze, and the late nights. You're getting back on track with your food, sleep, and training. You're going to start seeing that therapist I helped you find last year. And you're going to show up for your teammates like you used to. Have I missed anything?"

"No, you got it all." He sounds surprised. If I didn't like Slade so much, that would irritate me. I've put in the work perfecting my skills over the years and am more than competent.

We finish up our conversation and I get ready for my meeting with his teammate. Mostly though, my mind is pretty much focused on only one thing: that public display of affection between Callan and Penelope.

I've never had to share Callan. He may date and sleep with a lot of women, but his heart has never been involved with any of them. Not even when he dated Lisa Reynolds for an extended time right after I turned twenty-two. I might protest at the idea of him spoiling me whenever he tries to, and I might protest whenever he wants to take over and manage situations in my life, but now that I'm presented with the idea of him searching for his forever bae, I suddenly feel all kinds of feelings over him not doing those things for me anymore because he's doing them for another woman.

3

OLIVIA

"I DON'T KNOW why you're having a breakdown over this dress," Blair says to Sasha just after seven p.m. Monday night, her tone a little sharp and a lot exasperated. "It's fucking stunning and I've never seen you look more radiant."

I make eyes at her and mouth, "Stop it."

We've been at Sasha's place for nearly two hours and Blair's patience is disappearing rapidly. To be fair, though, she's displayed more patience than usual, so there is that.

"I can see you two in the mirror," Sasha says before gathering the tulle skirt of her dress and turning to face us. "I agree that this dress is stunning." She smiles at her dress designer who's here for the fitting. "What I'm unsure of is whether it's too over the top for me."

"Oh my god," I say as everything suddenly makes sense. "You're worried about what Rhodes's mother will say, aren't you?"

"No." She squishes her face. "Maybe." Her expression

turns positively forlorn. "Okay, yes, a lot. That woman is so mean. You know I won't be okay if she says even one little thing about me or my dress or my makeup or anything! Oh my god, I can't do this. I can't marry Rhodes!"

"Well, that escalated fast." Blair looks at me and motions with her hand. "This is all yours now. I should not be in charge of this."

The three of us have been friends since college and haven't found a life emergency we couldn't fix between us. However, Blair is not the one we put in charge when emotions spill over and run wild. She's the hard-as-nails one we go to when we need a good slap and help navigating a situation without letting our emotions interfere. Sasha is usually the one we go to when we want to sit in our emotions while I'm the one in the middle of the spectrum who mixes pragmatism with some feelings thrown in.

I walk to Sasha and take hold of her arms. "You *can* marry Rhodes and *will* marry Rhodes. In this dress. And he will love it as much as you do, and that's all that will matter. And honey, if there's one day in a girl's life that calls for over the top, it's her wedding day. You should have every single thing you want on your wedding day. I mean, you know my thoughts on you and Rhodes having Otis and Daisy in your bridal party. I'm still unsure why you're not."

I eye the two Pugs sleeping soundly on Sasha's bed. Otis and Daisy are the light of their lives and I'm pretty sure the only reason they nixed the idea of having them walk down the aisle with Sasha is because of Sasha's fear of what Marlene Barron would have to say about that.

"I am also completely behind that idea. Otis would make the best ring bearer," Blair says. "Fuck Marlene and all her boring ideas of how a woman should act."

"I agree. Otis and Daisy need to be in your bridal party," Nancy, the dress designer says. She's also a good friend of Sasha's and championed the whole family being part of the wedding from day one.

"While we're throwing out our thoughts, I also think you should consider giving Rhodes that lap dance we discussed a while ago," Blair says. "No one would ever forget your wedding."

Sasha's eyes fill with horror. "We discussed that while we were drunk. I'm not making our first dance a lap dance. Good god."

Blair shrugs. "Well, I might steal that idea in case I ever get married."

Nancy laughs. "I can actually imagine this happening."

"Okay, back to the matter at hand," I say. "We need to come up with a plan for how you'll handle Marlene because whatever you choose to wear or do, she's going to have something to say about it. Even if she loves it, she'll never admit it."

Nancy nods. "Truth. That woman might be the meanest woman I've ever met."

"Take her off the guest list." Blair's not even kidding. It's exactly what she'd do.

Sasha presses her lips together at Blair. "That's not a helpful suggestion, Blair."

"Isn't it, though?" Blair asks. "I think it might be the most helpful suggestion of the night so far. But since I know you'll never entertain it, I can also suggest I sage her down as she enters."

Sasha frowns. "Sage her down? What?"

"Spiritual hygiene, Sash," Blair says, like that term should already mean something to Sasha. At our friend's blank look, she adds, "We've gotta take care of our energetic body. Burning sage or spritzing it will help cleanse the bad energy that Marlene brings to your wedding."

I fully expect Sasha to tell her no, but she doesn't. Instead, she seriously contemplates this idea before saying, "Maybe. We'll see how she is at the rehearsal dinner."

"Okay, so sage is on the maybe list." I bring everyone back to the plan we're making. "What else?"

"I've told you what to do," Blair says. "If you took my advice, you wouldn't need a plan."

I give her the look that says *not helpful* and move on to other ideas. "Have you brought this up with Rhodes? Perhaps you two could have a signal you give when you're feeling overwhelmed by his mom, which lets him know to intervene and help you out."

"He knows how I'm feeling," Sasha says as she thinks about this idea. "I'll talk to him about a signal."

"You know that man will do anything for you," I say softly.

Sasha smiles. "Yeah, he will. I just hate that I need him to."

"Isn't that part of what a marriage is, though?" I say. "Knowing all the little intricate ways your partner needs you and also knowing exactly what they need in certain moments."

We get into a discussion about just how deeply

Rhodes knows all of Sasha's distress signs and how he always helps her through her anxious moments. This leads us back to the dress she's concerned is over the top and in the end she decides this dress really is the one for her.

"Thank fuck," Blair says after a half-hour conversation. "Now, can we order dinner? I'm starving. And Rhodes and Callan will be here any minute, and you guys know they get hangrier than me when we keep them waiting for food after they've been to the gym."

"Wait," Sasha says. "I want to talk to Olivia about the dress she's wearing to my wedding."

I groan silently because my dress selection has become a debacle that I don't want to add to Sasha's worries. "My dress is sorted." I fake smile. "It's gorgeous and I love it! And Blair's right about the guys. We need to order food."

Blair gives me the look that says *that was way too much and no one is buying it.*

Sasha gives me the look that says she's absolutely not buying it. "I feel responsible for this and I have a solution."

"Why do you feel responsible?" I ask.

"Because if I hadn't just gone along with Rhodes's mother's ridiculous stipulation that he only have his brother as his groomsman and I only have my sister as my bridesmaid, you'd be in the bridal party and wearing a bridesmaid dress."

"Good god you worry too much," Blair says.

Sasha ignores her. "I have a dress I've never worn that I think would be perfect for you."

"Ahh, Sash, have you taken a look in the mirror lately?" I ask. "There's no way I'll fit into one of your dresses. These curves would blow it out before I even got it on."

She smiles brightly. "Nancy can fix that! I want you to try it on now and let her work her magic. It's going to look amazing on you."

Before I can stop her, she's retrieved the dress from her closet and is forcing it upon me. And Blair is encouraging her.

"Stop it," I mutter to Blair when Sasha leaves the bedroom to take a call and Nancy goes to the bathroom. "There's no way this dress can be altered to fit me."

"I think it can. Just try it. Nancy's like a magician when it comes to dresses. You know this."

"I know you're being difficult tonight."

"I'm hungry. We all know I can never get hungry or bad things happen. And I also don't want to be dragged through the city for weeks while you search for a dress. I think this one might work."

I look at the dress again. It's a soft pink chiffon dress that is flowy and super feminine. In my opinion, though, the long slit that falls from mid-thigh level revealing one leg almost completely is maybe a little too much for a wedding.

"You don't think it's too sexy for a wedding?" I ask.

"No. Just try it on so I don't have to starve tonight."

"Fine. But I'm pretty sure this will not be the dress I wear to the wedding."

I change into the dress and Blair is in the middle of fighting with the zipper at the back when Sasha returns.

"Oh my god, that color is perfect for you!"

I meet her gaze. "The color might be, but there's no way we're even getting close to my boobs fitting in this."

The dress is strapless and my breasts are spilling out of it every which way.

"A different bra will help."

"Different boobs would help. A bra can't solve everything on its own."

"Olivia!" Nancy calls out from the living room. "Your phone is ringing."

I smack Blair's hands away from the zipper, which is never going to go up, not even if she keeps trying. "This dress isn't going to work."

Sasha moves in close and stops me when I attempt to take it off. "Please let Nancy see. She'll let us know if she can alter it."

One of my downfalls in life is Sasha when she asks something of me that I really don't want to give. She's the sweetest, most thoughtful, and caring person I know, and rarely asks for anything. I can't say no when she does.

"Okay," I agree and gather the dress around me so I can go check my phone. "Just let me take this call and then Nancy can have a look."

I pass Nancy on the way out to the living room. She eyes the dress that barely covers me and nods as she walks past me. I think that nod means she can fix the dress and the feelings I have over that tell me that I hope she can't. This is not a dress a guest should wear to a wedding. It's too revealing for a wedding and I'm unsure why Sasha is even suggesting it.

Putting those thoughts on hold, I squeeze my arms close to my sides to keep it in place while I locate my cell phone and find a missed call from Slade. A text from him comes in right as I'm about to return his call.

SLADE

My dick has appeared all over the
internet and I need you to remove it.

He texts me a link to a website and I laugh out loud
when I read the name: www.inmybigdickera.com.

OLIVIA

Send me a list of all the sites where it
appears and I'll take care of this.

SLADE

That's the only site.

OLIVIA

You said it was all over the internet.

SLADE

It is!

Men. Honestly.

OLIVIA

I'm on it.

"Liv," Blair says, joining me in the living room. "I'm
going to order Thai for dinner. Are you good with that?"
She comes closer. "And what are you staring at so
intently?"

I show her the text from Slade with the dick link.
"Some days, I wonder what will become of the human
race. I mean, why are people wasting their time with this
kind of stuff when we've got big problems to solve?"

"The human race is fucked, babe. We know this.
Don't bother wasting your time wondering about that."
Blair's a lawyer too and her client list has some of the

biggest assholes in this city on it. She's always been jaded when it comes to people, but I've watched that deepen over the years because of her work.

She taps the link and her eyes flare at what she sees. "Wow, Slade's hung." She taps away some more at my phone before saying, "Ugh. So is Hunt." She looks up at me. "God could have gifted him with a personality instead." Hunt is the guy at her work that she's currently at war with. I think she should just have sex with him and get him out of her system but she swears she couldn't think of anything worse.

"Two things. One: you don't believe in God. And two: don't ever tell me you don't want to have sex with him again. This just proves you're fixated on him."

"It proves nothing."

I arch a brow. "He was the guy you searched for first."

She arches a brow back. "And we both know the guy you'd search for would be Callan, yet you tell me all the time you just want to be his friend." She hands my phone back to me. "I'm going to order dinner."

With that, she leaves me alone with the thought that she's put front and center in my mind. Callan's dick. I could throttle her right now because I wasn't thinking about that before she mentioned it. And now that I am, I can't think about anything else.

I type his name into the search bar and immediately a dick appears. A big dick.

Holy. Fuck.

This dick is erect and purple-red and veiny, and has a hand wrapped around the base like he's about to stroke himself.

I'm staring at it in complete silence when a deep voice

sounds from in front of me. "Ace. What happened to meditation tonight?"

I jump at Callan's voice and a complete calamity ensues.

I fumble with my phone in my haste to get out of www.inmybigdickera.com and get his dick out of sight. My arms that were holding my dress in place shift as I reach for the phone that's falling to the floor. Falling between me and Callan. With said dick still on the screen. This, though, is fast becoming the least of my concerns because also falling to the floor is the dress that's doing a god-awful job of covering my body.

Callan steps forward and bends to retrieve my phone, to which I exclaim, "No! Don't."

I bend at the same time and when he lifts his head to look at me after I practically scream at him, he comes face-to-face with my boobs. The dress is down around my waist and I'm internally berating myself for choosing the bra I chose today. It's a black plunge bra that is all thin black straps and flesh colored mesh. I love it because it makes me feel sexy and feminine. Callan's staring at it like his eyes are glued to it, and while that's generally the point of this bra, I'm experiencing conflicted sensations right now.

I've wanted his eyes on me like this forever and god, does it feel good. Like, all the way down in my belly good. But also, it's happened so awkwardly and nothing will come of it, which means this will become a memory that won't feel good whenever I remember it.

Hastily reaching for the dress, I attempt to pull it back up. This gets Callan's attention and he tries to help me. If I thought things were already awkward, I had no idea of the levels of awkwardness we could descend into. Now it's not only his eyes on me, but also his hands. On my boobs. All over my boobs. Everywhere. And not in a sexy, hot way, but in a *let me cover you up* way.

"Fuck," he curses once I've got the dress back in place.

I look down at his hands that are still covering my breasts. "I think I'm good now."

He immediately removes his hands like he was touching something burning hot. Then, he picks up my phone and hands it to me, his blue eyes holding an emotion I can't get a proper read on.

When he doesn't say anything, I blurt, "They're just boobs, Callan. You've seen lots of them in your lifetime."

Goodness, this is painful. I have no idea what's happening but there's an energy sitting between us that's new and unfamiliar and bewildering.

He appears lost for words, but finally he asks, "What's with the dress?"

"It's hot, right?" Blair says as she saunters into the living room. She's looking at me like she's planning something wicked that I won't like very much.

Before Callan can answer her, Rhodes strides into the room too, his eyes coming straight to mine. "Did your boy tell you who he just met?"

My boy.

Nope, I wanna say, *not my boy. I wish, but it'll never happen.*

"Who?" I ask, grateful for the change in conversation.

Rhodes rattles off the name of Callan's favorite pitcher from the baseball team he never stops thinking about. I barely pay attention though because all I can think about is the fact I need to get this dress off me.

When Rhodes finishes his monologue about how they met the guy and what happened after they got talking, his brows wrinkle at me. "What the fuck are you wearing, Liv?"

Such a great question. And one that leads me into saying, "Something I should never have agreed to try on."

With that, I scurry from the living room into Sasha's bedroom and announce, "We're done with this dress and neither of you will ever convince me otherwise!"

Sasha and Nancy stare at me like they want to argue with me but obviously my tone was clear enough that they got the point because they don't. Instead, they just glance at each other and then leave the room like they came to a silent agreement to do so.

After I change back into my clothes and hang Sasha's dress in her closet, I join everyone in the living room. Rhodes is leading a conversation about the baseball player they met. Blair is sitting on a sofa looking like she may kill someone if her dinner doesn't arrive soon. Sasha and Nancy are hanging off every word Rhodes utters and Callan appears only half invested in the conversation.

He meets my gaze when I stand across from him in the group, his eyes flaring a little, which is his signal to me that Rhodes is talking a lot and that he wants to be done with this conversation.

The wild energy that's been racing through my veins since the moment he caught me staring at that dick photo settles at that gesture. He's moving on from the moment and I, for one, am relieved about that. I don't know what that weird current between us was, but I'm happy to leave it behind and get back to normal.

"Rhodes." I cut in on what he's saying. "Have you decided what wedding gift to get Bobby and Karen?"

A pained expression fills his face. "Did Sash tell you about that?"

I laugh and briefly catch Callan's thank you smile. "She and Callan have both told me how ridiculous the registry is, and yeah, Sasha told me you're having a coronary at the price of everything they want."

Rhodes is filthy rich but he's also frugal and, so far, has refused to part with any of his cash for a gift. The wedding is coming up in three weeks though, so time is ticking. Both Sasha and Callan are highly amused over the entire affair and I enjoy listening to their latest update on Rhodes's most recent outburst over it.

"There's nothing on that registry under five grand, Liv. I'm not fucking spending that kind of money on that asshole. The only reason we're going to the wedding is because Sash likes Karen." He looks at Callan. "Have you bought something yet?"

Callan shakes his head. "No."

"But you will?"

"Yeah. For Karen. She deserves it for putting up with Bobby."

Blair wades into the conversation from the sofa. "Remind me how you guys know this couple."

"From college," Rhodes says. "Karen was in one of our classes in freshman year. She's a cool chick, but she's always chosen assholes. I give this marriage a few years at the most."

Sasha frowns. "Don't wish that on them, babe."

Rhodes looks down at his fiancée. "I'm not wishing

anything on them. I just don't think she'll put up with him for long."

"Are you taking the lovely Penelope to this wedding?" Blair asks Callan. "I saw that PDA photo of you two on Insta today."

Callan scowls, which catches all my attention. He's not generally a scowler. "No."

His *no* catches all of Blair's attention and she leaves the sofa to join us. "So, who will be your plus-one now?"

"I'll find someone."

"Haven't you got like a million weddings to attend this season?" she asks.

"He's got nine," I say. "It's insane."

Blair eyes me. "You've got a few, too, right?"

"Yeah." I groan. "I dedicated a good hour all up today to narrowing down my candidates to ask to be my plus-one. And I'm still not convinced I want to ask any of them."

"Who's on the list?" Sasha asks.

I rattle off a list of five names to which Blair pulls a face and says, "Surely you've got better options than those guys. You should let me make this list for you. Straight off the top of my head, I'd say to ask William Bronson."

"Fuck no," Callan says without taking even a second to think about it.

Blair's brows lift. "Oh? You've got feelings about him being Olivia's plus-one?"

"He's an asshole who can't keep his hands to himself," Callan says.

"Maybe Liv would enjoy those hands all over her," Blair says.

Callan's eyes bore into mine, an intensity blaring from them that I've never seen. "You wouldn't."

Whoa.

I guess his feelings about William Bronson are very strong feelings. I'm getting vibes like the ones he was throwing off when he got in that fight with Slade last year.

"Who do you suggest?" Sasha asks.

"None of the assholes on her current list," he says.

"There weren't many better options than that list." I frown. "And none of them are assholes."

"I've got ideas," Blair says.

Callan gives her a look that says he doesn't think her ideas would be any good and then looks at me. "I'll come up with some names for you."

Rhodes takes this moment to wade on in with a bomb of an idea. "Why don't you two just be each other's plus-one for the summer? It seems like a no-brainer to me."

"No, that would never work." The words are out of my mouth before my brain even gets a minute with the idea.

"Why not?" Blair asks. Very fucking fast, may I add. I've no doubt this was where she was heading. Probably giving Rhodes the idea without anyone even noticing. She's sly like that, my other best friend.

I make eyes at her. They're so subtle no one here would pick up on them, but she and I are well-versed in making these eyes that say *shut the hell up right now*.

"Yeah, why not?" Rhodes waits for my answer like he thinks I've actually got a valid one.

Callan? He's over there thinking about this. I can see it on his face that he's reaching the same conclusion as

Rhodes, which means I need to double down on coming up with a reason he'll buy.

Being his plus-one is a terrible idea. The worst idea in all the history of ideas. Not because I don't want to spend that kind of time with him, but because doing so will be hard for me.

Over the years, I've accepted we will never be together in the way I'd like. Being his best friend is both the greatest thing in the world and at times the worst. It's hard in the moments when he shares his greatest successes with me and I wish I could share them on a deeper level. And in his lowest moments when I wish I could do more for him. And every moment in between where I have to keep my hands and my mouth and my heart to myself.

A summer of weekends spent together at weddings would be filled with so many of these moments. Add in the romantic sentiments and desire to find my life partner that a wedding always stirs in me, and it's a recipe for heartache.

I'm still racing to land on a plausible reason why it wouldn't work when Callan says, "It's a good idea, Ace. We've got three weddings in common already. Rhodes is right, it's a no-brainer."

My heart is pounding against my ribcage as every set of eyes comes to me, waiting for my agreement.

Oh, Jesus.

There's no saying no now. When Callan sets his mind to something, he always makes it happen.

Blair's lips pull up. Just a teeny bit, but I see them and I shoot her a quick glare. Then, I smile at Callan. "Okay, let's do this."

4

CALLAN

"WHY ANYONE WOULD CHOOSE to get married at ten a.m. is beyond me," Sasha says during the pre-wedding dinner that Bobby and Karen hold on the Friday night before their wedding. They had their wedding rehearsal dinner last night so they could have this dinner tonight. Bobby insisted every wedding guest attend. This meant I had to push my way through a hectic afternoon of work meetings, reschedule a work dinner, and fight through traffic to arrive in Long Island on time. I couldn't give a shit what time people get married; I only give a fuck that I was forced into this dinner.

"I don't think I'd choose that time," Olivia says as she reaches for her glass of wine, drawing my gaze to her bare arm. "I want the morning of my wedding to be relaxed and I don't think an early wedding would allow that."

"And who issues a wedding day schedule?" Sasha appears extremely confused about the timeline we were emailed during the week.

"I've never received one," Olivia says. "But I'm not mad about it."

"That's because you're the queen of being organized," Sasha says. "It feels very bossy to me."

I barely pay attention as they continue discussing the schedule. Rhodes checked out of the conversation five minutes ago when he had to leave the table to take care of a work problem and Olivia's bare skin has me checking out now.

Truth be told, I've struggled to check *in* on any of the conversations the four of us have had since I arrived an hour and a half ago. Olivia came earlier with Sasha and Rhodes, and when I knocked on the door of her hotel room, she answered it wearing the sexy black dress that's the cause of all my current problems.

If I didn't know better, I'd swear she glued it to herself.

It's fitted everywhere but cinched hard at the waist, accentuating those luscious curves that I've been unable to remove my eyes or thoughts from for three long weeks. Ever since that conversation with Penny at Bradford's wedding.

At least this dress covers her breasts. Unlike that pink dress I walked in on her wearing at Rhodes's condo a couple of weeks ago. Fuck. That memory is burned into my brain and I've revisited it more times than I care to admit.

She laughs at something Sasha says and leans back against her chair while bringing both her hands up to scoop her long brunette hair off her shoulders and tie it into a ponytail. I'm fucking mesmerized. It's as if I've never seen a woman tie her hair up. My gaze traces every single movement before finally settling on her sun-kissed face.

"Are you okay?" she asks, concern creasing her face. "You've been quiet and seem distracted."

I'm distracted as fuck but I'm not about to tell her that. I pull at my tie that I'm still wearing and loosen it before undoing the top couple buttons on my shirt. There was no time to change when I arrived. We were straight into drinks and then dinner. "Work kicked my ass today, but I'm okay. Don't worry about me, Ace."

Her features smooth into a soft smile. "I always worry about you. That's my job." She glances around the restaurant before leaning in close to me, placing her hand on my thigh, and whispering against my ear, "Bobby and Karen just left, so this means we can too. And I have the perfect thing for you up in my room."

Christ.

If she knew the shit running through my mind right now as to what she could give me up in her room, she'd be shocked. Fuck knows, I am.

Olivia is a touchy-feely person. Always has been. With me, anyway. And I've never thought anything of it. I can't begin to count the number of times she's placed her hand on my thigh. Tonight, though, it's as if she's wrapped her hand around my dick because that's where I'm feeling it.

I almost choke on my words when I say, "What is it?"

She inspects me like I'm sick. "Are you sure you're okay?" Her fingers curl into my leg while she studies me. "What's going on, Callan?"

Rhodes saves me when he comes back to the table and announces, "The bride and groom have finally fucked off." He eyes Sasha. "Time to go, baby." Then, to me and Olivia, he says, "We'll catch you guys at the wedding."

Olivia looks at him. "What, no early morning break-fast with us before the wedding?"

Sasha stands. "Very funny, Liv. You know I'm not cut out to get ready for a ten-a.m. wedding *and* show up for breakfast with you guys all in one morning. We can't all be queens at managing our time like you."

"You should build Sasha a spreadsheet," I say once we're alone.

Olivia narrows her eyes at me. "I can't tell if you're being serious or making fun of my planning methods."

I grin and reach for my glass of whiskey. "You know I fucking love your planning methods."

"Yes, but you've got that cheeky look in your eyes that you get when you're making fun of me."

"I'm amused at the thought of you trying to manage Sasha. You have to admit that you're very dedicated when you're trying to help someone, and we both know Sash has even less skills when it comes to personal manage-ment than I do. She'd be running to Blair within twenty-four hours begging for her help to manage *you*."

She smacks me lightly before pushing her chair back to stand. "You're lucky I love you, Callan Black. Also, you better be on my side if this ever happens. You're the only person I know who can handle Blair when she goes into Blair-battle Mode."

Olivia has told me she loves me almost as many times as she's put her hands on my body. I've always taken it for granted and never really stopped and thought about the words when she's said them. Tonight, they're like a direct hit. They pierce through all the noise in my brain and settle inside my soul in the most confusing way.

I've wanted her friendship and the platonic love that comes with it for as long as I can remember, but now, there's something more to it. Something I don't want to get too close to because if I do, it'll fuck everything up that we have. And that's not something I ever want to do. I want Olivia in my life for *life*; taking our friendship further would land us in a tangled mess of feelings that could end everything.

As we weave our way through the tables to leave the restaurant, I push all that down and do my best to ignore it. I also do my best to avoid all the couples who try to stop us on our way out. This is the problem with knowing too many people, and while I'm usually up for a conversation, I'm not tonight. I just want some time by myself so I can figure out how to get through this weekend because as much as having Olivia as my plus-one for the season sounded like a no-brainer at the time, I've very quickly realized tonight that it may have been a grave error in judgment.

Olivia's cell phone starts ringing while we're standing at her hotel room door. She's busy fumbling in her purse for her room keycard and mutters something about hockey players having a knack for calling at the exact wrong moment. Just as she stabs at the phone to answer the call, it stops ringing.

She looks at me. "In my next life I won't even know what hockey is, let alone know any of the men who chase pucks around for a living."

"Slade?" She's working with three hockey players now, but Slade's the one who gives her the most hell.

"Yes. He's called me ten times today. Ten!"

"Jesus." I bite my tongue because there's a fuckload more I could say but I know she won't want to hear any of it.

She sighs as she taps the keycard to the door and opens it. "Hayden's gotta be happy with the billable hours, but the emotional work with Slade is equal to double those hours really. I asked him to only call me in the case of an emergency this weekend, so I'll quickly return his call just to make sure he's okay."

I follow her in and survey the room. Olivia is the tidiest person I know but this room looks like a bomb hit. Her suitcase is on the bed with clothes strewn half in and half out. Other clothes lay in piles on the bed, and fuck me, two lacy bras are on the very top of those piles. One is black and one is red, and I've never wanted to see a bra on a woman as much as I want to see that red bra on Olivia.

While she calls Slade, I reply to a few emails that need to be taken care of tonight and ask my assistant to follow up on a couple of others. I try hard to remove my eyes from that red bra while I do this but I appear to have developed a multitasking skill that I've never had before and astound myself with my ability to tap out an email while committing the lace of that bra to memory.

When Olivia finishes with Slade and says, "Now, I know you're not a fan of any kind of tea, but I have an herbal tea for you that I really want you to try," I shove my phone in my trousers and say, "Hit me with it." At this point, I'd drink tea all night long if it meant my mind was distracted from bras and bare skin and that sinful black dress I've imagined peeling from her in a million different ways.

Her brows gather together right before she plants her hands on her hips and says, "Okay, so now I know there really *is* something wrong with you. In all our years, you've never once easily submitted to tea."

The tie that I loosened at dinner suddenly feels like it's strangling me. Between Olivia standing in front of me the way she is and using words like submit, I'm fucked. I'm generally a straight thinker and rarely find myself with chaotic thoughts. Right now, my mind is a wreck I can't even begin to make sense of.

"It's been a fucker of a day at work. If tea will help me unwind, I'm all for it."

Keeping her hands on her hips—fuck me, those hips —she shakes her head. "No, I'm not buying that anymore."

"Anymore?" I'm fighting to keep up with this conversation because all I can think about is how much I want *my* hands on her hips.

She finally drops her hands. "You've been off for weeks. Brushing my concern aside whenever I bring it up. Ever since you slept with Penelope, to be honest. I'm worried you're in denial over your feelings for her."

"My feelings for her?" I'm only half paying attention because I've moved on from her hips and am now preoccupied with her earrings. *Christ.* I've never been engrossed with a woman's earrings before. I'm telling myself it's the sparkling diamonds that drew my gaze but that's a lie. My eyes are all over her neck, her jawline, and the skin where they meet near her earlobe. What I'm *actually* engrossed in is thinking about kissing her there.

And about inhaling that vanilla and coconut scent she loves to wear.

"Yes, Callan, your feelings. I think you've checked out on them. Dissociated maybe. I think you've been so busy these last few weeks because you're trying to distract yourself from her."

I am distracted. She's got that right. Wrong woman, though. And my current distraction is wondering what perfume she wears. I'm stunned that I have no clue. I know a thousand things about Olivia and her preferences but I've never learned her favorite perfume.

"I don't have any feelings for Penny."

"Are you sure? Because that was definitely when you got weird. That weekend you spent with her. And we never did discuss that photo of her groping you while practically sitting on your lap in a restaurant. The one that was posted on Insta. That's proof that something's going on."

"How do you figure that?"

"You've never even come close to doing something like that in public. Well, not that I know of, anyway." She cocks her head and looks at me questioningly. "Have you?"

Fuck.

I've always known women overthink shit, but I've never known Olivia to. It was this side of her that appealed to me as a kid. I liked having a girl friend while not having any of the drama that girls often brought with them. She's intelligent and rational, and always approaches situations with logic. This line of thinking she's engaging in is absolutely not logical.

"Sleeping with Penny and spending the weekend with

her was a lapse in judgment. I've never had feelings for her and I never will, Ace. I'm not dissociating or in denial."

This does not put her mind at ease like it should. She doubles down on her worry and looks at me with tenderness. "You can tell me anything, Callan, and I'll always support you and be there for you."

Be there for me? "I'm not sure what you think is happening in my head, Liv, but you're probably wrong. Work has distracted me for weeks, which you know. And now the German deal looks like it might fall through, so I'm busy trying to ensure that doesn't happen. I'm tired because it's affecting my sleep. And on top of that, I still haven't heard back from Ethan, which has pissed me off."

"Are you depressed?" she blurts. The wild look in her eyes says she really didn't want to ask that question but couldn't not ask it.

"Fuck, no." I move closer to her, wanting to reassure her and take all her worry away. "I'm definitely not depressed and I'm sorry I've been giving off vibes that made you think that." I frown. "Have you been worried about that for weeks?"

She bites her lip in the most adorable way. "No, but yes," she says slowly before launching into her reasoning. "I've been worried about a lot of things because we haven't been talking like we usually do. You feel distant. I even wondered if you'd finally developed a sex addiction. It was so unusual for you to sleep with a friend and then to do that whole"—she gestures back and forth with her hand—"PDA thing in the restaurant, and you just didn't seem to want to talk about it, which was the most unusual thing of all. I don't think there's anything you and I have ever avoided talking about. It felt like you were shutting down on me and, honestly, Callan, don't ever do that to me again. I don't cope well when we're not talking about everything."

"A sex addiction?" My mouth curves up in amusement because it's highly fucking amusing knowing she went there.

She arches a brow. "If the shoe fits."

"Fuck, I don't have that much sex."

Still with the brow arch. "You really do."

"I haven't had sex in three weeks."

Her brow arch is replaced with a hint of worry again. "You haven't slept with anyone since Penelope?"

"No, but don't make that into something it isn't. I'm completely feelingless when it comes to Penny. I've just been too busy."

She doesn't appear convinced but she lets it go. "Okay, you need this tea more than I thought you did. It's supposed to help with relaxation and sleep. And I also bought you a sleep mask that's infused with lavender that I'll give you before you leave. Hopefully that will help your sleep too." She puts her hands all over me while directing me to the armchair in the corner of the room. "Good god, your muscles are tight. We should see if we can book you in for a massage first thing tomorrow."

"No, I'm not getting up any earlier tomorrow morning."

She forces me into the armchair. "Okay, then take off your shirt and I'll give you a quick massage while the tea brews."

Without waiting for my response, she turns and makes her way to the kettle and sets to work boiling water and preparing the tea. My eyes are locked on her body the entire time. I'm un-fucking-able to look anywhere else.

Olivia has given me more massages than I can remember, but tonight, that's not happening. No fucking way am I letting her hands anywhere near me. I'll drink this tea and then get the hell out of her room to the safety of my own. Thank Christ we didn't book the two-bedroom suite she originally found for us. I'd agreed to it but someone else booked it before Olivia could.

Mercifully, my phone sounds with a text, giving me something to do other than thinking indecent thoughts about her. I'm replying to an email when she places the cup of tea on the low table in front of me. She's eyeing my shoulders with intent and I'm about to tell her I don't want a massage when her cell phone rings.

"If that's Slade again, I may throttle him," she mutters. "That guy doesn't understand the meaning of emergency."

I'm instantly annoyed every time I hear Slade's name and now isn't any different. There's just something about him that rubs me the wrong way. He has no care for Olivia's personal time and that pisses me off.

"Ignore the call if it's him."

"I can't ignore him. I'm paid *not* to ignore him."

"Well, maybe you and Hayden need to revisit your contract with him and insert a clause that protects your personal time."

She gives me a pointed look. "I think you of all people can understand that personal time doesn't always come into it when work is involved. I imagine that whatever you just did on your phone while I made your tea was for work."

She's got me there, and since I never want a repeat of what happened the last time I got in the middle of her and Slade, I let this go. However, my brain doesn't let it go and I stew on it while she takes the call.

Olivia's worked with a lot of assholes in her time and none of them have irritated me the way Slade does. I only have to see his name in the news and my chest tightens with annoyance.

I'm all the way down in this irritation when Olivia laughs at something Slade says. It's at this point I know I've reached my capacity for being with her tonight. I take hold of the cup of tea she made me and stand. "I'm tired. I'm going to drink this in my room and go to bed."

She frowns. "Okay, but—" Slade says something that pulls her focus back to the call, to which she says, "Sorry, Slade, can you give me a second?" She meets my gaze again as she shifts her phone away from her face. "This won't take long. I want to try and massage some of those knots out of your shoulders."

"My knots can wait. I'll book a massage in for tomorrow." I nod at her cell. "Don't work too late. You need sleep too." She likely needs it more than I do. She's worked a million hours this week.

This earns me a smile. "Okay. Let me know what time your massage is so we can coordinate breakfast together."

I'm in my own room fifteen minutes later when there's a knock on my door and I find Olivia on the other side, in her pajamas, with her hair falling down over her shoulders and her glasses on.

Holding the sleep mask out to me, she says, "You forgot this."

I take the mask while barely looking at it. That's because I'm staring at the mint candy stripe pajama shorts she's wearing and the cropped pink top that sits tightly against her breasts and doesn't cover all her stomach. If I thought the sexy black dress from dinner was hell on me, I had no idea what was coming.

We've got ten more weddings to go and I've just decided I may need to cancel all of them. There's no fucking way I'll survive this season if I have to spend it with Olivia killing me like she has tonight.

5

OLIVIA

"CALLAN'S BEING WEIRD THIS WEEKEND," Sasha says over cocktails at the wedding reception on Saturday. "I seriously just watched him avoid a woman who was desperately trying to give him her number. Have you two got a deal that says he can't sleep with anyone at all the weddings this season?"

I eye my best friend who is currently at the bar talking with Rhodes and another guy. "No." I look back at Sasha. "We didn't discuss it but he can do whatever he wants."

"And you can do whatever you want, right? Because if so, there's a guy here who hasn't taken his eyes off you and I'm pretty sure you haven't even noticed."

She's right, I haven't noticed, and that's because the only guy here I have noticed is Callan. He's wearing a new suit and holy hell, it should be illegal. The way he fills out those trousers causes me to forget that breathing is a thing.

I shrug. "Sure, we can both do what we want, Sash, but I'm not really looking at the moment."

She crosses her legs and settles in for the conversation I know she's wanted to have for weeks. Sasha lives for romance even more than I do and is a diehard matchmaker. The idea that a woman isn't currently looking isn't an idea she would ever entertain. "Tell me why. It's been a couple of months since you and Jensen broke up, and it's not like you were heartbroken, so why the break from dating?"

I sip some of my Cosmo and glance at the twinkle lights strung above us while gathering my thoughts. I'm not entirely sure why I've been reluctant to put myself back out there and I know any sign of hesitation will give Sasha the in she's looking for to take charge. I need to be clear with her that I'm not open to matchmaking right now.

Placing my glass on the table, I give her a look that I hope conveys how seriously I feel about this. "I'm not sure why I'm taking a break. I just know I need it. I'm almost thirty and all the guys I've dated up to now haven't been right for me. I need a minute to assess and figure some things out."

Rhodes walks past me to sit next to Sasha as I say this. I sense Callan slipping into the seat on my other side and turn to find him looking at me intently, like he's wondering something about me. Sasha wasn't wrong when she said he's being weird today. I keep catching him watching me like this and I don't know what to make of it.

Rhodes draws my attention when he asks, "What kinds of things do you need to figure out, Liv?"

I groan inwardly. This is the last conversation I want

to have with the group. "There's a lot to work out. Mostly, I want to narrow down exactly what I'm looking for in a man."

"Well, I don't think that means you need to stop dating," Sasha says. "I think we discover things about ourselves through other people. The more guys you date, the faster you'll learn what you do and don't want."

Callan makes a noise and I could swear it's a grunt, which is odd because I've never heard him grunt. "The more guys she dates, the more assholes she'll meet."

Sasha fixes a dirty look on him while I try not to laugh. This is *not* the conversation Sasha was looking for.

"Fair point," Rhodes agrees and I keep smiling.

Sasha elbows her fiancé. "Not helpful, babe."

"It's true, though," Callan says.

"So, what, she should just sleep her way to finding her true love rather than date?" Sasha arches her brows at Callan waiting for his response.

I turn in time to see his features darken.

"She should take things as slowly as she wants," he says.

"*She's* sitting right here in between all of you," I remind them. "And she's not interested in dating or sex at the moment."

Rhodes looks positively horrified. "You're off sex too?"

"I'm just taking a break, Rhodes."

"For how long?" He still looks pained like he could never imagine taking a break from sex.

"For as long as it takes me to figure things out."

A text comes through on my phone and I gladly check it while the three of them have a conversation about abstinence.

HARPER

> Livvy!! I got engaged!! I'll call you later
> but I wanted to share the news with you
> right now. And I want to ask if you'll
> consider being my wedding planner
> since I won't be back in New York before
> the wedding and our moms both insist
> on us holding the wedding there. Please
> say yes! I know you've never planned a
> wedding before but there's no kind of
> planning you don't excel at. Love you xx

"Oh my god!" I look at Callan. "Harper and Landon got engaged!"

He smiles. "Good for them."

"She wants me to plan her wedding."

"Who's Harper and Landon?" Rhodes asks.

"Harper is Olivia's cousin," Sasha says. "She and Landon live in Paris." She looks at me. "Will you say yes?"

"I don't know. It's such an important day in her life. I'd hate to mess it up."

Callan touches my arm. "You won't mess it up, Ace."

I meet his gaze and read between the lines of what he's saying. The only person in the world who knows all my fears and hurts and regrets is Callan, and he's reading me perfectly. He knows I already feel responsible for a tragedy in my family when we were children and that since that day I've done everything in my power to ensure Harper is happy. "I might," I say softly. "So many things could go wrong."

"So many things could go right. If anyone can plan a wedding, it's you. I'll help in any way I can."

Callan has always been my protector and he's not letting me down now. I know he absolutely means it, and that he would walk through fire if I asked him to. I also know he wouldn't make this kind of offer for very many people. It isn't that he's not kind, helpful or thoughtful; it's that helping plan a wedding, or anything really, isn't where his skills lie. Planning an event is actually his idea of hell, so this means the world to me.

"You might regret that," I say, keeping hold of his gaze.

"I don't think so." He's watching me like he's got all the time in the world for me. Like he wants to make sure I'm okay.

We're in the middle of this moment when Rhodes says, "I agree with Callan. If anyone can plan a wedding, it's you, Liv."

I break eye contact with Callan to look at Rhodes. "Thank you for saying that."

"I agree with the guys. You will make an excellent wedding planner," Sasha says before leaning into her fiancé. "Now, it's time for you to dance with me, babe."

I smile at the way Rhodes accepts his fate without argument and leads Sasha to the dance floor. I then turn my entire body to face Callan. "Thank you for offering to help. I don't know if I'll say yes, but if I do, I'll definitely be calling on you. Even if just for moral support."

"I'm here for whatever you need." He glances at my empty cocktail glass. "Would you like another drink?"

"Yes, please."

While he's at the bar, I check my emails to make sure nothing urgent has come in that I need to attend to. I reply to a few before getting stuck on one from Mace Hawkins. I've been working with him for a few weeks now and while I like him, I don't like dealing with the problems his soon-to-be ex-wife has caused. Mace has emailed through a new problem that's reared its ugly head and I feel exhausted by the entire situation as I read the email.

"You look like you want to throw that phone across the room," Callan says when he comes back to the table with our drinks.

I glance up at him. "That's because I do. And I can't say I've ever wanted to do that before."

He reaches for my phone and gently takes it out of my hand before placing it face down on the table. "Take a break, Liv. God knows you deserve it."

"I honestly wish I could, but social media makes it so I can't." I reach for my phone. "I'm really sorry, but I have to take care of something that can't wait."

His features cloud. "Slade?"

For the life of me, I can't figure out exactly what Callan has against Slade. He took a dislike to him very quickly when I first worked with the guy late last year, and his dislike only seems to be intensifying.

"No, it's Mace Hawkins. Gossip accounts have posted stories overnight about his wife trying to sleep with some of his teammates since they broke up. The stories have hinted that this has driven a wedge between Mace and the team. This is on top of the other stuff he's dealing with because of Katie's drama with Penelope." I sigh because I struggle to wrap my head around this kind of high-school-style drama. His team's general manager has told him to fix the problem and he wants me to get to the bottom of it so we can put a stop to it. This means I'm going to have to wade into the drama, which has me questioning crisis management as a career. Going back to straight law is looking more appealing every day.

"I thought the stuff between Katie and Penny was sorted out. Didn't Katie give Penny's diamonds back?"

"She did, but it doesn't seem to have settled Penelope's beef with Katie. I think that's what I have to get to the bottom of if I'm going to have any hope of helping Mace. He just wants to get on with his life and get back to being on good terms with his team."

"And you think I'm crazy for not wanting a relationship. This is the kind of shit I'm avoiding."

I refrain from rolling my eyes. "This type of problem isn't usual in a relationship and you know it." Callan's got baggage a mile long thanks to his parents' marriage. We've discussed it at length many times and I've gently suggested he work through this in therapy. He'd rather stab his eyes with a hot, sharp stick than go to therapy.

"Don't be so sure of that, Ace. Some of the things I've heard guys say they've had to deal with when a relationship goes sour blows my mind."

A waiter walks past with a platter of cheeses and I lean across Callan and motion to get the man's attention. Once he's on his way over, I lean back and say, "What kinds of things? I think you're making this up."

"What, so I can win this argument?"

The waiter joins us and I fill a small plate with an assortment of cheeses to share. Once he leaves, I place the plate on the table between us and carry on the conversation. "Yes! Your competitive streak knows no bounds." I pick up a piece of cheese and offer it to Callan. "Try this and tell me if it tastes any good."

He takes the cheese as he says, "I'm not making this up. Marc told me last week that Tina vandalized his car after they broke up. That was right before she sent movers to their condo and took all their belongings." Pointing at his mouth, he says, "This cheese is good. It's got that sharp bite to it that you love."

"Ooh." I pop the other piece of the same cheese into my mouth. "Let's be real about those two, though. They're not an example of a healthy relationship."

"Healthy relationships don't seem to exist, Liv."

"That's not true. Look at Bradford and Kristen. That's one of the healthiest relationships I've ever seen."

"That's fair, but again, not the norm."

"A relationship is what you make it. You can't convince me otherwise." I select another piece of cheese. "You don't win this argument."

He grins. "Says you."

This time, I do roll my eyes. Then, I stand. "I'm pretty sure we'll still be arguing over this when we're old. I wonder if you'll be sad and lonely then because you were stubborn and didn't try new things like relationships."

He keeps grinning. "I won't be sad or lonely, Ace. I'll still have you keeping me company while arguing with me over things like this."

A few minutes later, I'm on the phone with Mace and seriously contemplating leaving crisis management behind. But then, I admit to myself that's only because this particular crisis involves Penelope Rush, and if there's one woman I wish I'd never heard of or met, it's Penelope.

"So, wait," I say after he details what he's learned today, "this all stems from a comment Penelope made to Katie about why you two broke up?" Apparently, Penelope told Katie "It's no wonder Mace is done with you. Have you seen the size of your ass lately?" Katie then swiped her diamonds in a fit of anger and hurt. Penelope wasn't satisfied when she gave them back and went on to start spreading lies about Katie sleeping with Mace's teammates.

He releases a frustrated breath. "Yeah, but it's not true. I didn't leave Katie because she put on weight. We broke up because I'm a dickhead and cheated on her."

"Okay, here's what I'm going to do," I say before outlining my plan to send a cease and desist. "If it's okay with you, I'll call Katie and get all the information I need from her."

"Yeah, I've told her you'll probably have to do that. She's ready for your call." He exhales another long breath. "What a fuck up. If I could go back and change everything I did, I would."

As a lawyer, I keep my personal feelings to myself. They don't come into my work. Not even when I'm thinking *yes, what a fuck up that we all could have avoided*. "I'll keep you updated, Mace. Hopefully, the cease and desist will put a stop to this."

"And if not?"

"If not, we have other avenues we can take. One step at a time. I'll be in touch."

I'm on my way back to Callan when I run into Sasha.

"Who's that woman Callan's talking to?" she asks, nodding toward a table that's three over from ours.

Callan's sitting with a blonde woman, deep in conversation. He looks like he's held captive by her. "I don't know," I say as I experience the jealous churning in my stomach that I only ever feel when I see Callan with another woman.

"Hmmm, they seem very cozy." She eyes me. "At least

he's not acting weirdly anymore. I was worried about him when I saw him fight that other woman off earlier."

I'm busy staring at him, noting the way his eyes are fixed intently on the blonde, and only vaguely hear what Sasha says.

I hate this. I hate that even though I made peace years ago with the fact I know he'll never be mine, I still have these jealous feelings. I just want them to go away and never return. They're useless and unproductive. All they do is remind me I'm a twenty-nine-year-old woman hung up on her best friend, who has a past littered with failed relationships, awkward dating moments, and bad sex.

"Okay." I loop my arm through my friend's. "It's time we had a drink."

Sasha looks at me with confusion. "We already have."

I shake my head. "No, we sipped a few cocktails. Now, I'm ready for a real drink."

Sasha glances in the direction I'm staring and suddenly connects the dots. She tightens my arm in hers and nods. "I agree. It's time for a drink."

6

CALLAN

"Have you seen Olivia?" I ask Rhodes after I finish my conversation with Lana Smith.

"Yeah, she's on the dance floor with Sash. They've been into the whiskey."

I look at the dance floor that's three tables away from us. The 16-piece orchestra are currently playing a song I don't know. The lyrics suggest it's about a toxic attraction. Olivia's hips are enjoying the hell out of the song. "How much whiskey?"

Rhodes eyes his fiancée. "Enough that I know I'm in for a good afternoon." He chuckles as he looks back at me. "Either that or they're both gonna pass out by three p.m."

Olivia isn't a big drinker. At the most, she usually only has a couple of cocktails when she drinks. If she switches to whiskey, something's up, and it generally ends with her intoxicated. If the way she's dancing is anything to go by, she's close to or has reached intoxication levels.

It makes me wonder what happened in between her

leaving me to make a work call and now. I got sidetracked talking with Lana who has helped shed some light on why my German deal has taken a bad turn, so I missed Olivia coming back from her call.

While I'm thinking about this, Peter Hudson moves behind Olivia and begins dancing with her. I tense at the sight, not fucking liking the way he's bending to whisper something in Liv's ear, or the fact his hands are on her body.

"Easy, tiger," Rhodes says, and when I meet his gaze, I find him watching me with a knowing look.

"I don't like that guy for her."

"You don't like any guy for her."

"Not true. I liked Jensen for her."

"You liked the fact *she* didn't like him."

"She was in love with him, Rhodes. Have you forgotten she dated him for almost a year?"

"She was nowhere near in love with him, and the fact you think she was tells me you're deeper in denial than I thought."

"Jesus, Olivia thinks I'm in denial over Penny, and now you think I'm in denial over her and Jensen. What the fuck are you talking about?"

"For an intelligent guy, you're fucking clueless when it comes to Olivia. You're losing your shit over her dancing with another guy because *you* want to be the guy she dances with."

"I can dance with Liv anytime I want."

He shakes his head like he's dealing with an idiot. "Yeah, you keep telling yourself that, Callan. One day, you'll wake up and she'll be married and you'll be left wondering why the fuck you didn't wake up to yourself sooner." Sasha waves at him to come and dance. With one last glance at me, he says, "I hope you pull your head out of your ass soon. You and Liv are meant to be together."

He strides toward the girls leaving me with that bomb.

The fuck?

Liv and I are friends and that's worth a hell of a lot more to me than a romantic relationship. I will go to the ends of the earth to protect our friendship, and while my fucking brain seems intent on imagining doing filthy things to her, there is no way I'll risk what we have for sex.

I watch her with Peter for another moment before deciding he has to go. I don't trust him. If given half a chance, he'll rip Liv's heart out and trash it, and I won't have that.

Olivia blesses me with a smile when I reach her. It settles in my bones like all her smiles do. "Callan," she gushes and I grin at her loose lips.

"You got into the whiskey, Ace?"

Her smile grows as she extricates herself from Peter who's glaring at me. "I blame Sasha. All I said was that it was time we had a drink. She's the one who insisted on lots of drinks."

I catch her when she stumbles, pulling her into my arms. "Why do I find that hard to believe?"

She pouts. "You think I'm the bad influence?"

"I think you're both the bad influence when you get together."

Peter, who's long forgotten, interrupts. "Well, I'll just go, shall I?"

Fuck, he's a whiny bastard.

I look at him. "Sounds like a great fucking plan."

Olivia smacks me playfully, bringing all my attention back to her. "That was mean."

I bend my mouth to her ear. "Yeah, and I don't regret any of it. He's an asshole you're better off without."

She presses her body hard against mine and I have to contain my groan of approval. "See, you get it. I'm better off without a guy right now. I don't know why Sasha has so much trouble believing that."

The very last thing I want to be thinking about is Olivia with another guy, but I'm unable to stop myself from saying, "What's really going on there, Ace? What's with the abstinence?"

She loops her hands around my neck as we sway to the music. "Sex is bad."

"I beg to differ."

She giggles. "That came out wrong. God, I'm drunk."

She's fucking cute when she's like this. "Yeah, you are. What did you mean?"

She lets out a sigh. "I'm tired of bad sex. I'm just gonna stick to giving myself orgasms for a while."

Christ.

That's material I don't need.

"You've never told me you were having bad sex. With Jensen do you mean?" Olivia has never given even a hint that she was unhappy with her sex life.

"That's because you're over there having the greatest sex of life. All the time. Every time. And I'm over here begging to be fucked right. I'm not sure if it's me or them but finding a guy who knows how to give an orgasm is harder than passing the bar exam."

Olivia rarely uses terms like "begging to be fucked right." To say I'm into it is a massive understatement.

"It's not you." There's no way it's her. Olivia is one of the most sensual women I know. She's in touch with all her senses and I have no doubt she'd bring them all into the bedroom in the most erotic way.

She gives me soft eyes while tightening her grip on my neck. "You say that because you have rose-colored glasses for me. You think I'm perfect at everything. It might be me." Her brows tuck together. "Although, in fairness to me, my analysis of the situation is that the responsibility lays with all parties involved, so if the guy can't help me out, that's not on me." She looks at me questioningly. "Right?"

"Fuck, you're cute." The words slip from my lips before I can stop them. She is, though, and I have an overwhelming urge to tell her in so many ways just how cute, and beautiful, and smart, and right she is. Somehow, I manage to keep all those thoughts to myself, but it's the hardest thing I've had to do in a long time.

Olivia's eyes grow wide and she stares at me in silence for what feels like minutes but really is only a moment. Then, she blinks like she misunderstood and carries on. "I'm right, aren't I?"

"Of course, you're right. Where's this doubt coming from?"

"You should try having sex with a guy and see how your confidence handles it."

"I'll pass, so how about you fill me in on what you mean."

She inhales a long breath before releasing it. "I only had two orgasms with Jensen and that was because I helped him out. When I tried to help him learn what I needed, he had the audacity to tell me he knew what he was doing and that if it didn't work for me, that was my fault. With Todd, I came once and he never cared enough to notice when I didn't. With Martin, I never orgasmed and he told me it was too much work to even try to get me there most of the time. Rationally, I know they were just lazy, because I have no trouble orgasming when I do it myself, but lots of bad sex all adds up to a girl not feeling good about herself. Well, for me anyway. Rational thoughts don't always come into it when sex is involved." She stops talking before adding, "I just want a man to care enough to spend time on my needs like I do for him. And I don't think it's a bad thing to have to learn together, but guys seem to get all hung up on it when I try to initiate that kind of discovery."

Fuck. Me.

I would be all in on that kind of discovery. Hell, I'd let her be my teacher anytime she wanted.

"And here I was thinking we shared everything." I slide a stray hair from her face and tuck it behind her ear. "I seem to recall you saying just last night that you don't cope well when we're not talking about everything. What gives, Ace? Why have you never told me all this?"

"You're so sure of yourself when it comes to sex. I don't have that confidence and I'd rather not analyze all of it with anyone."

"We don't have to analyze it. I can just listen while you unload. If you *had* told me all this before, I would have made sure you knew there are guys out there who would be happy to learn together."

"Are there, though? Because I've dated a lot of guys

and haven't gotten the vibe from them that they're that kind of man."

Olivia *has* dated a lot of guys. She's only given her heart away three times, but there's been a lot of dates that went nowhere. I know because I've sat through the analysis after each of them with her. She might not have wanted me in on the sex analysis, but she's brought ice cream to my condo a lot for the date debriefs.

"I promise you there are."

"Well, I'm still taking a time-out. I need to lick my wounds after Jensen and gather myself before trying again. And as for sex, I'm sticking with Ricardo. He never lets me down."

"Ricardo?"

"He's my Spanish lover." At my confused expression, she elaborates, "I like to fantasize about making love under the sun in Spain with a hot Spanish guy who spends hours eating me and fucking me until I beg him to stop." She grins. "I named my vibrator Ricardo."

I don't think I'll ever eat pussy again without thinking about Olivia. Or handle a vibrator without thinking about Ricardo.

One wedding in and my ruin is imminent.

"Liv!" Sasha bumps hips with Olivia as she drunkenly yells her name over the music. "It's time!"

Olivia's eyes light up. "I forgot! Yes, let's do this!"

"Do what?" I ask, immediately concerned as to what these two are planning.

Rhodes lets go of his fiancée with a look of defeat and as Sasha and Olivia grab each other's hands and start weaving their way through the crowd on the dancefloor, he leans in and says, "They're doing shots."

"Jesus, is Sasha as drunk as Olivia?"

His brows lift as he nods. "Yep. Neither of them needs a Three Wise Men. I tried to talk Sash out of it but you know what they're like once they've got some booze in them."

I do know. They forget just how much they've already consumed. "Looks like you were right about them passing out early."

He nods. "I just hope the hangover isn't as bad as the last one Sasha had when these two decided shots were the best thing of life."

That was about six months ago and Olivia told me she was done with shots forever after she took a day to recover from the worst hangover she's ever had.

I scan the bar until I find her. She's laughing with Sasha as the bartender makes their shots, and I think about everything she's just shared with me. I feel like a real asshole for being oblivious to it all. I've never gotten the vibe she was withholding information, but maybe I've just been so self-absorbed that I missed the signs.

"I ten out of ten don't rate a Three Wise Men," she says when she returns. Pulling a face, she adds, "I like whiskey but not that much at once."

"Oh my god!" Sasha exclaims as a new song starts. Grabbing Olivia, she says, "I love this song!"

I eye Rhodes and we exchange a *fuck me* glance. We both know where this afternoon is ending.

An hour later, I've got Olivia tucked safely under my arm with her head resting against my chest as I guide her down the corridor from the elevator to her hotel room.

"I don't feel good," she complains, her voice filled with regret. "Why did you let me drink so much?"

I chuckle. "We both know that when you decide to do something, I haven't got a shot in hell at changing your mind."

"That's not true," she mumbles into my jacket.

I use her keycard to open her door and then get her to the bed where she collapses in a heap. The suitcase that was on the bed last night is now on the floor with her clothes lying in a cluttered mess around it.

"What's going on with your suitcase?" I ask. This mess is so unlike her.

She lifts her head to glance at it. "You."

I shrug out of my jacket and hang it over the back of a chair. "Me?" I undo the top buttons of my shirt as I watch her and wonder if she'll give me an answer that makes any sense.

She rests her head on both her hands and curls into a ball. She looks like she's wishing for death. "I'm in a flap and it's all your fault. This season was not a good idea. Doing weddings with you is too much, but Blair got her way and here we are, and I'm all messy."

I still. "What do you mean that this season was not a good idea?" Fuck, she's drunk and I'm taking advantage of the situation, but I need to know if what I think she's saying is what she's actually saying.

She flings an arm in the air in my direction while she mumbles into her hand. "That suit is too much. I can't think straight. I want to take it off you."

My mouth goes dry.

Fuck.

I back up against the desk and grip it hard to steady myself.

Fuck.

I'm lost in this disclosure when Liv lurches forward off the bed and rushes into the bathroom. When I hear her vomiting, I head in there to make sure she's okay.

She hears me come in and tries to get me to leave. "I'm okay. You don't need to—" Her words are cut off when she vomits again.

I move behind her and gather her long hair that's hanging loosely in soft curls into my hands. The last thing anyone wants is their hair coated in vomit.

"Ugh," she groans as she straightens and reaches for a washcloth, fumbling and unable to pick it up.

"Here, let me get it." I take it from her and flick the faucet on so I can wet it.

She places the toilet seat down and sits.

I glance at her as I let her hair go and wet the washcloth. "Are you okay?"

"I think so."

I turn the faucet off and crouch in front of her. "Do you want to wash your face or do you want me to?"

She takes the washcloth. "I'll do it."

I grin as she smooshes the cloth to her entire face at once.

"How long do you think it'll be before you do shots again?"

From behind the washcloth, she says, "Never. I'm breaking up with shots."

"What about whiskey? You breaking up with it too?"

She removes the washcloth. "Whiskey and I are done." She stands, wobbly on her feet. A moment later, she brushes her teeth, all the while swaying and grasping the vanity to hold herself up.

I stand behind her in case she needs help staying upright but she manages not to fall.

When she's done with her teeth, she wets the washcloth again and places it to her neck as she turns to face me. Her dress only covers one shoulder and she runs the cloth over her bare shoulder and down that arm, while slurring, "It's so hot in here."

My eyes follow the washcloth but instead of stopping when it reaches her wrist, I allow my gaze to drop lower, down to where the slit of her dress has the fabric divided and falling either side of her leg. Her thigh is in full view and how I didn't notice it sooner is beyond me, but now that I have noticed it, my gaze is stuck.

Jesus, it's not like I haven't seen Olivia's legs before. We grew up swimming together every summer and still swim whenever we get the chance. I've seen her in bikinis, in shorts, in skirts. I've seen this leg a thousand times, but it's like I've never laid eyes on it in my life.

"Callan."

I glance up and find her watching me intently. "Yeah?"

She studies me silently while she puts the washcloth down and brings her hand to my chest, resting it on the bare skin where I've undone my shirt buttons. Our eyes are locked so fucking tightly that I know I couldn't unlock them even if I tried.

The air is still, holding its breath like I am while Olivia slowly glides her fingers over my skin. Her touch is like fire to my soul and I inhale sharply.

The desire in her eyes is undeniable.

Fuck.

Our friendship flashes through my mind. Twenty-one years could be undone in a moment.

"Ace." My voice is low. Rough.

She doesn't break eye contact. "Don't you ever think about it?"

I swallow hard, fighting the urge to give her the truth. The way she's looking at me, the way her hand is still on my chest - it's almost too much to handle.

"Think about what?" I ask, my voice barely above a whisper.

"Us," she replies, her fingers tracing patterns on my skin. "You and me."

Twenty-one years.

Twenty. One. Years.

I can't fuck this up.

But *fuck*, her touch is unlike any other.

I want her.

I want her more than I've wanted anyone and that's a holy fucking revelation I'm not ready for.

"You don't know what you're saying, Liv. You're drunk."

She grips my shirt with her other hand and then curves her fingers over my abs. "You wouldn't be bad at sex. You'd let me show you how I like it."

It's a good thing she's drunk. I'm so fucking hard for her now and that's the last thing I need her to be aware of.

She kills me with a sexy smile when I don't respond to what she says. "You would, wouldn't you? You'd be more than happy to sit back and watch while I touch myself and show you my favorite things."

I'm going straight to hell for allowing her to keep talking. A decent best friend would have put a stop to this as soon as it started. Not me. I want to let her keep going. I want to hear all the ways she likes to be touched. I want to beg her to describe in detail how she prefers to be fucked.

"Liv," I start but she cuts me off.

"I know. We're friends and I'm not your type. But a fantasy never hurt anyone. I'm not even a little bit sorry I touched you. It'll give me something to help Ricardo do his job." She presses both her hands to my chest. "I think I need to go to bed because the room is spinning."

My hands are instantly on her arms. "Do you feel like you're going to pass out?"

She leans into me and puts her head on my chest and murmurs, "Always my protector."

When she doesn't answer my question or lift her head again, I scoop her into my arms and carry her to the bed. By the time I get her there, she's snuggled into my chest and it's astonishing how fucking much I like that.

After I place her on the bed, she cracks her eyes open. "I can't wear this dress to bed, Callan."

I stare at the burnt orange dress she's wearing. I only know that's the name of the color because we had a ten-minute conversation about this dress today. I know more about dress rules for wedding guests than I ever needed to know. Right now, I wish I knew the accepted rule for helping your best friend remove a cocktail dress when she's too drunk to do it herself.

"I'll get your pajamas."

"No, just help me get this off." She rolls onto her stomach and says into the bed, "Undo my zipper."

Christ.

Straight. To. Hell.

I should have called Sasha the minute Liv started putting her hands on me.

Except she's out of action so I can't really be blamed for letting this happen.

I lean down and without taking my time I unzip the dress. She rolls onto her back and wiggles around a bit, shimmying the dress down her body. When it reaches her feet, she gives it a little kick and it lands on the floor, at which point I collect it and hang it in the closet. I do all of this without looking at her body even though that's the only place I want to look.

"Okay," I call out from the closet, "I'm gonna go. Call me if you need me."

"Callan, wait. I need you."

I close my eyes and beg for guidance. I don't know who the fuck I'm begging, but surely one of the gods that people worship is around and can help a guy out.

When I go back to Liv and find her lying sprawled on her stomach again, I know I've seriously pissed the gods of the world off and am now being punished. She's wearing a thong. A fucking thong of all the underwear she could have chosen for today. And hell, her ass is fucking perfect. I try like fuck not to dedicate time to it but I'm no saint. It's fast becoming apparent that it's in my DNA to do the opposite of what I should do when it comes to Olivia.

"What are you doing?" I ask when I realize she's trying to reach something across the bed.

"I need my phone charger so I can plug it in on this side of the bed."

Before I see it coming, she's lifting herself up onto her

knees. In the process, she shoves her ass in the air and I get an eyeful of body parts I should never have seen.

"Fuck, Liv, let me do it." I'm around the bed faster than I've ever moved and have retrieved the charger. Less than a minute later, it's plugged in on the other side of the bed with her phone connected. I then pull the sheet up and cover her from head to toe before sternly saying, "Don't move from this bed. Go straight to sleep and don't get into any more trouble."

I shove my fingers through my hair and exhale a long breath as she scrunches her beautiful face up at me. "Why are you cranky Callan right now?"

"Because it's been a long weekend and I'm tired. Go to sleep. I'll see you in the morning."

The last thing I hear before her hotel door room clicks closed behind me is her cute little snore. And fuck me, I even find her gorgeous when she snores.

7

OLIVIA

"I don't think meditation is for me," Blair says on Monday night as we walk home after finishing the meditation class she insisted on attending with me.

"I agree. And if I get kicked out of this class because of your behavior tonight, you will never hear the end of it."

"In my defense, I was unaware cell phones aren't allowed in a meditation class. That's on you for not advising me."

I roll my eyes as we round the corner into my street. "You're the smartest woman I know. There's no way you weren't aware that meditation means no phones and no talking."

She shrugs. "Sasha told me she took a call during the class when you forced her into going."

"And that's why Sasha is also barred from my class. You're both banned as of this minute."

My cell phone notifies me of a text and I check it immediately because I'm waiting on something for work. After I read the text, I look at Blair. "I'm quitting my job."

"Penelope again?"

My chest feels like everything inside it is tightening in one big knot. "Yes. That woman is one of the most conniving, scheming, calculating, dishonest women I've ever met."

"What's she done now?"

She says *now* because Penelope has been angering me all day and Blair's the one I've texted each time to vent to. I think it's the main reason she told me she was joining my meditation class tonight; she was worried my sanity was almost out the window.

"She responded to my cease and desist with a request for more information, which is bullshit even though I expected it. And now my name has started popping up on gossip accounts."

She frowns. "Your name? Why?"

I show her the Instagram post that Slade just sent me.

@thetea_gasp

Besties! WTF is happening over at New York Power HQ? Three of their players are out of control and their teammates are turning against them #gasp The latest word on the street is that @macehawkins is on his way out thanks to his ex who has gone cray cray since he dumped her. Mace is still cash IMO and we'd be sad if the team boots him, but we've all seen men fall over lesser things, so it's not looking good for him. And then there's li'l old @sladesullivan who can't catch a break. His ex was spotted on the arm of another player over

the weekend and he full lost his grip on life for a hot minute #gasp which we bet is only causing even more issues between teammates. Boys, maybe it's time to dump the girl you hired to fix your shiz. @olivialancaster is so mid these days. You can both do better.

Blair looks up at me. "You think Penelope is behind this?"

"I know she is."

"How?"

"She called me this afternoon and used some of these words during the conversation in which she threatened me."

"Threatened you how?"

The knot in my chest pulls harder. "She said I'd live to regret getting in the middle of her business, and that she hoped I wasn't too attached to my career."

"That bitch." Blair has the look in her eyes that she gets when she's ready to go to war. And she would if I asked her to. Blair would walk through hell for her inner circle.

"I don't have time for this. Running around after these guys is one thing, but having to watch my back because I've stepped in drama is a whole other thing." I rub my temple. "And trying to think about any of this while dealing with this headache is too much. Not even meditation helped!"

"You've *still* got that headache? I hate to say it, but I don't think whiskey is the life for you."

It's not! I want to wail. My hangover from the weekend has been next level. Yesterday was atrocious and I'm actually not sure how Callan didn't end our friendship with all the whining I did. Today has been only slightly better. And if I wake tomorrow still feeling ill, I swear I'll crawl in a hole and never come out.

"I agree. It ruined a good weekend."

She stops walking and turns to face me. "Okay, we need to talk."

I take in the serious expression on her face. "Oh God, you're not going to tell me you think my headache isn't from my hangover but rather from something far worse, are you? I don't think I have it in me to hear that you think I'm dying."

She stares at me with disbelief for the longest moment. "This is why you and Sasha are such good friends. You both worry about dumb things."

"It's not dumb. Not when there's a thirty-nine percent risk of a woman developing cancer."

She continues staring at me while slowly shaking her head. "You are the very reason why the internet should never have been created."

"I am the very reason why people like you will live longer. I learn how to mitigate the risk and pass that information on. Thanks to the internet. You're welcome."

She rolls her eyes. "Your headache is from the whiskey. I have zero doubt about that. I also have zero doubt that you're keeping information from me."

"What information?" I work hard not to bite my lip which is one of my tells when I am in fact keeping information from someone.

"I want to know what really happened between you and Callan over the weekend. That story you gave me about nothing happening was bullshit. You forget that I always know when you're lying."

Blair grilled me about the weekend, wanting a blow-by-blow of every little thing. She hasn't come out and said it, but I know she's convinced that all the weddings Callan and I attend will somehow bring us together. The last thing I want to do is fuel that belief, so I told her I got drunk and went to bed early. I didn't tell her anything else I remember from that night.

My headache takes this very moment to pound harder against my skull, and I blame this for my inability to withhold information a second longer. "I woke up on Sunday morning wearing only my underwear," I blurt, "and I have a vague recollection of Callan helping me undress."

"Well, that's boring. Anything else?"

My eyes go wide. "That's *not* boring! I was wearing a thong that covers practically nothing."

"I'm one thousand percent convinced that Callan has seen a thong or two in his life," she says dryly.

"Yes, but he's never seen my thong or the ass it wasn't covering."

"Your ass could do with some action of the Callan type. I imagine it was a fun night for all. What else aren't you telling me?"

I bite my lip. Blair's brows arch at that and I know there's no turning back now. "Apparently, I told him all about my sex life and how bad it is. I can't remember that, but I do have flashes of memory that make me think I said something about him not being bad at sex and that he'd let me show him all the things I like a guy to do to me."

Blair's eyes sparkle. They literally glitter with glee. "That's my girl. Have you guys talked about that?"

My eyes go even wider than before. "I can never ask him about that part of the conversation! I'm horrified to think I might have said that to him."

She laughs. "We both know that if there's one thing Callan loves to talk about, it's sex. I imagine he enjoyed you saying that to him. Okay, so to recap, he likely undressed your drunk ass and put you to bed. He then drove you home yesterday and told you he knows all about your sex life, but he didn't tell you he undressed you or that you said lewd things to him?"

"Yes. All of that."

"And he's not weirded out over the weekend like you appear to be?"

"No, he's being normal. So, maybe he didn't undress me and maybe I'm making that conversation up in my head."

"Let the record show that I, for one, hope you did say that to him."

"Let the record show that there will be no more whiskey. Ever."

"That's what you always say. I don't believe you anymore."

"You should believe me. My ass believes me. It never wants my best friend to have to see it again."

"How I managed to find the prudiest prude of a best friend, I shall never know. Asses are on display everywhere in the world. Also, what a lovely gift to give your best friend. I hope he appreciated it."

"My ass is special to me. It will never be on display for the world to see."

Affection softens her gaze. "And that is one of the things I adore about you. While the world is throwing its morals away left, right, and center, I love knowing that my best friend is holding onto hers tightly. It gives me hope that maybe we're not as doomed as I think we are." She nods at my phone. "What did Slade have to say about that Insta post?"

"He apologized for his blowup over the weekend and that it's caused people to think badly of me. I never saw the day coming where Slade Sullivan would apologize for his bad behavior."

"You should have. You always work your magic on these guys. Whoever runs that Instagram account is an idiot for listening to any of this gossip."

"They'll realize their error soon enough."

Blair nods knowingly. "Yes, they will." She knows I have my ways of dealing with this kind of thing. I wouldn't be a good crisis manager if I didn't.

My phone alerts me to another text and I want to throw it away, much like I wanted to at the wedding on Saturday. I don't want to read one more email, text, or Instagram post today.

> **KRISTEN**
>
> Please tell me you're still coming tonight. I just got my period and have no supplies! And neither does Ingrid. I'm hoping you can bring me something.

"Oh, shit!" I look at Blair. "I forgot I told Callan I'd drop by his parents' place tonight to say hi to Bradford and Kristen who just got home from their honeymoon."

I tap out a reply to Kristen.

I'll be there soon and I'll bring you
supplies.

I love you even more now.

I smile at her text. I met Kristen last year when she
was in the middle of the scandal that her marriage to
Bradford caused, and I felt an instant connection with
her. She's got a vulnerability about her that I like. She
puts her heart out in the world even when she's trying so
hard to guard it. I like people like that.

"Okay, I've gotta cancel on our tea date, I'm sorry."
Blair is my one and only friend who loves tea as much as
I do and we'd planned to go back to my place and drink
some while doing face masks.

She waves me off. "Don't worry about me. I'm gonna
go home and get Bob out."

A memory crashes into me and I stare at her with
wide eyes. "Holy shit, I think I told Callan about Ricardo
when I was drunk. I think I detailed my Spanish fantasy
for him. I really am never drinking whiskey again."

She grins. "I hope you did. That would have been
another wonderful gift for him."

Ten minutes later, I've walked to Callan's parents'
condo and spiraled all the way down into thoughts about
the things I might have told him while I was drunk. I'm
not a prude, even if by Blair's standards I am, however I
don't tend to get into conversations about my sexual
fantasies. My sex life is the one area of my life I don't feel
confident in and I feel awkward talking about it.

By the time I arrive at his parents' home, I'm all up in

my mortified feels and am glad that Callan isn't the first person I see. I need a moment to shake off these feelings before I see him.

His mom, Ingrid, greets me when I step out of the elevator, and pulls me in close for a hug. "How are you, darling? And why haven't I seen you for weeks?"

I adore Callan's mother and often drop by to spend time with her, especially since my parents live in the same tower. She's loved me like a daughter since the day her sons took me under their wings when I was eight and I think of her as my second mother. "I've been busy with work. I've only seen my parents once in the last few weeks too. You weren't home the night I visited them."

She gives me a gentle smile. "Your mom told me you're going to help Harper plan her wedding. I imagine that will take up a lot of your time."

Gage wanders over. "Harper's getting married?"

"Yes, in six months, and she's asked me to plan it because her mother wants the wedding to be held in New York rather than Paris."

"I bet her mother does." Gage is one of the most perceptive men I know. Most people think he's a rich, self-absorbed asshole but I know that while he can be an asshole, he's more attentive to others than most people. He notices everything about people and cares deeply for those he's brought in close. He understands exactly why my aunt wants Harper to get married in New York. I imagine he's also already put it together in his mind why I've said yes to being the wedding planner.

Callan and his family know my history with my cousins, but Gage is the one who was there on the day tragedy struck. My youngest cousin was killed in a hit and run while I was supposed to be looking after her, and Gage witnessed it all. I was ten, he was eleven, but he stepped into much older shoes that day when he helped me live through each harrowing second. And he's never stopped watching over me, making sure I'm okay, because the guilt I've carried has been heavy.

Harper's mother became a helicopter parent after her youngest daughter's death and Gage knows this, which is why he's looking at me with understanding right now.

Not wanting to talk about this too much, because I know Gage always wants to challenge me on the guilt I still feel, I smile brightly at Ingrid and say, "I love this new hair color! Did you end up changing to a new hairdresser?"

She touches her shiny brunette hair that now has summer highlights. "No, I stayed with George and I'm glad I did. I think he's been going through something with his boyfriend the last six months and that's why he was so distracted and misunderstood what I asked for each appointment." She catches sight of Kristen coming our way. "Gage and I will leave you two girls. Can I get you a drink, Olivia?"

My headache reminds me that the last thing my body needs is alcohol. "No, I'm good thanks."

Gage gives me one last glance of *this conversation isn't finished* before leaving with his mother.

I smile at Kristen as I take the period supplies out of my purse and hand them over. "I can't wait to hear all about your honeymoon."

"You're a lifesaver. Also, I'm coming back as a man in any future lives I have to live. Bradford can take a turn as the woman next time." She holds the tampons up. "Let him deal with this hell!"

"I'd love to see Bradford deal with a period," Callan says when he comes to stand with us.

His arm brushes mine as Kristen excuses herself and I'm instantly aware of a new tension between us. A vibration that speeds my heartbeat and shoots electricity through my limbs. Callan's eyes, deep and intense, hold mine in a magnetic gaze, suspending time around us. A rush of heat blooms at the base of my spine and radiates outward, making my skin flush with warmth.

I have no idea what's happening. Surely I'm imagining it.

But it's right there, in the way his gaze drops to my throat. In the way his eyes linger there. In the way heat flares between us.

I'm lost, floundering in this moment when he finally glances up and says, "I was beginning to think you weren't coming, Ace."

Butterflies in the thousands unleash themselves in my stomach and the air is sucked from my lungs at what I see in Callan's eyes. He's looking at me like he's been waiting for me. Like I'm the only reason he's here. *Like I've completed his day.*

I steady myself, because I think that if I don't, my knees may just give way. "It's been a day." Those are the only words I can manage. In fact, they may be the only words I utter tonight if the current state of my brain is anything to go by.

I'm bewildered.

And I think perhaps still drunk.

That's the only reason I can come up with for

thinking Callan's looking at me differently than he's always looked at me.

Concern flashes across his face. "What happened?"

We spoke at our usual time of eleven this morning but haven't spoken since. It's unusual for me to choose Blair to vent to, but because all my problems are because of Penelope, I haven't wanted to drag Callan into it. So, he is unaware of any of the hell she's causing me.

I bite my lip, trying to figure out what to share with him.

"Liv," he says, his voice low and deep. "Don't keep stuff from me. What's going on?"

"Damn you for knowing all my tells," I mutter softly, to which he simply raises his brows and waits. "Ugh. Your friend, Penelope, is what's going on."

More brow arching. "*My* friend?"

My arm flies up all by itself in a wild gesture I'm unable to control. "Yes, *your* friend. I have no idea how you can't see her true colors. She's spreading lies and rumors, causing problems for me and my clients. And she's had the audacity to demand more information from *me* as to what she should cease and desist. Honestly!" I stop talking abruptly, having already said more than I intended.

Callan's jaw clenches and anger darkens his gaze. "Tell me exactly what she's done. And don't leave a single thing out."

Holy god, the intensity blazing from him is unlike anything I've ever seen.

When I stall because I'm so struck by that intensity, he growls, "Olivia."

I blink.

Callan has never used that growly voice on me. Never ever *ever*. And I can't deny how much I like it. I can't deny how much my body likes it.

I launch into an account of everything that has transpired today and he listens intently. When I get to the end, I say, "I will still be your friend if you ever decide you want her to be your plus-one again but you should know that I won't be a fan of that decision."

"I won't ever make that decision."

I feel immediate and immense relief at that.

"I'll call her tomorrow and find out what the hell game she's playing at," he adds while I'm still processing my relief.

"Oh god, no. Don't do that."

"I'm not just going to stand back and let her attack you." The ferocious determination in his voice reaches out to me and pulls me further into his web. Callan has always made me feel protected and safe; those feelings are heightened by his desire to stride into my problems and solve them for me. But I can't let him do that. I need to protect him. Goodness knows what she'd do to him if he pisses her off too.

"You *can* stand back. I don't want to put you at risk."

"You're not putting me at risk."

I step closer and touch his arm. "Please don't get involved. This is my work and I have to handle it appropriately."

His eyes search mine for the longest moment. "Okay. But if she pushes this and it hurts you, there's not one thing you can say that will hold me back."

My heart melts.

I'm still convinced I'm imagining the shift in vibe

between us, but for now I'm choosing to indulge in the butterflies fluttering wildly in my stomach.

This is what it would feel like to be loved by Callan.

Deep intense affection.

Next level attention.

Steadfast protection.

I'm beginning to question if I could actually survive being with him because right now I'm finding it hard to breathe while he looks at me the way he is.

8

CALLAN

OLIVIA IS GLOWING. She wasn't when she arrived, but she is now. Actually, the glow in her cheeks is more of a blush, and fuck if I don't like that pink on her.

Hell, there are a lot of new things I like about her. Far too many to count and they've all been messing with me since Saturday night when she got drunk and asked me if I ever think about us being together.

I've gone round and round with this for days, wondering if this is new for her too. I've not seen any evidence in our friendship that she's thought about this previously, but then there are things she's not felt comfortable telling me before, so I'm questioning everything.

She woke with a fucker of a hangover yesterday and no memory of the things we talked about or of the fact I helped her out of her dress. Knowing she's a private person when it comes to her body and would be mortified over the knowledge I undressed her, I kept that to myself. I also kept most of our conversation to myself.

I'm un-fucking-sure what to do here, but I know for certain that if we get our feelings out in the open, we won't ever be able to put them back in their box. And our friendship would never be the same.

"Thank you," she says after I tell her I'll honor her wish for me to not get involved in her situation with Penny.

I meant it when I said nothing would hold me back if Penny hurts her. I've never felt so sure of something as I am of this. Or felt a decision so deeply in my bones. Olivia is precious and there's no fucking way I'll allow anyone to cause her pain.

A text comes through for me and I'm stunned when I see my brother's name on the screen.

ETHAN

I got your text. I'm out.

"What is it?" Olivia asks after I read the message. My face must show my disappointment.

I meet her gaze. "Ethan's out for the Alps."

"Oh, I didn't realize you guys were still talking about doing that."

I shove my phone in my trousers. "We weren't, but I was hoping he'd pull his head from his ass and let shit go so we still could." My words taste as bitter as they sound. Before he left New York, Ethan and I had been making plans to highline in the French Alps. Since I haven't been able to get an answer out of him for months, I figured he'd changed his mind but I still held a glimmer of hope.

"I'm sorry. I know you were looking forward to that."

"I'll still do it."

Her eyes widen a little. "Oh. Okay." She pulls her

bottom lip between her teeth. "Are you still planning on doing it at that place that has 400-foot cliffs?"

"You're thinking of the canyon in Utah where we train. The Alps is higher."

"That's so high, Callan. What if you hurt yourself?" Now, her eyes go wider. "Oh god, you're not going to do it alone, are you? Is that even possible?"

Fuck, her worry is endearing. "I'd never highline alone, Ace. I'll find someone to do it with. And there's no need to worry. You know I believe in safety all the way."

I've been slacklining for five years and moved onto highlining two years ago. Walking ropes up high is the greatest challenge I've ever found in life. It pushes me physically and mentally and helps me shed fears as I progress to greater heights. I credit the sport for my success in business. The mental levels it pushes me through helps me do the same in my work. I know Olivia worries about it but I train hard and take all the safety precautions I can.

"I know, but that doesn't make it any easier when I know you're walking across a thin piece of rope over a canyon with a 400-foot drop. I much preferred it when you slacklined in a park and I brought you ice cream to celebrate no broken bones. If you survive the Alps, it'll be on you to bring *me* ice cream to celebrate the fact I don't have to order you a coffin."

I chuckle. "I promise you I won't require a coffin."

She gets a bossy look about her. "You better not, Callan Black, or you will incur my wrath for eternity when I get to heaven and hunt you down."

"Are you threatening him again?" Bradford asks, joining us with a smile on his face.

"Yes, because he needs a good threatening," Olivia says.

"Before you get too engrossed in that, are we all still planning on heading to the Catskills next month?"

"Yes," Olivia says before rattling off the date. "Tell me that weekend still works for you and Kristen."

"I think so. I'll check with her and let you know."

"I'm praying it does. Wrangling you and your brothers is hard work, and settling on that date took over a month of back and forth with everyone," she says.

"We like to keep you on your toes." He grins. "I'll make it work, Liv."

"Are my sons giving you grief?" Mom asks when she joins our group.

"Always," Olivia says but the affection in her tone reveals how much she likes wrangling our family.

"Well, you've got me now to help you plan these weekends," Kristen says to Olivia while coming to stand next to Bradford, an adoring look in her eyes as she gazes up at him. The day he married her instead of Cecelia was a good fucking day. I shudder to think of what would have become of family vacations with that dragon woman along for the ride.

"This makes me very happy," Olivia says. "Between work being super busy, planning a wedding for my cousin, and attending a million weddings with Callan, it'll be great to have your help."

"How about I take charge of coordinating the guys while you plan everything else? I don't want to step on your toes, though, so whatever you need me to do, just let me know," Kristen says.

"When she says 'coordinate', I'm almost certain she means 'boss'," I say.

Olivia grins at me. "Which is exactly the right word for what you guys need." She looks at Kristen. "Thank you. I would love you to be in charge of bossing the boys."

I turn silent while Mom, Olivia, and Kristen talk about the trip and the spa Olivia wants to visit. Olivia is radiating with the kind of beauty that can't be dimmed. Not even a hangover and five straight hours of complaining like she did yesterday can lessen it. And while physically, she's the most beautiful woman I know, so much of what makes her beautiful is her soul. Her way of loving people and caring for them. I've always been drawn to this, but now, I'm captivated by it.

I could watch her with my family for hours. Hell, I could watch her for hours period. It wouldn't matter what she was doing, I'd happily dedicate myself to taking in every single thing she did. But watching the way she listens intently to my mother; seeing how she encourages Kristen when she appears uncertain; observing how she expresses her interest in everything being said; and receiving a smile or a sparkle of her eyes every once in a while throughout the conversation, *this* is something I could do day in, day out.

The thing about all this that confuses the hell out of me is that none of this is new. This is what she's always done, and somehow, I've never seen any of it the way I'm seeing it now. I've never *felt* it the way I'm feeling it now.

The conversation shifts and changes, and Bradford and I offer our thoughts every now and then as to what we're interested in doing during the weekend away. When the topic of hiking comes up, Mom mentions a trail she's heard about. She drags Bradford and Kristen to her computer to show them while I reach for Olivia and hold her back so I can talk to her about the week ahead.

"I have to fly to LA tomorrow and depending on how my meetings go there, I may need to go to Vancouver after that," I say. "So, I may not be able to meet with your contractor on Wednesday." After getting quotes from five contractors, Olivia's remodel is beginning this week and I want to meet the guy she hired. After much deliberation and encouragement from this particular contractor, she decided to also remodel both her bathrooms. I'm concerned the guy is rushing the job. I want to meet him so he knows I'm watching his work and looking for any corners being cut.

She waves me off. "I've got this, Callan. I know you're worried about this guy, but I looked into his work history. His work is high quality. I don't foresee any problems."

"I know you did, Ace, but I still want him to know there will be repercussions if he screws you over."

She smiles. "I appreciate you looking out for me. You can come over and meet him when you get back."

"Trust me, I'll be over the minute I get home."

"When do you think that will be?"

"Hopefully by Thursday, but it may be Friday. I might be pushing it to get to the Hamptons on time Friday." The second wedding we're attending is for a couple we've both known for years. They've invited their guests for a welcome party that kicks off at lunchtime on Friday.

"Oh god, me too. I've got a day of interviews lined up for Slade and I think I'm going to have to hold his hand during them. If so, I won't arrive until late Friday afternoon, which sucks because I was really looking forward to the spa afternoon with the girls."

I push my irritation with Slade down and try to ignore it even though I'm doubtful I can. "We'll take the helicopter, so that will help."

"Yes, and I'll do everything in my power during the week to convince Slade he doesn't need a babysitter."

I'm more than grateful when Hayden takes this moment to cut in on our conversation. It was on the tip of my tongue to tell her what I think of a grown man being unable to handle his own shit.

"I hate to do this," Hayden says to Olivia, looking as regretful as he sounds, "but can you give me ten minutes so we can go over something that's come up for Bradford."

"Sure," Olivia says before leaving with him.

I watch her until they disappear down the hallway that leads to Dad's office where I imagine Bradford and Dad are waiting for them. Hayden is Bradford's lawyer and from what I heard them talking about earlier, they're working on mitigating any headaches that arise from the disgrace Bradford's ex-fiancée has recently found herself in. Besides being investigated for tax fraud thanks to a tip off from Bradford, her ties to a crime boss have been made public, along with rumors of complex financial crimes she's supposedly committed. Her offices were raided today, and while Bradford's not linked to her anymore, he and Dad want to ensure his name isn't smeared.

"So, you're finally opening your eyes," Gage drawls as he hands me a whiskey.

"Huh?"

He nods in the direction of where Olivia went. "Liv."

I throw some whiskey down my throat. "What are you talking about?"

"I saw how you're looking at her tonight."

My gut reaction is to tell him to fuck off, that he's imagining things, but after weeks of being tied up in knots over my feelings, I've reached the point where I need to talk about it. "I don't know what's happening, but I'm pretty sure I'm about to fuck things up between us."

He watches me over the rim of his glass while he takes a sip. "What's happening is what was always going to happen. I'm only surprised it's taken this long."

I frown. Rhodes said something similar on the weekend and I haven't been able to get that conversation out of my head. "Liv and I have never been attracted to each other, Gage."

"Yeah, you have. Why do you think you've fucked your way through New York and never been interested in a relationship?"

"Fuck, is this going to be one of your therapy sessions? I'm out if it is." Gage likes to dissect people and I'm in no mood for that tonight.

He ignores me and carries on. "Why do you think the only relationship you've had was at the same time that Olivia fell in love for the first time?"

I take another gulp of whiskey. "You're connecting things that aren't connected."

"You hated watching her with that guy so you found yourself a girlfriend to distract you."

I want to tell him he's wrong, but my gut is insistent there's some truth in what he's saying.

He watches me closely while I work my way through

a million thoughts. "You're in love with Olivia, Callan, and you always have been. But watching Mom and Dad fucked you up and you're shut down on relationships because of what you fear marriage does to people. Take another look at their marriage and you'll see what's possible when two people work at a relationship."

Kristen waves him over to where she and Mom are looking at something on Mom's laptop, leaving me alone with that bomb.

Jesus.

My parents didn't marry for love. It was a marriage of convenience to bring their two families together. It was a long-term project to build power so they could eventually get a son into politics. They brought five sons into a marriage that was filled with turmoil and we all paid the price for that. Not that I was aware of much of this during my childhood. I was a happy child but I always sensed trouble and I sure as fuck knew it took a lot of effort to get my parents' attention for the first decade of my life.

Some light was recently shed on that. It turns out my father cheated on my mother just after I was born and so they were both preoccupied with that mess for years. Looking back, I can see how that played out in our lives. Gage wasn't wrong when he said I use my parents' marriage as my reason for avoiding relationships. They may be happy together now, but I can never unknow the deep unhappiness we all lived through when they were fighting all the time.

I do love Olivia.

As a friend.

And that's all it can ever be.

9

CALLAN

"I'M ON MY WAY!" Olivia says just after one p.m. on Friday afternoon. "If everything goes to plan, I'll only be five or so minutes late for the spa."

She sounds breathless like she's been running, which I highly doubt. Liv wears heels everywhere. And also, she's not a runner. She swears running was created by the devil.

I don't think too much about this, though, because I'm currently staring at the queen bed in our suite. It's *our* suite because the hotel screwed up and didn't book a room for me. When this mistake was discovered upon my arrival, they fixed the problem by giving us an upgraded suite. With only one bed.

I pull at my tie to loosen it and bring my focus back to my conversation with Olivia. "I'll see you when you get here."

It's been a long week of rumination for me while I was away for work. After trying to put all the thoughts from my mind that Gage stirred up, I soon came to the realization that I can't put Olivia out of my head. She lives there permanently and with ease.

She's there when I wake every morning and wonder if she slept well.

She's there when I get dressed and imagine what it would be like to share a bedroom with her. When I imagine watching her dress, fix her hair, apply her makeup.

She's there when I come home from a long day and think about how much I'd like to come home to her.

And she's there first thing in the morning, mid-morning, at lunch, mid-afternoon, and throughout the night when I'm playing out all the ways I'd peel her clothes from her, kiss her, and make her come.

This queen bed may be the death of me.

After we end our call, I look through the welcome basket Charlene and Joe had delivered to the suite. I find an assortment of gifts inside, including T-shirts, a sleep mask, a candle, chocolates, a bottle of champagne, and fruit. I open the envelope that has information inside regarding the spa afternoon Olivia's attending. I don't intend on reading it once I see what it's about, however at the very top, written in bold is a message that Charlene would like all the girls to arrive earlier at 1:45 p.m. so they can give the therapists their massage requests.

I pull out my phone and send Joe a text.

CALLAN

> I can't make golf at 1:30 now. Can we push it back half an hour?

JOE

I'll check with the guys and get back to you. If not, just come late.

If there's one thing I know about Olivia's visits to the day spa, it's that she has many preferences. Since she won't be able to arrive early to detail her requests, I'll make sure the therapists have the information so she can just go straight into her massage and get what she wants.

I spend the next half hour working. I then dress for golf and make my way down to the day spa where I find at least twenty women crowding the small reception area.

"Callan!" Charlene greets me with the widest smile I think I've ever seen. She pulls me in for a hug and squeezes me tightly. "Where's Olivia?"

"She'll be here soon but not in time to let the therapists know her massage preferences."

"Oh, that's okay. We'll figure it out when she gets here."

I step to the side when a bunch of the women propel themselves forward, squeezing more people into this space than it was made for. Once they move past us, I say, "No, I know what she'll want, so I can let the therapist know."

Surprise nudges Charlene's brows up. "Really?"

"Yeah." I glance around the room taking in the number of women in here. They're all wearing matching pink T-shirts that say *Bride Squad*, white retro pearl heart-shaped sunglasses, and hair accessories that also alert me to the fact they're part of the bride squad. It's hectic and noisy. The sooner I get out of here, the better.

"Wow. That's impressive. Joe wouldn't have the first clue as to what I like."

The woman behind the reception desk waves me over. "Hello, Sir. What can I do for you?"

"My friend is coming in for a massage and I want to give you her requests."

"Absolutely. What's her name?"

"Olivia Lancaster."

"And what kind of massage would she like?" She lists five different options.

I shake my head. "No, none of those. She prefers a therapeutic massage with Swedish style strokes, but the pressure needs to be in between Swedish and deep tissue."

"Okay." The woman makes a note and then smiles. "Thank you. I'll be sure to let our therapist know."

When she glances at the next person in line, I say, "She has other preferences I'd like you to note as well."

"Oh. Okay, what are they?"

"She doesn't like patchouli."

The woman nods. "I'll make a note."

"She doesn't like it when the therapist puts essential oil in the space under the table near her face."

"Okay."

"She prefers more time spent on her feet than her legs and arms."

"Right."

"She doesn't like her scalp being massaged with oil. She'd prefer the therapist to wash her hands first."

"Yes."

"Right, that's it, I think. Please don't let her know I

told you all these things. She would never ask for all this and would be horrified that I did."

The woman smiles. "Your wife is a very lucky woman to have such an attentive and caring husband."

Before I can correct her, Charlene takes hold of my arm and pulls me to the side. "Can you do me a favor?"

"That depends."

She grins. "Smart man not to commit before you know what I want but this will be easy. I've got a surprise for Joe after he finishes golfing but it won't be ready until five p.m. Can you please make sure he doesn't come back until then?"

I agree to her request and leave the chaos of the spa to head out for the game of golf with the boys. On my way, I shoot Olivia a text.

CALLAN

Enjoy your massage, Ace.

OLIVIA

OMG I can't wait! I need it after this week. You should have booked one too! I don't think that massage you got last weekend even scratched the surface of your knots.

CALLAN

Fuck no. I just saw how many women are lining up for a massage. It's bedlam.

OLIVIA

Where's the Callan I know? The one who would happily surround himself with that many women? LOL!

She has no idea.

No idea that the real reason I haven't had sex for weeks is because I only want to have it with her.

CALLAN

> One other thing: the hotel screwed up my reservation and have put us in a suite together. I've left a room card at reception for you.

I've spent the last hour thinking about it and have decided I'll take the couch tonight. There is no way I'll be able to lie next to her and not want to fuck her.

10

OLIVIA

I stare at the bed.

The only bed in the suite.

Holy shit, *no*.

I need my own room.

This suite might be lavish with its soft, thick carpet that makes me feel like I'm floating, its chandeliers, and its cream and gold touches, but it won't do. The man at reception told me they don't have any more rooms, though, so what I really need is a new hotel.

The fact Callan didn't mention that there's only one bed must mean he doesn't have any problems with it. I imagine he could sleep next to me all night without a care in the world.

God.

Why did I let Blair convince everyone that being Callan's plus-one for an entire season was a good idea?

She must go.

When I get home from this weekend, I'm giving her her marching orders.

We can no longer be friends.

Or, maybe all I need to do is sage her.

Yes, I'll try that first because she really is a good friend. Except for this one inconvenient little part of her that thinks Callan and I should be together.

"Ace."

I didn't hear Callan come in and I jump at his voice. "Jesus, you just gave me a heart attack! Why do you have to be so good at being all stealth-like?"

His lips quirk in amusement while he walks to the bed and drops his cap on the other side of where I'm standing. I guess that's the side he's claiming. "You were staring pretty hard at this bed. Were you busy planning the demise of the person who fucked up my reservation?"

"What? No. I'm okay with sharing a room with you."

He gives me a long glance like he's trying to figure out if I'm lying. "I'll take the couch."

I eye the couch. "God no, Callan. That thing looks rock hard. It will put your back out."

"I don't mind."

I make a face at him. "Don't be silly. You're not sleeping on the couch."

He doesn't argue with me but I know that doesn't mean the argument is finished. Callan can be stubborn when he wants to be.

"How was your massage?"

"It was the most amazing massage I've ever had." I cock my head at him. "Apparently, I have my husband to thank for that."

"I asked them not to tell you that."

"They told me you gave them a list of my preferences." Warmth spreads across my chest as I think about the fact Callan not only remembers how I prefer a massage but that he took the time to go and detail this information for the therapist. "Thank you. And you should know I didn't bother to correct them that you're not my husband, which means that any woman here who doesn't know us thinks we're married. The receptionist made a big deal to anyone who would listen that my husband is the dreamiest husband ever. Sorry about that." I'm not really, though. I could get behind keeping up this charade.

He bends to untie his shoelaces and my eyes run down his body, taking in every inch of him. He's wearing navy golf shorts and a white polo, and I have trouble looking away from his tanned calf muscles. Not to mention his thighs and ass that his shorts are sitting snug against. My imagination is doing a fantastic job of picturing what's under those shorts.

"They can think what they want," he says before straightening and toeing off his shoes. "Are you still keen to go to the party tonight?"

Joe and Charlene are holding a party by the pool and while I told Callan I was excited for it, the massage has relaxed me sufficiently that all I can think about is an early bedtime and lots of glorious sleep.

"Are you?"

"I don't care either way."

I think about the bed and suddenly sleep isn't as appealing. I'm intent on Callan sharing the bed with me so the couch doesn't hurt his back, but sleeping together is the last thing I want to do. I'm going to be a hot mess with him lying right there next to me.

"Let's go to the party and see what we think. We can leave early if we want to."

He nods his agreement. "Do you want the shower first?"

"No, you go first. I'm just going to close my eyes for a second."

He grins. "We both know what that means."

Yes, usually that's the signal for *I'm actually going to sleep*. But not now. "Nope, not today. I want ice cream by the pool under the moonlight. If you come out from the shower and I'm asleep, wake me."

An hour later, we arrive for the pool party. I'm lost for words when I see what Charlene and Joe have created poolside. Canopies of fairy lights are strung across each of the three pools while candles of various sizes are grouped and scattered amongst floral installation art around the edge of the space. Bar tables and stools are sprinkled throughout for people to sit at, along with lounges that invite more intimate conversations. Waiters mingle, offering champagne and platters of food. It's the bar across the pool from us, though, that captivates me. It's a brilliant fusion of installation art and functionality. Vibrant, striking blooms grab attention, bursting forth from below, draping above, and cascading from counters and shelves. Animated conversations and laughter fill the air as people gather around. Every detail meticulously designed, every ornament carefully placed, the bar infuses the surroundings with the most enchanting romantic ambience I've ever encountered.

I clutch Callan's arm. "I need to think bigger for Harper's wedding. This is amazing!"

He eyes a waiter. "You need to think about eating. I heard your stomach rumble in the elevator."

"Oh my god, you did not just say that. Don't you know there are some noises a man is supposed to ignore?"

He ignores *that* and waves the waiter over. Taking a napkin from the man, he places it in my hand and proceeds to pile canapés on it. He then piles even more on another napkin for himself before thanking the waiter.

I look at his mountain of food. "I see you're even hungrier than I am."

"No, I ate late this afternoon. Most of this is for you." He lifts his chin at my napkin of food. "When you finish that, I'll get you some more. If that rumble I heard is anything to go by, you're going to need a lot more."

"If I eat all this and then more, I won't fit dinner in."

"Don't be so sure."

I playfully smack him. "You started the weekend off well with the massage, but you are fast going downhill."

There's a subtle shift in his gaze as I touch him. The tenderness I see is familiar yet carries a distinct depth, evoking the same fluttering sensations he awakened in me earlier this week. "I don't want you to starve, Ace."

My butterflies need their radar checked. I've spent years searching for a man to wake them up and it has to be said that not one of the men I've had a relationship with has excited them as much as Callan is.

"Have you ever known me to starve?" I try to ignore all the butterflies, which is a pointless endeavor. That look in Callan's eyes has them convinced their excitement is warranted.

"No, and I don't want to see it now." He's glancing around the party like he's looking for something.

"What are you looking for?"

He continues scanning. "More food. Surely they've got more variety than what you have now."

I reach for him to gain his attention because he's super intent on all that searching for food he's doing. "I have more than enough here. Stop looking and have something to eat."

He meets my gaze before eyeing the canapés in my hand. "Are you sure? I can go find you something else."

"Callan. Stop. I'm perfectly happy and nowhere near starving. I promise you."

He gives me one last questioning look before letting it go.

We're halfway through eating and discussing Callan's work trip to Vancouver when I spot Penelope Rush standing on the other side of the pool near the bar. She's with a group of women who are all laughing at something. Penelope's the only one not laughing. Instead, she's glaring at me.

I return her glare.

She's pissed off with me because I won our battle this week when I had every social media post that contained lies about my clients and me removed. I used the law and won, and it was the greatest *fuck you* I could have given her. Slade's interviews went well today and I've already seen a few positive social media pieces about him. And Mace is on track with his team who are happy with the way we've worked on his reputation this week.

Mean girls don't always win and Penelope doesn't like that one little bit. She's used to getting her own way.

"Olivia! Callan! It's so good to see you both."

I'm pulled from my thoughts about Penelope when a woman Callan and I know through Rhodes joins us. Callan's not a fan of Larissa but he pastes a smile on his face. "Larissa. How are you?"

She inches closer to him, smiling like he's the only man here. Curling her fingers around his forearm, she purrs, "I'm well. How are you? I've been hearing a lot about your company growth these last six months. It's so impressive."

"We're doing okay," he says.

"Oh, hush. You're doing more than okay." She squeezes his arm and looks at me. "He's so modest, isn't he?" Before I have even a second to reply, she turns back to him and carries on. "I've been meaning to call and chat with you about a charity gala I'm helping plan. You'll be one of our invited guests and I want to give you the date ahead of time so you can pencil it in your calendar."

"You can email my assistant and she'll make sure it gets on the calendar."

"Oh, Callan, no. I'll call you and we'll set up a dinner so I can tell you all about it."

I've always suspected Larissa was interested in Callan but this is the first time she's made a move on him. He's usually able to extricate himself from situations like this while still allowing the woman to feel good about herself, however some women are over-the-top insistent when it comes to forcing him to commit to a date and it appears that Larissa might fall into that category. I know he'll put his foot down if she refuses to take no for an answer, but I also know he won't feel good about doing that.

As he opens his mouth to reply, I step closer to him

and slide my arm around his waist. Smiling sweetly at Larissa, I say, "I'm sorry, Larissa, you mustn't have heard the news." I make sure to really lean into him. "The only woman Callan's having dinner with these days is me."

Larissa goes still and glances between Callan and me. Her features wrinkle in confusion. "Oh. Really? I thought you two were just friends."

Callan puts his arm around me as I say, "Nope, not anymore." I place my hand to his chest and look up at him with what I hope Larissa will consider adoration.

She processes this slowly before finally saying, "Well, I always wondered if you two were having some benefits on the side. It sure did seem like it."

It did?

I don't have time to contemplate that any further before Callan says, "It was great to see you, Larissa."

She gets the message and glides away after saying goodbye to us both.

I drop my hand from Callan's chest and am about to step away from him when he tightens his arm around me and drops his mouth to my ear. "I owe you for that, Ace."

I'm not sure if it's his gravelly tone, his warm breath on my skin, or his proximity, but one of those things ignites my longing for him. My skin warms and my tummy flutters as I look up into his eyes. "Anytime."

His gaze locks on mine. "I'm pretty sure one of your favorite songs just started playing. We should dance."

Those flutters in my stomach intensify. I'm beginning to wonder if my radar *isn't* off. Callan's eyes hold heat and he's looking at me in the way I've always wanted him to.

I give him a flirty smile. It's on my face before I can stop it. "You just want to see me shake my ass." The song he's referring to is one I've been known to let loose with and really get my dance on to.

His eyes smolder. "Guilty as charged."

With that, he takes hold of my hand and leads me to the dancefloor while I wonder what the heck universe I'm living in.

I think Callan might really want to see me shake my ass.

11

CALLAN

OLIVIA HAS NEVER BEEN MORE beautiful and I've never been more bewitched. I can't take my eyes off her tonight. And I'm fast moving toward being unable to keep my hands off her too.

We've been dancing for a half hour, possibly longer, and she's so fucking radiant. She's wearing a pink strapless dress that is fitted down to the waist where it billows out into a ruffled skirt. Strappy silver heels complete her outfit, but what really finishes the look so stunningly is her glow. Every inch of her is lit up with happiness and she exudes the kind of confidence that makes it look like she owns the dance floor.

I'm not the only guy who thinks so.

Three men have tried to dance with her but she's made it clear to all of them that she's with me, and hell if I don't like that. It's not lost on me that I'm feeling a level of possessiveness I've never felt. I have no idea what I would have done if she'd said yes to any of those guys.

When the current song ends and the next one starts,

her eyes blaze brightly and she reaches for me. Her fingers curve around my waist and she pulls me close. "I love this song!"

I lean my mouth down to her ear as my hand finds her hip. "You love every song."

She laughs and her eyes sparkle some more. "Not true! If they suddenly started playing that country music you love, I'd evacuate the dance floor."

"It was one song, Ace." This is what I get for turning up the sound on a country song once while we were driving home from a weekend away. She's never let me forget it.

Her grin is infectious. "That's what you say. I think you listen to country in secret because you're ashamed."

I smile as I shake my head. "Keep it up and I'll be sure to treat you to country all the way to the Catskills next month."

Her fingers dig into my waist as she tightens her hold on me. "Maybe I won't drive with you. I might go with Kristen and Bradford."

"If you think I'll allow you to drive with anyone but me, you're dreaming."

A subtle blush spreads across her cheeks and surprise sparks in her green eyes. "Are you trying to boss me, Callan Black?"

"I'm not trying. I *am* bossing you."

I can't be sure because it's difficult to hear over the music, but I would swear her breath hitched.

I spot Larissa on the edge of the dancefloor. "Larissa is watching us, so we need to convince her that you like me more than you like Ricardo."

"Oh my god!" The blush on her cheeks turns a deeper

shade of pink. "I *did* tell you about Ricardo! I wasn't imagining that!"

So, she does remember this. I've wondered all week if she recalls more about last Saturday night than she's let on. "What else do you remember?"

She hesitates before confessing, "I think I told you about my Spanish fantasy." There's uncertainty in her gaze. Maybe some nervousness. Liv doesn't openly discuss her sex life, not even with me. I get some of the details but I realized last weekend just how much she hasn't shared with me. "Did I?"

Fuck.

Her vulnerability and softness turn me on.

"Yeah, you did." My mouth brushes her ear. "And it was hot as hell."

This time, I clearly hear her intake of breath and it reminds me of what I'm putting at risk here.

I didn't intend on flirting with her like this tonight. Hell, I left our suite earlier intent on sleeping on the couch and continuing my denial of whatever this is between us. But somewhere between then and now, I veered off track. I think it was the moment she smacked me during our conversation and told me I started the weekend off well when I arranged her massage. It was such an insignificant moment but I was suddenly aware of my desire for more like it.

I want to share hotel rooms with her; make plans together; ensure she's always got everything she needs; and banter with her so I can encourage her eye rolls and playful responses.

I want to be the man who doesn't ignore her stomach

grumbling with hunger. The man who fills a thousand plates of food for her.

But I am my father's son in more ways than one and who's to say I wouldn't take what Liv and I could have and fuck it up?

She pulls her head back and stares up into my eyes, slowing time between us. There's a question in her eyes and I know exactly what it is because it's the same one I'm wrestling with. *What's happening here?*

I suck in a breath when her hand moves around from my waist and skims over the edge of my abs.

Fuck.

I want her hands there. Now, tomorrow, the next day.

Her fingers move over my abs like they're mapping them. Fuck, I want that too. I want her to know every line, every ridge. "I told you that I thought you'd be good at sex."

I don't take my eyes off her. "I'd let you teach me how you like it."

Her lips part slightly as her breathing turns shallow. "You held my hair while I vomited."

"I did."

"No man has ever done that for me before."

"You've been dating the wrong men, Liv."

That slows her down. Her eyes search mine more deeply while my words work their way into her soul. "You undressed me." It's a statement but I hear the question in her tone.

"Yes." I snake my hand around her hip and splay my fingers across the small of her back. "You told me you couldn't wear your dress to bed. You were very demanding."

"Oh god." Nervous laughter spills from her. "I'm sorry."

"Don't be." I try to stop my next words from landing between us, but they're out of my mouth before my brain gets a say. "You own some sexy underwear, Ace."

Her body sways into mine and my gut tightens. She's in this with me. *So* fucking in this. "I can never drink whiskey again. You should make sure of it."

I apply slight pressure to her back, forcing her harder against me. "You can count on me. But you should know that out of every moment we've ever shared, that afternoon is at the top of my list."

She blinks like I've just said something she can't wrap her head around. I see the moment she decides to put a stop to everything. After all these years of being her best friend, I know the sequence of events when Olivia compartmentalizes things. I see her mind working as she opens a box, puts what doesn't work for her in it, and seals it closed.

She removes her hand from my body and steps back. "It was a crazy afternoon." She gives me wide eyes and a smile that doesn't reach her eyes. "So much fun, but seriously, that hangover was the absolute worst."

I want to tell her I can't compartmentalize what's happening between us any longer. I want to tell her I'm going fucking crazy from not telling her that she's on my mind every second of every day. But I don't. I keep it all to myself and let her have what she needs.

"No more whiskey. I'm on it."

Her smile grows but it still doesn't find its way to her eyes. "Something else I need you to remind me of is that the first time a girl wears new shoes, it should not be to a party."

"Why not?"

"They should be worn for short periods to begin with to break them in." She looks at her shoes. "I should have worn these to a lunch or dinner a few times so I was splitting the time between standing and sitting. I think I'm going to have a blister after tonight."

I glance down at her shoes that are some of the sexiest, strappiest heels I've ever seen. "Have you got other shoes for tomorrow night?" From what Joe told me yesterday, they've gone all out and are putting on a wedding reception no one will forget anytime soon.

"Yes." She gives me an apologetic look. "I think I need to call tonight quits or else my feet will go on strike for the rest of the weekend. But you can stay if you want. You don't have to leave just because I am."

Fuck, I've pushed her too far. Liv is a runner when it comes to men. I've watched her do it with every relationship and almost every date that looked like it could turn into something more. She reaches a point where she lets fear control her and ends things before more is demanded than she thinks she has to give.

There's no fucking way I'll let her run from me. I'll deal with my feelings on my own and not force them upon her if that's what it takes to keep her in my life.

In an effort to lighten the mood and bring us back to normal, I say, "I better come with you in case your feet die on the way back to the suite and you need someone to carry you."

Now, her eyes crinkle. "See, this is why you're my best friend. You always make the needed sacrifices for me."

Right.

Best friend.

I got carried away there for a minute.

We search for Joe and Charlene to say goodbye but fail to locate them. Olivia's manners make it so she doesn't want to leave without finding them, however her feet are clear in that they've had enough.

We've almost reached our suite when her phone rings. I know the ringtone to be the one she reserves for Hayden. Not a good sign when her boss is calling at this time on a Friday night, especially when he knows she's away for the weekend.

"Hey," she answers the call. "What's up?"

We continue walking down the corridor as she listens to what he has to say. I make out the fact that something's wrong but have to wait until she ends the call to find out what's happened.

"It turns out that while I managed to have Penelope's lies all taken down, they've done the damage I guess she was hoping for." She releases an angry breath. "One of our biggest clients, who I work closely with, has expressed his concern over my work on a contract we're currently finalizing."

My own anger at Penny surges. "And?"

"And so now I have to spend time tonight working. It's a lengthy and complex contract which I've put a lot of hours in on already, but Hayden wants me to go over it again just to be sure everything's in order. I don't blame him, but if I run into Penelope tomorrow, I can't be held accountable for my actions."

I frown. "Penny's here?"

"Yes. I'm not sure how you missed that fact tonight."

I refrain from telling her I didn't see Penny or any other woman besides Larissa because the only woman I'm looking at these days is her.

We reach our suite and I follow her in and watch as she takes her laptop to the workspace in one corner of the living room and sets herself up at the desk.

"Did you bring tea with you?" I ask.

She glances up as she takes a seat in the large chair that at least looks like it will offer her some comfort while she works late. "Yes."

"I'll make a cup for you. It's in your suitcase?"

Her lips spread out in a smile and she nods as she leans back into the chair and exhales a long breath. "Thank you."

God, she looks tired. This bullshit that Penny created has exhausted her. I've known this all week but being so far away, I was unable to support her except with texts and phone calls. But even then, we've both been so busy that we had little time for either, and when we did call, we were lucky if we got ten minutes of conversation.

"Is there anything else I can do to help?"

She sits forward and opens her laptop. "No."

"Are you hungry? We didn't eat much. I can go find you something."

"I'm not hungry." At my expression that says I don't believe her, she adds, "I promise to tell you the very minute my stomach threatens a growl, at which time I will allow you to go on a mission to find me all the food in the lands. Until then, you should go into the bedroom and put your feet up. You need rest after your hectic week. But mostly, I need to get this work done and it will take me longer if you're hovering like you are."

She's right; I am hovering. And that's not something I've ever done for a woman. Well, except for Liv. I try to do this for her whenever I can but since she prefers to be the one who watches over her loved ones, I rarely get the chance.

I continue watching her while she starts typing. "I'll leave you alone but I want to know the minute you need something. Let me look after you tonight."

She looks up mid-typing, her features softening. "You say that like I never let you look after me, which we both know isn't true since you had to do a lot of looking after me last weekend."

"We also both know the only reason I got to do that was because you were drunk."

"Okay," she says haltingly like she really doesn't want to be agreeing to this. "I'll let you know when I get hungry or thirsty or when I need your ear for whining. Honestly, it'll probably be whining that I'll need and then you'll regret forcing me into this."

I shake my head at her inability to relinquish some independence. Then, lifting my chin at her, I say, "Do your work. I'll bring you tea in a minute."

After taking tea to her, I head into the bedroom and shower. I then lie on the bed and flick aimlessly through Netflix in search of something to distract me from Olivia. Finding that kind of distraction is proving a hell of a task and if I know anything right now, it's that I'm in for a long night.

12

OLIVIA

I STARE at Callan who has passed out. The television is blaring with a horror flick, which is highly concerning. Callan never watches horror and the fact he was makes me wonder again if he's going through a sex-addiction crisis. Or possibly a pre-thirties crisis. I'm honestly not sure which would be worse. On one hand, a sex addiction can have a devastating effect on your life and lead to depression and other addictions. Yes, I researched this during the week and discovered that eighty-three percent of sex addicts have concurrent addictions. Eighty-three percent! However, having a crisis in your twenties surely has to mean things are dire. Your twenties are meant to be some of the best years of your life.

Yawning, I remind myself that it's late and I should put these thoughts aside for another day. It's just past one a.m. I need a shower and sleep. But first, what I really desperately need is a debrief with Blair on everything that happened between Callan and me today.

I pad back out into the living room, locate my phone, and tap out a text.

OLIVIA

Are you awake?

She calls me instantly. "Something's happened, hasn't it? Tell me everything. I have snacks prepared."

I can't even with her. But also, I have so many words for her and they all gush out unfiltered. "I found out that I did tell Callan about Ricardo and also that I thought he'd be good at sex. He did undress me. He told me tonight that I own some sexy underwear. We danced for a long time and it wasn't the kind of dancing we usually do. He's been acting differently and I'm pretty sure he was flirting with me tonight."

"Why are you whispering?"

"Because the hotel messed up his reservation and ended up putting us together in a suite!"

"Oh." I literally hear her brain working. "Oh! Wait, is there only one bed? Tell me there is. That would make every hellish thing I had to live through today worthwhile."

"I really want to ask you what hellish things happened today but that will have to wait. I'm having a moment over here that you need to talk me through. And don't just say that Callan and I are meant to be together. Please give me some advice I can action because I'm flailing and so confused right now. He's my best friend and none of this makes any sense to me. "

"I'm still waiting to hear about the bed situation. Don't keep a woman hanging."

"Yes, there's only one bed."

"This is the best news of the year."

I roll my eyes. "Okay, but can we please get back to the flirting situation? I need your guidance on this."

"No, you don't, Liv. If you think he was flirting, he was. And I don't doubt that he was."

My pulse quickens.

I think he was too.

And I flirted back a little too. Until he told me that last Saturday afternoon was at the top of his list of favorite moments with me. It was then I decided I was completely misreading the situation. Now, I'm not so sure. He probably just meant he had a lot of fun because of how drunk I was and the crazy things I said to him.

"I'm going to tell you something that you can't use on me later if I change my mind, okay?"

"Tell me first and then I'll decide on my answer."

"You are the worst," I mutter before launching into my confession. "I do want to be more than Callan's friend."

"I already knew that."

"No, you didn't."

"Liv," she says with some exasperation, "We all know that."

I walk out onto the terrace to get some fresh air. Staring up at the stars, I think about all the years I've spent working hard to hide my feelings from everyone. I'm a twenty-nine-year-old woman and some days I feel like a sixteen-year-old teenager. I'm tired of feeling that nervous energy all the time.

I sigh. "Okay, so everyone knows. Do you think Callan does?"

"If you'd asked me that before last weekend, I would

have said no. But who knows what you said to him while you were drunk. Maybe he does."

"It doesn't make any sense that he was flirting."

"Why not?"

"Because I'm not his type."

"Honestly, where do you come up with this stuff? I don't think Callan has a type."

"He does, and it's not me. I've never seen him with a brunette with hips and boobs. Have you?"

"Yes. You."

"The time he spends with me doesn't count."

"It really does." When I begin to protest, she cuts me off. "I would bet a million dollars that if Callan was given the choice between spending a week on an island with you or a week of sex there with someone else, he'd hands down choose you. Liv, he wants to be with you. He just hasn't admitted that to himself yet." She pauses before adding, "Flirt with him tomorrow and see what happens. I mean, you guys have got that bed all to yourselves; you should make the most of it."

I really want to do that.

And also, I really don't.

"What if I've misread everything? What if I let him know how I feel and things turn awkward between us because he doesn't feel the same way? I wouldn't survive any damage that might do to our friendship."

"Oh, babe. You guys would find a way to work through that. You've been friends for too long not to. What if he does feel the same way? What if you two never brought your feelings out into the open and then you reached eighty and both admitted you felt the same way? I think regret for a lifetime of what could have been would far outweigh a little awkwardness you might have to deal with now if he doesn't feel the same way."

She's right. I know she is.

And yet, there's so much uncertainty in all this for me. I don't cope well with uncertainty.

I take a deep breath. "Okay, I'm going to think about this."

Blair groans. "You've been thinking about this for twenty million years. Now is the time to stop thinking and start doing."

"And people pay you tens of thousands of dollars to fix their legal problems all while having no clue you can't count."

"You're right. It's been thirty million years."

I roll my eyes while smiling. "I do love you."

"There was never any doubt. Now, go get some sleep."

"Wait, what hellish things happened to you today?"

"It was just work. Hunt. If I end up in jail for murder, please represent me and make sure the court knows he got what he deserved."

I spend another ten minutes on the terrace after we end our call. I think about Callan and a lifetime of friendship with him. I replay tonight in my head, remembering the heat in his eyes, his hand on my body, and the way he made me feel every time he bent to say something close to my ear.

I'm not imagining anything.

Callan was flirting with me tonight and god it felt good.

Twenty minutes later, after a quick shower, I slip under the bed covers. Callan stirs and rolls to face me.

"Ace," he murmurs, his voice husky from sleep. "Did you get all your work done?"

I shift onto my side, trying to ignore how sexy he sounds when he's just woken up. "No, but I got through a lot of it. I'll have to finish the rest tomorrow." My eyes get used to the darkness in the room and I make out his face. "You were watching a horror movie."

He smiles, his eyes on mine. "There's never anything I want to watch. It's all shit."

"So, you settled on horror? You hate horror."

His smile shifts into a grin. "I'm proving you wrong and showing you that I can try new things."

"And? What did you think? Any good?"

"I'm not changing my earlier statement that it's all shit."

"I think you should give romantic comedies another go."

He groans. "I've sat through enough of those with you. I'm not looking to change my thoughts on them."

"But you laughed through the last one we watched."

"It had some funny moments. A few at most. I'm not giving them another shot."

I curl my legs to my stomach, trying to calm the whirlwind inside. Callan and I have never shared a bed but it's something I've dreamed about. I've imagined lying side by side with him like this a thousand times. My imagination fell short; this reality is beyond my wildest dreams.

Callan's closeness is electric and my body yearns to press against him. His scent fills the air, so uniquely his and familiar. Pine needle and sandalwood from his body wash mixed with peppermint from his shampoo. I know these fragrances so well that if he were in a crowd, I could find him blindfolded by scent alone.

"What are you thinking?" he asks when I turn silent.

I want to tell him I'm not thinking because his nearness has short-circuited my brain. Actually, no, I *am* thinking. I'm thinking about how much I want to get to know the curve of his lips more intimately. With my fingers, my mouth, my tongue. I'm thinking about how much I want to run my fingers through his hair. About how I want to grip it and pull it while he puts those lips on me and makes me come. Because he *would* make me come. I have no doubt about that.

"Liv."

"I have to tell you something," I blurt before I can stop the words.

"What?"

Holy god, am I really going to tell him how I feel?

Is now the exact right moment to do that?

My heart bangs around in my chest like it's trying hard to get my attention.

Nerves take hold of my entire body.

I can't tell him.

It will change everything we have.

Maybe ruin it.

I can't, I can't, I can't.

My heart moves up into my throat.

She desperately wants him to know that she's his.

"Ethan texted me." Where those words come from, I have no idea, but my nerves instantly settle. My brain resumes normal functioning. My body relaxes away from high alert.

"When? Why?"

"This morning. He wanted to check in on you after he told you he wasn't going to the Alps."

"So he texted you? He'd rather ask you how I am than come straight to me?" Anger laces his words and my heart hurts for him. For both of them. Callan and Ethan have always been inseparable, but now, their relationship is so fractured that I worry it may never be the same again.

I reach out and place my hand on his arm. It's an instinctual move, one that wouldn't have caused me any second thoughts before tonight. But with everything that happened between us today, I'm acutely aware of the way that one action charges the air between us.

Keeping my hand on him, I say softly, "He's worried about you."

"That's bullshit."

"No, it's not. It's the truth."

"How the fuck do you figure that? I've barely heard from him in almost a year. That's not the actions of a person who's worried about me."

"It's the actions of a guy who's hurting and working through some deep stuff." I wiggle closer to him. It's like I need to leave no space for his hurt to disappear through the cracks. When Callan hurts, I do too, and I have this desperate desire to wrap every ache of his up and tend to it. "I think Samantha destroyed Ethan. And I don't think he knows how to heal from that."

"Running away doesn't fix shit, Ace."

"Sometimes, I think it helps." At the look on his face that says he's about to tell me how wrong I am about that, I gently squeeze his arm. "I agree that it doesn't help forever but I imagine the space Ethan got by leaving might have been good for him for a while. He's always had problems with your dad, and he's felt lost in his relationship with your mom. I think the reason he's never been single is because he's looked for women to fill a void. I'm hopeful this time away will help him figure some things out and find himself."

Callan inhales a long breath, rolls onto his back, and exhales the breath. He stares up at the ceiling for a long time before looking back at me. "Ethan's lucky to have you."

I smile. "Well, let's be honest, you all are."

I expect him to grin and banter about me being a smartass, but he doesn't. Instead, he turns serious and says gruffly, "That's the fucking truth."

Callan steals all my words and all my thoughts with that. It's not just what he says, but the way he says it and the way he's looking at me. The air between us is now completely wired and I don't know what to do with all my feelings and desires.

Thankfully, Callan takes charge. "Okay," he says, pushing up off the bed. "It's late. I'm going to let you get some sleep."

"You're not sleeping on the couch."

He glances down at me. "Yeah, I am."

I sit up. "No, you're not. And if you do go to the couch, I'm coming with you and will sleep on the floor next to you."

Even in the dark, I can make out the combination of frustration and amusement on his face.

When he appears to still be trying to figure out a way around this, I say, "You know I will, Callan, so just get back into bed."

With a shake of his head and one last moment of hesitation, he stops fighting me on this. He finds his pajamas and gets changed in the bathroom. Once he's settled next to me again, he says, "If you snore, I'm leaving and you're not following."

"Oh my god, I do not snore! Wait, do I?" We may not have slept in the same bed before, but we've slept in bedrooms next to each other. If he's heard me snore before, that means I do snore and I do it very loudly. I'll be mortified if he answers yes to my question.

He turns his face to mine. "Yeah, you do."

My eyebrows hit my forehead. "How loud am I? Do I snore all night? Or just a little bit during the night? Like, is it just when I'm really tired? Jesus, Callan, why have you never told me this?"

He chuckles. "Calm down. I've only heard you once and that was last weekend when you were drunk."

"I fell asleep while you were still in my room?"

"Yeah, you were snoring by the time I got to the door to leave."

"Loudly?"

He watches me silently for a long moment before answering me. It feels like he's maybe stalling while figuring out his answer. This makes me wonder if he's trying to figure out how to soften the blow when he has to tell me I snore like a freight train. Finally, he says, "No. Your snores are soft and cute. I was just being an asshole when I threatened to leave if you snore. I could listen to you sleep all night."

And there go my butterflies.

The whirlwind starts up in my belly again and in an effort to force it into submission, I resort to my standard method of gaining control in my life. "We need to set an alarm. You've got breakfast with the guys in the morning and I know you'll want to get a run in before that. And I've got a lot of work still to get through." I reach for my phone. "Is six good for you? Or do you want to get up earlier for your run?"

Callan is slow to reply and I feel his eyes on me while I'm grabbing my cell. When I turn back to him, he's got the look on his face that says he's deep in thought over something. The way my butterflies zero in on that look is like something I've never experienced. You would think I was a teenager about to be kissed for the first time with the way they're carrying on.

It turns out I was right about my butterflies' radar being off. The only thing Callan was deep in thought over was the alarm time. I get a sinking feeling in my stomach when he says, "Six is good."

Maybe I actually was off base about Callan flirting with me tonight. I'm beginning to think I'm rusty when it comes to flirting. After almost a year dating Jensen and then months of no dating, it's been a long time since I've had to read the cues when it comes to a man.

"Six it is." I set the alarm and then roll to face away from him, wiggling as close to the edge of the bed as possible. "Sleep well."

"Night, Ace." The bed dips as Callan rolls over too.

This may be the longest night of my life. Between all the overthinking I'm now engaging in about flirting cues and my hyperawareness that the man I want is lying right next to me, I don't see a lot of sleep in my near future.

I'm two thought spirals down on this when Callan

says, "For the record, if Penny fucks with you tomorrow, I won't stand back and watch it happen."

I stop drawing air into my lungs.

The tone in his voice is *everything*.

It's the kind of tone I'm sure every woman wants to hear from their man.

Callan wants to protect me and I love him for that. I just have to remind myself of one thing: he's not my man. He wants to protect me because that's what he's done since we were kids.

I pretend I'm asleep. It's safer this way. The alternative is to throw myself at him like my heart is demanding, and that could end very badly. Callan and I have decades of friendship ahead of us and I'm still not convinced he wants anything other than that. What I am certain of is that what we have now is the best thing in my life. I'd rather have this than not have him in my life at all.

13

CALLAN

I WAKE LONG before Olivia's alarm on Saturday morning. Hell, I'm not convinced I even fell asleep during the night. I spent most of the night lost in my thoughts about her. About the fact she was lying next to me rather than being where I really wanted her, in my arms. My filthy imagination ran wild. I thought about doing things to her that a best friend should never do, let alone imagine.

I throw the bed covers off just after five a.m. and head into the bathroom to change into my running gear. Olivia doesn't stir. Fifteen minutes later, I'm on the beach. Running is one of the best ways I've found to clear my thoughts and help me focus. This morning, I use my run to force Olivia from my mind and think about work instead.

My assistant, Abigail, emailed overnight to let me know a key investor has pulled out of my German expansion. She's aware of the Plan B I've devised for this exact scenario and has already put its wheels in motion. That plan involves me wooing an American investor who has an extensive network in Germany and could play a pivotal role in our move into Germany. It looks like I may need to alter my calendar to fit in a trip to Florida to meet with this investor, which is a pain in my ass because my schedule is already so tight. However, the German market is lucrative, so I'll do what it takes. I spend time while running, mentally rearranging my schedule, and figuring out how to fit it all in.

I return to the hotel suite at six thirty and find Olivia gone. She's likely in the gym or out for a walk. It's her preference to work out early in the morning. She hasn't returned by the time I'm dressed for breakfast, so I leave her a note letting her know I'll be back around two p.m. to get ready for the wedding ceremony. I want to give her space to finish her work today without the distraction I know I'd provide if I was in the suite with her, so I'll spend the time after the breakfast working in the coffee bar downstairs.

Breakfast is a long affair with Joe and his friends. Halfway through, when I'm feeling irritated to be here, I admit to myself that I would normally be enjoying this time with the guys, and that the only reason I don't want to be here is because I want to be with Olivia. It's a mind-fuck. One I've never experienced over a woman before.

The only times in my life that I've thought about being somewhere else like this has been when I've thought about the sex I knew I was going to have. With Olivia, it's not sex driving my thoughts. I'm imagining watching her fuss over her hair and makeup. Talking with her. Asking her how she feels over this work situation she's in. Making sure she's okay. And while these are all things I've done with her in the past, I feel a deeper level of interest in all of it. I want to be the only man she allows into her space to see and know these things.

Fuck me.

These are not the kinds of thoughts I ever pictured myself having about a woman.

I manage to immerse myself in the last half of the breakfast. I learn that Joe and Charlene were friends for about a decade before anything happened between them. I also learn that the surprise she arranged for him yesterday centered around her sharing the news that they're going to be parents.

I contemplate this for many hours after breakfast while I should be working. The only couple I know who took a friendship further ended up mortal enemies. Their breakup was long, messy, and devastating to both. That was after a relationship that only lasted six months, off the back of a friendship that spanned five years. I've always figured that if two people were meant to be together, they wouldn't have wasted time being just friends first. Discovering more about Joe's relationship today has made me question that.

Maybe, for the right people, a friendship builds a strong foundation first. One that helps them stand strong together when everything around them is in chaos.

Olivia and I have helped each other through some chaos. We've supported each other, held each other up, and quieted the noise of the world for the other when it's become too loud. The question I keep circling back to is this: could we still do all of that if we added in the extra layers of a relationship?

Living with each other.

Being in each other's space twenty-four-seven.

Tolerating habits, moods, quirks.

If the answer to all this is no, there's no point putting our friendship at risk.

But fuck if I can't stop thinking about being with her.

I return to our suite and am barely two steps inside when Olivia comes running out of the bedroom. She almost crashes into me on her way to the sofa where a pile of clothes and makeup have been dumped.

She comes to an abrupt stop, a stressed look in her eyes. "I lost track of time. I'm running so late now. Do you need a shower? Because if you do, we've got a problem."

It's unusual to see her in this frazzled state. Olivia's the person I can always count on for calm order.

I frown. "What happened?"

She returns my frown. "Huh?"

"This." I gesture at her wild energy. "What's caused your stress? Fuck, was it Slade? What's he done now?" That fucking guy is always doing something dumb that heaps more work onto her plate. If I could remove him from her life permanently, I would, and we'd all be a lot better off for it.

Her frown deepens. "What? No, he hasn't done anything. I just got caught up in the contract I was working on and didn't realize the time. Now, we've got less than an hour until the wedding and I'm nowhere near ready."

I narrow my eyes at her, still not convinced Slade hasn't done something. "Was it one of your other clients? Is there something I can do to help?"

The lines smooth from her face and her features soften. "There's nothing you can do, Callan, but I appreciate you wanting to." She glances at the mess on the sofa.

"Actually, you could collect all my cosmetics and bring them into the bathroom for me while I figure out which dress I'm going to wear."

"You brought more than one?"

She's already at the sofa gathering her clothes. "Of course." She says that like everyone in the world except me knows that a woman would, of course, bring multiple dresses to choose from.

"Why are all your clothes and cosmetics on the sofa?" I ask as I help her.

She doesn't stop what she's doing but she does glance at me, her brows furrowing. "Why are you asking so many questions?"

"Because I'm fucking bamboozled as to why you'd bring everything out here."

"I'm bamboozled as to why you're using a word I've never heard you use." She stops and stares at me. "It's a pre-thirties crisis, isn't it?"

"What?"

"All the weird things you've been doing and saying the last month...it's not a sex addiction crisis, it's a pre-thirties crisis."

My lips twitch. "You're fucking cute when you're conjuring up shit about me."

She blinks and stares at me some more like I just said something very confusing to her. "I'm trying to figure out what's going on with you."

I want to say, "It's you! You're what's going on with me," but I don't. Instead, I say, "I can assure you I'm not in crisis, but I'm certain *you* will be if you don't hurry up and get ready."

With that, I take her makeup into the bathroom,

calling over my shoulder, "I just need a quick shower and shave. You go first."

She joins me. "Okay, so this is where our problem lies. The lighting in this suite is bad and there's no way I can apply my makeup or do my hair in the living room or bedroom. Honestly, we're paying a fortune for this suite. They'll be hearing from me as to my suggestions for what to improve."

I only just rein a grin in. I fucking adore her nerdy attention to details. "So, what you're telling me is that you'll be applying makeup in the bathroom while I'm showering."

She worries her bottom lip with her teeth. "That's gonna be awkward, isn't it?"

"Not for me."

"I'll try to give you as much privacy as I can."

I can't fight my grin a second longer. "Have I ever struck you as a man who requires privacy?"

That gorgeous pink blush I love colors her cheeks. "Well, I'm going to give it to you anyway."

Fuck.

The urge to pull her into the shower right now and strip her is overwhelming. I had no idea how much modesty turns me on. Or maybe it's just because it's coming from Olivia. Either way, I need to put space between us, otherwise she's going to learn really fast just how much I'd prefer no privacy in this bathroom.

"Don't spend a second worrying about me. I'm easy with whatever needs to happen to get you to the wedding on time."

Liv has the fastest shower I've ever known her to take. I'm sitting on the sofa replying to an email when she comes into the living room with a towel wrapped around her. I'm engrossed in what I'm doing so am slow to glance up. By the time I do, she's bending to pick up something she dropped. Thanks to the tiniest towel known to mankind, I'm treated to an eyeful of the backs of her legs and a hint of ass.

Christ.

I'm instantly hard.

If I thought last Saturday was difficult to get through when she begged me to undress her, I had no idea what was in store for me. I only just made it through sleeping next to her last night. Now, I have to make it through getting ready with her, attending another wedding and reception with her, and surviving another night lying in the dark with her while my imagination does its fucking best to kill me with a running porn movie of all the ways I could spread her legs and bury myself in her.

"Shit." She straightens and looks at me. She does this so fast that there's no way she doesn't catch me checking her ass out. I'm sure it's only her mild panic that's scrawled across her face that stops her fully processing that. "Have you seen my earrings?"

"No."

When I look at the earrings in her hands, she shakes her head. "Not these ones. I had another pair out here but now I'm not sure where they are." Her panic is clear in her voice too.

I stand and move to her. Placing my hands on her upper arms, I say in the calmest voice I can muster, "I'll look for them while you get dressed. We're not going to be late, okay?" Olivia's dedication to always being on time for everything is legendary. I can't recall one event she's ever been late to. I also can't recall ever seeing her descend into anxiety like she is right now.

She nods but it's a jittery nod at best.

"Ace," I say, gently tightening my grip on her. "What's next? Hair, makeup, or getting dressed?"

"Makeup."

"Ok, good." I turn her and walk us into the bathroom. "You do that while I take a quick shower. I'll find your earrings once I'm dressed, and if you need help with anything else, I'm your guy."

She takes a deep breath and nods. This time, it's far less jittery but it's evident she's still running on anxiety.

I undress and jump in the shower. For Olivia's sake, it's a good thing the bathroom is massive. The vanity and mirror are spread so far along one wall that it's almost like she's in another room to me. My back is to her while I shower and I don't turn once even though I want to spend the entire time facing her, watching her, and having her watch me.

I stay silent while we're both in the bathroom. I want to give her space to deal with the wired energy consuming her. After I shower and then dress in the bedroom, I get to work locating her earrings. It only takes me a couple minutes to find them. They'd fallen under the desk in the living room.

"I've got your earrings." I step back into the bathroom and instantly suck in a breath at her beauty in the mirror.

Olivia has always been the most beautiful woman in the world to me, and I've always thought whoever she ended up marrying would be the luckiest guy around. Not only because of her beauty but also because of every other quality she has. Today, she's breathtakingly beautiful and I'm momentarily lost for words.

She turns to look at me after I make the announcement about her earrings. "Thank you!"

I place them on the vanity near her. As I do this, I notice the makeup line along her jaw. From previous conversations we've had, I know that line isn't something any woman wants. *You have to blend, Callan!*

Moving closer until our bodies are almost touching, I bring my hand up to her jaw and lightly brush my finger over it. "You've got a makeup line, Ace."

She stills, her eyes boring into mine. The air between us thickens, heavy with anticipation and tension. We both feel it. The pull. The desire. The awareness of what we've been dancing around.

Her hand meets mine. "Thank you."

When she touches me, it's like every touch I've ever experienced no longer exists in my memory. I'm a blank slate and the only touch I know is hers. The only touch I *ever want to know* is hers.

"You look different."

"I've done my eyeshadow differently." A hesitant smile crosses her face. "Do you like it?"

"I like it a lot."

The hesitation leaves her smile as she takes her time with that compliment.

Every second I wait for her response feels like an eternity. The hush that surrounds us is a delicate symphony of nerves and expectation. I didn't plan on leading us to this moment but we're here now and I'm desperate to know if Olivia will run again or if she'll fall into this with me.

Her smile grows and her eyes sparkle. And then, *fuck me*, she flirts with me. Blatantly, in a way that no one could misinterpret. "You look different, too." She casts an appreciative eye down my body before meeting my gaze again, her eyes all sexy as she adds, "You should wear this suit every day of your life."

"I'll have you know this is a tux, not just a suit. This wedding is a black-tie event after all, and as such I went to great lengths to meet the dress code."

She rolls her eyes at my teasing. I would do many things to have that from her every day for the rest of my life. "You give a man a little bit of knowledge and he thinks he's Einstein."

I grin and shrug. "If the shoe fits."

Her hands come to rest against my chest. "I hope you brought a bow tie."

"I have a good teacher. She made sure I know the requirements."

We turn silent for a long beat, simply watching each other. Enjoying each other in a way we never have. Then, she pats my chest and says, "I have to finish my makeup and hair."

"How are you wearing your hair today?"

She takes her time before answering, like she's weighing something up. "How do you think I should wear it?"

My heart slams into my chest.

I want her to ask me that question a million more times throughout our lives.

I smooth her hair behind her ear, letting my hand linger there. "I think you should wear it however you were planning, but if you had no plans yet, I love it when you curl your hair and leave it down."

"I had no plans," she says softly. "I'll curl it."

I have zero desire to go to this wedding now, but I manage to pull myself away from her so she can finish getting ready. I head back out to the living room and occupy myself by mindlessly scrolling Facebook, which isn't something I ever tend to do, but right now, it's all I have the brain capacity for.

When Olivia appears in front of me wearing a stunning strapless navy gown and asks me to help her zip it up, I fumble with my phone, almost dropping it.

She turns as I stand and I'm presented with her bare back that I've seen a thousand times but that I could swear I've never laid eyes on even once.

We don't speak while I slowly slide her zipper up, however there are so many words between us.

We're doing this.

I feel like I've stepped out onto the highest, longest highline in the world and am taking steps I've not trained for.

When she turns back to me, I take in the curls falling softly around her face. "You look beautiful, Ace."

"Thank you." She smooths her hands down her dress over her stomach. "This dress is so tight that I may not be able to eat dinner or dance." She draws in a long breath. "Actually, I may not be able to do anything except stand there and pretend I can breathe."

I'm instantly alarmed. "What about the other dress you brought? Can you breathe better in it?"

"No. I've gained some pounds in the last few months. None of my dresses fit me better than this one."

"I saw a dress shop downstairs. Let's go and buy you something that isn't going to kill you."

I'm already making a move to leave when she curls her hand around my wrist. "Callan, stop." She laughs gently. "I was being dramatic when I said I wouldn't be able to eat or dance."

My gaze drops to her dress. It is quite fitted. It's beautiful but all I can think now is that she's going to be in pain for hours. "If your stomach rumbles from hunger because you can't eat, we're leaving the reception and getting that dress off you."

I realize what I've said when heat flares in her eyes.

She steps closer, our bodies almost touching. "And if that happens, I might just let you take charge without arguing with you."

My hand is on her hip before I can stop it and I'm issuing orders like I never have. "You need to go and get my bow tie. It's on the bed."

Surprise flashes across her face. "Well, hello, Mr. Bossy."

"Now, Liv." I need a moment to myself. Otherwise, my mouth is going to be on hers and there's no way we're making it to the wedding.

I don't know if it's my gruff tone or if she reads the situation perfectly, but either way, she leaves me to do as I've said.

I exhale a long breath and rake my fingers through my hair. The feelings running through me are foreign; the desire, unlike any I've ever known. Liv and I aren't going to make it through this day without me putting my hands and mouth on her.

She returns with the bow tie and a look in her eyes

that says she's got plans I'm going to like. Coming right to me, she takes control of getting the bow tie on me. The record should show that I would let her take charge of this job any time she wants. Especially if she does it in the slow, sexy way she does it today.

She makes securing a bow tie the best kind of foreplay I've ever engaged in. When she's finished, she smiles up at me as she rests her hands on the vest I'm wearing. "I've always liked a bow tie and vest on you."

I make a mental note to find as many black-tie events to attend with her as possible. "As much as I wish we didn't have to leave now, we'll be late if we don't get going."

"I know. Just gimme a second to get my shoes and do one last check of my hair and makeup."

My eyes are all over her as she walks away from me. Thoughts of what we're doing crash through my mind. Red flags wave madly, trying to warn me of the possible consequences. I'm not paying attention though. Not anymore. Every fiber in my being wants this. Wants Liv. And if she tries to run tonight, I'm not having it.

14

OLIVIA

CHARLENE IS A BEAUTIFUL BRIDE. And Joe only has eyes for her. I swooned my way through the wedding ceremony, constantly leaning in close to Callan to give him a running commentary on all my thoughts. He dropped his head to the side every time to listen to every word and offered his thoughts too.

This isn't new for us, and yet *all of it* is new.

Callan has barely taken his eyes off me since we left our suite. We're currently mingling under the tents that have been set up on the lawn for us to enjoy cocktails before dinner. Normally, I'd be admiring the soft cascading drapery and the flowers decorating the space, but all I can focus on today is the man who keeps putting his hands on me.

He steps toward me to allow a couple to walk past us, placing his hand on my hip as he does this. After the couple glides past, he keeps his hand on me and says, "Joe told me this morning that they'll have karaoke at the after-party tonight."

He's telling me this because I'm the karaoke queen. Anytime there's karaoke, you can count on me to get up on the stage and belt out a song. I'd happily stay on the stage and sing all the songs, but no one ever seems to want to let me. And the other thing I do whenever I indulge my love of karaoke? I make Callan sing with me. He hates karaoke but never lets me down. So, right now, he's watching me expectantly, knowing that this news will excite me.

It would if I wasn't already excited by his attention. By that hand of his that's *still* resting on my hip.

Neither of us has brought up what's happening between us. I've gone to a few times, but then the moment passed thanks to the wedding providing distractions everywhere. Callan knows a lot of the wedding guests, which means that while I have most of his attention, I haven't had much time alone with him.

For the first time in our lives, I have no idea what he's thinking. We're definitely flirting. I'm acknowledging that now. But I desperately want to know his thoughts about it. Everything happening is both thrilling and a little terrifying because I can't help but wonder what will happen if we take things further. I can't help wondering how Callan would deal with sleeping with his best friend.

"Ace." He draws my attention back to him and I find him watching me closely. "What are you thinking? You're a million miles away."

As I stare into his blue eyes, I think about a lifetime of having him watch me like he is now. Like the only thing in the world that's important to him is my answer to his question. It's intoxicating. And special. And it makes me think I should not be terrified of all the feelings swirling between us.

I take a deep breath.

It's time for me to be as confident in my ability to handle whatever happens with Callan as I am in every other area of my life.

"I'm thinking how much I like your hand on my hip."

His hand immediately curves tighter over my body as he moves into me. He takes his time though before saying, "Do you remember asking me if I ever think about us last weekend?"

I swear my heart stops beating for a second. "No. But I wish I did." My hand reaches for his shirt, pressing to his abs while wishing for skin-to-skin contact. "What did you say?"

"I didn't answer you. I told you that you didn't know what you were saying because you were drunk." His gaze drops to my lips for a moment before finding my eyes again. "If you asked me that question now, I'd tell you that I can't stop thinking about us."

We're in the middle of this moment when Joe's father announces to everyone that we're moving into another tent for dinner. The look in Callan's eyes tells me that he plans for us to stay right where we are and continue this conversation. However, we get swept up in the moving crowd and are unable to do anything but go with them. On our way, a couple we both know start talking with us and the moment is lost.

When that couple drifts away to their table, I curl my fingers around Callan's arm. "I really want to get back to our conversation, but I need to use the bathroom before dinner."

He nods and from the expression on his face, I know he has every intention of finishing that conversation. "Do you want me to get you a drink?"

"No. I'm not chancing getting drunk tonight."

He dips his mouth to my ear as his hand comes to the small of my back. "Smart, but a shame. I enjoy the Liv who gets drunk and shows me her ass."

Holy hell.

I enjoy the Callan who says things like this to me.

Before he can pull his face away from mine, I grasp his neck and turn so I can speak against his ear. "Maybe I'll show you my ass anyway."

I let him go, loving the look in his eyes as he straightens. It's heat and surprise all rolled into one. Then, without another word, I leave him, making sure to sway my hips as I walk away.

I'm a hot, lusty mess as I make my way to the bathroom. All I can think about is the fact I showed Callan my ass last weekend. That, and the fact he can't stop thinking about us.

Do we even have to eat dinner tonight?

Like, on a scale of one to ten, where does skipping the wedding reception sit for wedding guest etiquette?

Ugh. My manners and rule-following tendencies are my least favorite thing about me right now.

"Olivia."

I come to a dead stop at the sound of Penelope Rush's voice. Glancing to my left, I find her coming my way. *Why? What did I do to deserve this?*

"Penelope."

"I heard a little rumor."

"I bet you did." I seriously hate this woman, and I don't actively hate many people.

Her face pinches. "You really do think you're above all of us, don't you?"

Her question surprises me but I refuse to show it, and if being a good lawyer has taught me anything, it's taught me how to keep a blank face. And while I have no idea why she thinks this about me, I'm not getting into it with her. "I'm busy, Penelope, so can you just say what you came here to say?"

More pinching of that bony face. "Fuck you for being a bitch. I don't know what Callan sees in you, but soon he won't even be looking at you."

"Oh, really? Because?"

She steps closer with a look of triumph on her face. "Because soon, the only woman he'll be looking at is me. I doubt you know this, but Callan and I had the hottest sex. He and I have something special and when we take it to the next level, I'll ensure he leaves his old best friend behind. There's absolutely no room for you in the life he and I are going to build."

This woman is delusional.

"That's interesting."

She blinks.

And then she presses her lips together hard.

I don't think I gave her the response she was looking for.

"Why is that so interesting to you?"

I let my mouth curve up into the tiniest of smug smiles. Fuck her. "Because he just told me that he can't stop thinking about being with me."

Oh, she does not like that. Not one little bit. I see the

venom a split second before I feel it. "That's funny because you are so not Callan's type. Have you even looked in the mirror lately? He doesn't go for fat chicks, just FYI. I imagine your thighs might suffocate him."

And just like that, she manages to make me feel like I did all the way through high school. The self-loathing I've left behind thanks to hundreds of hours of therapy tries to rear its ugly head and my thoughts try to spiral into shame for being curvier than the world deems acceptable.

I don't manage a response before she gives me a satisfied smile and leaves after saying, "Don't worry. I'll be sure to take good care of him once he's mine. And good luck finding a new best friend. Oh, and a new job."

Shame is a mean emotion. A nasty, soul-destroying emotion.

I refuse to sit with it. Never again. So, I inhale a deep breath and walk the rest of the way to the bathroom while forcing that shame away. And once I'm finished there, I hold my head high and walk to the table where Callan's talking with two of the couples we're seated with for dinner.

He smiles at me as I slip into my seat and surprises me by placing his hand on my thigh. Dropping his voice low so only I can hear, he says, "You're going to want to avoid the couple to my right. Their patriarchal views will ruin your night. And I'd appreciate you saving me anytime it looks like they want to talk to me."

I may have decided never to sit with shame again, but that doesn't stop my brain from throwing a myriad of other feelings at me. Callan's hand on my thigh brings up old feelings of humiliation at the thought of being too big to be with a guy. Penelope knew exactly which barb to use when she mentioned my thighs suffocating him.

But just because feelings come up doesn't mean we have to let them in. It's in moments like this that I'm grateful for all the work I've done on my ability to self-regulate.

I'm healthy.

I'm fit.

And yeah, I've got curves, and an ass, and thick thighs.

And I'm as worthy of feeling good about myself as every other woman is.

Callan squeezes my thigh to pull me from my thoughts. "Ace."

I give him my full attention while also thinking about how much I love a thigh squeeze from Callan. It's hot and I'm feeling it all over my body. "I've got you. And honestly, you're not going to have time to talk with people during dinner. We need every second to strategize for karaoke tonight. I just heard in the bathroom that it's a competition."

He grins as he removes his hand from my thigh, which I instantly miss and wish he would put back there. "Jesus, they're ticking all your boxes."

I return his grin. I do love a good competition. "Yes, and you better step up. We must win this."

"What's the prize?"

I give him a pointed look. "You know that winning is the prize. Honestly, how have you forgotten that?"

His eyes flash playfully. "I just wanted to hear you chastise me."

I roll my eyes, shaking my head at him when he

simply continues eyeing me with amusement. I then launch into a battle plan for how we can win the karaoke competition tonight. I made sure to get all the details from the girl in the bathroom and I lay it all out for Callan.

He listens closely, hanging off my every word. When I'm finished, I wait for his response, and when it doesn't come straight away, I point at the look on his face, circling my finger and say, "Why are you looking at me like you think it's a bad plan? I know there are a lot of details in it, and that it's probably overkill, but—"

He cuts me off and stuns me into silence when he reaches for the base of my chair and jerks me closer to him. "I'm not looking at you like it's a bad plan. I'm looking at you like I can't fucking believe that I get to have you in my life. That I'm the one who gets to pull that plan off with you." He bends his mouth to my ear. "That I'm the one who gets to take you back to our suite and have you talk nerdy to me."

There is so much gravel in his voice and my core feels every word he utters.

Every. Single. Word.

"And Liv?"

I hold my breath. "Yes?"

"You're gonna let me kiss you and put my hands on you tonight. And if you want me to watch while you touch yourself and show me all the ways you want me to fuck you, I'll be more than happy to sit back and do that."

15

OLIVIA

THIS IS the best night of my life and I haven't even kissed Callan yet.

After his declaration earlier that he would be happy to sit back and learn how I like to be touched, I had to sit through a dinner with people I didn't care for. Callan was right about the awful couple next to him, and it turned out every couple at the table had their own version of nastiness. I had to endure all of that while thinking about having sex with Callan.

Then came the speeches, the dancing, the sharing of Callan with too.many.people.

I think we need to renegotiate our agreement to attend a wedding almost every weekend of this season. I think I'm all wedding'd out and that isn't something I ever thought I'd say. But when it comes to sharing Callan, I no longer want to do it.

The after party began an hour ago and we've sat through five karaoke performances so far. It turns out that there are some other hardcore karaoke lovers here tonight. I'm impressed with their efforts.

"You ready, Ace?" Callan asks as the current song comes to an end. We're up next.

I turn to him and assess his look. "We need to bad boy you up for this song."

He's amused. "How do you propose we do that?"

I eye his bow tie. "This needs to go." I reach for it and quickly remove it. "And your jacket and vest. They need to go too."

When he doesn't make a move to take them off, but rather just sits and watches me with that playful look I love, I say, "Quick. We have to get up on stage."

He relaxes back in his chair, all swagger and sex. "Feel free to take whatever item of clothing off you want."

I blink.

I did not expect him to do that. Or to look at me with fuck-me eyes.

But hot damn. I like all of it.

I slide to the edge of my seat and reach for him. Keeping my eyes firmly on his, I put my hands to his abs and run them up his body over his shirt and shrug the jacket off him. He sucks in a breath at my touch. The sound he makes is almost too much for me. If we weren't sitting in a crowd, I would not be able to keep my mouth to myself a second longer, and I don't think Callan would be able to either.

I remove his vest and we hang it with his jacket on the back of his chair.

"Better," I say, still looking into those blue eyes of his that are glued to mine like they'll be stuck there for life. "But we need to see some skin." *We really do need to see some skin.* With that, I undo the top two buttons of his shirt and gently press the shirt out into a casually-open, sexy look.

I lose myself in his bare skin and don't realize I've done that until Callan leans forward and asks, "We're good now?"

My eyes snap back to his. "Yes. Now, you're ready to pull off Joe Elliott."

"Joe who?"

"Oh my god, Callan, the lead singer of Def Leppard. How do you not know his name?"

He grins. "I'm just fucking with you, Ace." He stands and puts his hand out for mine. "Come on, let's go so I can beg you to pour some sugar on me."

I let him lead me up onto the stage where the emcee introduces us. Callan receives more high-pitched screams and cheers from the women in the audience than any man so far. As part of my battle plan to win this competition, I instructed him to perform like this is a gig, and he doesn't let me down. From the second he steps foot on the stage, he acts like he really is Joe Elliott. And holy hell, it has to be said that Callan Black could pull off being a rockstar.

The way he moves his hips is sinful and I squeeze my legs together as I think about him moving them with me later.

After he gives the crowd some attention, a hush falls over us as everyone waits for us to start. Callan strides to the front of the stage, microphone in hand, and utters the opening intro chant of "Pour Some Sugar On Me" in the sexiest voice known to womankind. How the hell did I not know he had that in him? When he gets to the last line of that chant, he turns and pulls me to him. By the time the beats merge with the guitar riff, Callan's got me in front of him, his hand on my hip, and is grinding against me.

This was not in my plan.

"I've got you, Liv. Just go with me," he says against my ear before he sings the next lyric.

I'm a little stiff at first. Mostly because *this was not in my plan*. But also, because I'm so turned on right now that it feels all kinds of wrong to be doing this in front of a crowd.

When Callan gets to the line about wanting to be my man, he brings his hand around to my stomach and holds me there while singing the lyric against my ear. At the same time, he thrusts himself against my ass, playing the bad boy rocker perfectly.

When I feel how hard he is for me, two things happen.

One: I forget we're up on a stage. It's just him and me now.

And two: I lose all my inhibitions.

I turn when it's time for me to sing, pressing my body to his, and grinding hard when I sing the line telling him to go all night. He grabs my ass when he sings about me being innocent. We sing the chorus together, letting each other go when we get to the end of it.

Callan struts his way across the stage, playing up to the crowd before starting the second verse.

His eyes find mine and he sings every lyric to me.

I then sing all mine to him.

The crowd no longer exists for either of us, which was

most definitely not in my plan to win, but by now, I just don't care.

I've already won everything I wanted.

By the time we get to the next chorus, I'm back in Callan's arms and we're dancing together like no one's watching.

It's sexy.

Far too sexy for this stage.

And it's full of so many promises of what's to come.

I'm staring into my best friend's eyes when the song ends. The crowd is going wild. Women are screaming Callan's name. I'm breathless and more turned on than I have ever been. And Callan's looking at me like he wants to *devour* me.

The emcee walks onto the stage and says something. I'm so lost in Callan's eyes that I have no idea what that is. Thankfully, Callan takes charge and ushers me off the stage. We head toward our seats, but instead of sitting to watch the rest of the performances, Callan guides me out of the after-party tent.

He holds my hand tightly in his and doesn't stop walking until we reach the elevator to go up to our suite. He jabs at the call button and the doors slide open. A second later, we're inside, but we're not alone. We stand at the back of the elevator and don't say a word.

Every second is torture.

If the way Callan's hand firmly grips mine is anything to go by, I think he feels the same.

The elevator finally reaches our floor and we exit. We're now alone and barely make it four steps down the corridor before Callan's got me in his hands and is forcing me against the wall.

"I can't wait another second to kiss you," he growls, his eyes all over mine.

He does wait another second, though, and I think he's waiting for me to signal that he should not. I grip his shirt and I see it in his eyes that that's all he needed.

We collide, Callan's lips crashing down onto mine with an intensity that takes my breath away. He hungrily devours me, his tongue sliding over mine, exploring, and claiming me.

We're wild.

Frantic.

Pushing.

Pulling.

Demanding.

As he deepens our kiss, he lets go of my face. He grinds his erection against me and groans while his hands roam my body. When he cups my breasts, he tears his mouth from mine and growls, "Fuck," while looking down at what he's doing. "Fuck, Liv, you're fucking perfect."

I thread my fingers through his hair when he bends to kiss the swell of my breasts. I curl a leg around his body and arch my back while the pleasure he's giving works its way through my body.

God.

This is everything I've ever wanted.

He spends an inordinate amount of time with my breasts, kissing and caressing me, and I die for every second of it.

I moan when he pushes my dress down so he can suck one of my nipples into his mouth. "Oh fuck..." I'm breathless with need. "That feels so good." I squeeze my eyes closed and pull his hair. I don't think anything has ever felt as good.

He cups both my breasts and splits his time between them before lifting his face. "We need to move this to our room, or else you're going to be naked against this wall in the next minute."

The door of our suite isn't even closed behind us before Callan has me against the wall again. He reaches behind me and unzips my dress. A second later, the gown falls to the floor and my bra isn't far behind it. And then Callan's mouth and hands are back on my breasts.

Oh, god.

I want to do so many things to him right now but I'm a hot mess of need and am struggling to figure out where to begin. I start with his shirt buttons, but my fingers can't move fast enough to satisfy that desperation. Before I can stop myself, I just rip his shirt open, to hell with preserving the buttons.

This gets Callan's attention. He lifts his face from my breasts, eyeing me with a look of extreme approval. Then, he's got one arm under my legs and one around my back, and he's carrying me into the bedroom as he says, "That's how a shirt should be removed."

He throws me onto the bed and then watches as I move myself up the mattress while waiting for him to join me. His eyes are *all over me*. "I feel like our first time should be slow and meaningful, but fuck me, Ace, I don't think I have slow in me."

Our first time.

"Our second time can be slow."

His eyes find mine as his hands go to his trouser

button. "Every time I imagined this moment, I took my time with you."

Holy fuck.

Every time.

"How many times have you imagined this?"

He slides his zipper down. "I've lost count."

My breaths slow as he undresses.

I drop my gaze.

I stare at his cock.

And holy fuck me.

"Breathe, Liv," he says as he moves on top of me.

I stare up into his eyes and put my hands to his abs. "You have a big dick."

His mouth spreads out into a sexy grin. "Yeah, baby." He brushes a kiss over my lips. "And I'm gonna learn all the ways you want me to use it." He moves down my body so he can kiss the skin between my breasts. "But first..." He kisses my stomach. "I'm going to take these sinful panties off..." He kisses the skin above my underwear and looks up into my eyes. "And I'm going to fuck you with my tongue."

I think I moan.

I can't be sure because I can't even think right now.

Callan positions himself between my legs, hooks his fingers into my panties, and slides them down so slowly I may die before he gets them off.

"I thought you didn't have it in you to be slow," I say once he's finally got them off.

He gives me more of that sexy grin of his. "I changed my mind." Then, the grin dies on his lips and he turns bossy. "Spread your legs for me."

In all of my fantasies of being fucked by Callan, I

never imagined him saying these words to me, but now that he has said them, I have no idea why I didn't picture it. They are so fucking hot.

I do as he orders and the sound he makes gives me so much pleasure. But nowhere near as much pleasure as when he grips my thighs, bends his mouth to my pussy, and licks me from one end to the other.

I grasp the sheets and squeeze tightly. "Oh, fuck." When he settles in and circles his tongue over my clit, I arch up off the bed and moan his name.

"Say that again," he growls as he lets go of my legs and brings his hands to my pussy so he can spread me open and push his tongue inside.

"Holy fuck, Callan...oh, *fuck*..." When I say his name again, he makes a guttural sound that vibrates through me, causing another wave of pleasure to consume me.

Callan knows what he's doing with a tongue. He licks and circles and fucks me with it like he was made to do these things to me. My entire body comes alive, my fingers gripping his hair, my legs wrapping and unwrapping around him, my back lifting off the bed over and over.

It's too much.

And yet, it's nowhere near enough.

Callan stops what he's doing so he can spread my legs wide. He rests one bicep on my left thigh while placing his forearm across my stomach just above my pussy, holding my body down. His other bicep holds my other leg down. "I'm going to make you come now and you're going to scream my name for me when I do." When I don't say anything, he demands roughly, "Liv, you're going to scream my name, aren't you?"

I tighten my fingers in his hair and nod. "I'm going to scream your name."

The look in his eyes says my answer pleases him. A moment later, he sucks my clit into his mouth and swirls his tongue around it over and over. Then, he rubs my clit, alternating between pushing his tongue and his fingers inside me.

My back tries to arch up off the bed but Callan keeps me where he wants me, flat on the bed. It's maddening in a very good way and it only takes me closer to the edge of my orgasm.

My eyes squeeze closed as every vein in my body and every nerve ending blaze with lust.

Callan fucks me deeper with his finger. Rubs my clit harder. Growls his pleasure.

I let go.

I come so hard the intensity of my orgasm is almost too much for me.

I've never known such pleasure.

I cry out Callan's name over and over while he draws every last bit of my orgasm from me. When I'm spent, he slows everything down and licks my clit with long, lazy strokes.

He releases me and moves off the bed. A moment later, I hear the sound of a condom wrapper. I open my eyes and watch him put it on.

"You were so fucking wet for me," he says as he moves on top of me.

I slide my arms around his neck. "That's because you practically dry humped me up on that stage."

He drops a kiss to my lips. "There was no practically about it. I *was* dry humping you. I couldn't keep my fucking dick away from you." He rubs his cock along my slit before pushing the tip in. "I want to do so many things to you right now. And I *am* going to do so many things to you. But I can't go another second without being inside you."

I circle my legs around him and push up to take him in further.

"*Fuck*." He drops his forehead to mine for a beat. "Do you know how fucking good that feels?"

"It'd feel even better if you'd just fuck me already."

"Jesus, you're a dirty girl, Ace."

I dig my fingernails into his back. "Just hurry up and get inside me." I kiss him, biting his bottom lip, which finally encourages him to just fuck me already.

He thrusts inside me and I swear I see stars.

With another one of his guttural groans, he pulls out and thrusts again. This time, he stays there while reaching for one of my legs from around him. He brings it up over his shoulder before thrusting deeper.

His eyes close as he rocks his hips, going even deeper.

"Holy god." I suck in a breath at how good that feels. Callan's dick is so big. I've never been so filled. And I've never had a guy take their time and go this deep.

His eyes open. "You okay?"

I nod and grip his shoulder. "Don't stop."

He brings his mouth down to mine and kisses me so thoroughly that by the time he's finished, I swear I'm ready to come again. Then, he drives his dick in again. This time, he makes sure to thrust his body so he rubs against my clit while fucking me. He does this a few times before slowing down and going deeper, rotating his hips, and then pulling back before doing that again.

He doesn't take his eyes off mine the entire time and this might be the most erotic thing I've ever experienced.

"You feel so fucking good, Liv," he says, his voice husky with desire.

I meet his thrusts while clinging to his biceps. I want to tell him how good he feels, how amazing this is, how I never want him to stop, but all I manage to get out is, "Just don't stop."

"I don't plan on it." He reaches down and rubs the area between my pussy and ass, spreading my wetness.

"Oh fuck." I bite my bottom lip. "Do that again."

His smile is so sexy, so lazy, so fucking beautiful. "You like that?"

I squeeze his arms. "Yes. Do it."

He steals a kiss before giving me what I want.

"Fuck, Callan." I close my eyes while he swirls that finger so fucking expertly. "I'm going to come."

He kisses me roughly. "You are so fucking beautiful. Come for me, Ace."

I'm so close, and all it takes is one hard, deep thrust from Callan and I fall over the edge. I orgasm with everything I have.

Callan slams inside me. He fucks me all the way through my orgasm and into the next. It doesn't take him long to come. He thrusts one last time and makes the kind of indecent noise that will forever live inside me. It's the kind of sound that tells me how good this is for him.

He drops his head into the crook of my neck and stays inside me after he orgasms. We're both breathing hard when he pulls out and moves off the bed to dispose of the condom.

I catch my breath while he's gone and gather myself

and all my senses. When he comes back to the bed, he brings me close, pulling my arm across his chest while I rest my head on his shoulder and hook my leg over his.

We're silent for a long moment that goes on for long enough for me to commence scrambling my way through a million thoughts.

I just had sex with my best friend.

Holy. Shit.

What the hell are we doing?

Holy fuck, holy fuck, holy *fuck*.

"Stop overthinking this, Ace." Callan tips my chin up to bring my eyes to his. "Talk to me." It's the gentleness in his tone that reaches me. And the care in his eyes.

I take a deep breath. "That was good."

His brows lift. "If good is your assessment, I've got work to do."

I smile as I feel the tension in my body ease. "Okay, let me clarify. You were up there with Ricardo."

Callan moves faster than I see coming and the next thing I know, he's got me on my back and is looking down at me with his hand curved around my neck. After kissing me, he says, "My goal in life from here on out is to make it so you forget all about Ricardo. And we're getting started on that in about half an hour."

I stare up at him. He's saying things that make me think this could turn into something for us, but I don't want to get ahead of myself. And while I really want to be the kind of girl who can just go with the flow, that's never been me and probably won't ever be me. I need to know where I stand. And I need that with Callan more than I've needed it with any man because there's so much more at stake here.

"What are we doing, Callan?"

I half expect him to throw out a flippant reply along the lines of "we're having sex, Ace," but he doesn't. He shows me why he's the man I've wanted for so long when he handles my question with the care I need him to.

"We're exploring our feelings, which I hope you'll continue to do with me."

I pull his face down to mine and answer him with a kiss that leaves me breathless.

When we come up for air, he says, "I'll take that as a yes."

"You should."

He watches me for a moment like he's settling his own thoughts. Then, he says, "I want to tell you I'm sorry that we didn't stick around to see if we won the competition, but I'm not sorry at all."

I wiggle my way closer to him, not that that's even possible since we're already skin to skin. But now, we're really smooshed together and his expression lets me know he's on board with all of this. "I'm pretty sure we won. I mean, I'm already over here figuring out how to get you your own band and begin promoting you."

"I like the idea of being a rockstar. I could get away with a lot of filthy shit like this." He gropes my breast and buries his face in my cleavage.

"You could get away with a lot of filthy shit like that even if you weren't a rockstar."

He kisses his way up to my mouth. "Good, because I intend on it."

My core clenches and I wonder if I'll ever be able to think straight again.

"Now," he says, "do you need food or a drink or

anything before I get started on learning all the ways I can make you scream?"

I tell him I want a drink. Mostly because I want to watch his ass while he walks out of the bedroom to find said drink. But also, because I need a minute to calm my heart down.

I just slept with the guy I've been crushing on for more than a decade.

He just told me he wants us to explore our feelings.

And I just had the best sex of my life.

16

OLIVIA

"Liv." Callan's deep voice fills my ears and I fight through my sleep to open my eyes and look at him. "Liv, wake up."

I blink a few times before finding Callan sitting on the edge of the bed looking down at me. I frown when I lay eyes on the white polo shirt he's wearing. "What time is it?" God, did I sleep through breakfast? It was after two a.m. when we fell asleep, so it wouldn't surprise me if I did.

"It's early," he says softly as he slides some hair off my face and tucks it behind my ear. "Just past seven. I have to leave, which fucks up our day I'm sorry, but there's no way around it."

I sit up, now concerned. "What's happened?"

His gaze momentarily drops to my breasts after the sheet falls away. "Fuck," he mutters, giving me his eyes again. "I really don't want to leave. I hope you know that."

"Callan. What happened?"

"Abigail called. The guy I'm hoping will invest in my

expansion into Germany wants to meet, and he can only fit me in today and tomorrow. I'll likely be gone a couple of days."

"Okay." I yawn. "How are you feeling about this meeting?" Callan's company, Black Asset Management, has nearly $300 billion in assets under management across the States and Canada. Expanding globally is his goal and while he's one of the most driven men I know, I also know he has his moments of doubt.

He smiles but doesn't answer me. Instead, he takes his time tracing his gaze over every inch of my face.

"What's that smile for? I'm tired and not at full capacity, and I don't seem able to read your mind anymore."

His smile only grows at that. "Good. I need to keep your interest somehow."

If only he knew.

I reach for his shirt. "Trust me, you have it. Now please tell me what's going on in your mind."

"I was thinking about how you're the only person besides my mother who ever asks me how I'm feeling about my work. I like that you do that. And in answer to your question, I'm feeling concerned that I'm not going to be able to convince this guy to invest. And if I don't, there aren't a lot of other options I like."

"Why do you need his money? You have enough of your own to make this happen."

"That's true. But I don't want to tie it all up in this."

"That makes sense. Just remember that you've pulled the impossible off many times. Options always come up when you least expect them."

He smiles again. Then, after another long moment of

him watching me silently, he says, "The helicopter will be ready for you whenever you're ready to leave. Please let me know when you get home."

I agree to do that before asking, "Where are you going?"

"Florida."

"Text me when you get there, okay?"

He curves his hand around my neck. "I will." Then, he pulls my face to his.

I put my hands to his chest and stop him, horrified that he wants to kiss me before I've brushed my teeth. "I'm not kissing you with my morning breath!"

He tightens his grip on me. "Liv."

I press harder to his chest. "No."

"Fuck, you're cute." He lets me go and stands. He then jerks his chin at me and when I frown in response, he says, "Up. Brush your teeth. I'm not leaving without a kiss."

I push the sheet off. "You just want to see me naked before you leave."

"Guilty as charged."

Having Callan's eyes on me while I walk into the bathroom naked will be the highlight of my day. I am sure of it. I change my mind when he moves behind me at the vanity and puts his hands on my hips while checking me out in the mirror, deciding this is the highlight. However, that moment is trumped when he turns me to face him once my teeth are clean and looks at me like he won't ever get enough of me. And then, when his mouth claims mine, I know this will be the absolute highlight of an entirely highlightable ten minutes.

Callan's kiss this morning is unhurried, like he has all the time in the world for me. His lips brush against mine softly to begin with, lingering long enough for me to inhale his scent and feel the warmth of his skin. Then, his hand comes to the nape of my neck and he holds me firmly while he opens his mouth and deepens the kiss. His tongue sweeps over mine, still unhurried, and so intimate that it makes my toes curl.

He keeps hold of my neck when he ends the kiss, his eyes searching mine, telling me how affected he is by me. He brings his other hand up to take hold of my face, his thumb lightly brushing over my jaw. "I'm taking you on a date when I get home."

My heart is all over the place. "I'd like that."

He traces his thumb over my lips while he watches what he's doing.

"You should go," I say softly even though it's the last thing I want him to do.

He nods absently. He appears lost in my lips.

"Callan."

His fingers tighten around my neck. "Fuck."

I smile. "That about covers it."

He bends his mouth to mine again. This kiss is rough. Hungry. Demanding. Promising. When he sees me next, I know to expect more of this.

Then, he's gone and all I can do is sit on the couch and let my mind run free with all my thoughts over what happened this weekend.

Somehow, I manage to get myself showered, dressed, and packed to leave. I fly out just before lunchtime. Callan texts while I'm in the car on my way to my condo to let me know he arrived in Florida. I stare at his message for the rest of the drive home.

We're going on a date when he gets home.

For the first time in his life, Callan isn't ending a friendship after sex.

17

CALLAN

CALLAN

The next time I have a meeting with an investor, I need to make sure I've had more than two hours sleep.

OLIVIA

Two? We went to sleep just after two a.m. I think your math is off.

CALLAN

You went to sleep at that time.

OLIVIA

Wait. You couldn't fall asleep?

CALLAN

I didn't want to.

OLIVIA

Did you do inappropriate things to me while I slept?

I LAUGH AND CALL HER.

"Where do you come up with these ideas, Ace?"

"If you knew half the things I've heard in my line of work, you'd know where I come up with these ideas."

"I hate to break it to you, but I didn't do any inappropriate things to you while you slept. Although, you should expect that going forward now that you've put the idea into my head."

I hear the smile in her voice when she says, "So, how did your meeting go?"

"It was long and not at all productive. I've left him with some information to look over before we meet again tomorrow afternoon."

"I'm sorry you were so tired."

"That was my own fault. I may not have done anything inappropriate to you, but I did spend all that time thinking about it."

"Oh, god." She's all breathy, which only gets me harder than I already am.

I've struggled to remove my thoughts from Liv today, which likely also contributed to my meeting not being as successful as I would have preferred. I was distracted as well as tired. Right now, I'm fighting with myself over talking dirty to her or being a gentleman. I'd fucking love to wrap my hand around my dick while telling her to touch herself, but more than that, I want to hear how she is.

"How was your day?" I ask.

She gives me a rundown of the things she did to prepare for the week ahead. Liv's Sundays always consist of meal prep and work prep. I sit up straight when she mentions Slade Sullivan.

"Back up," I say. "Why was Slade calling you on a Sunday?"

"We were going over the interviews he's got scheduled for the week."

"And he couldn't have done that with you tomorrow?"

"Callan." She laughs gently. "My work is like yours. It doesn't stick to a Monday-to-Friday schedule. You know this."

I do. I also fucking know this Slade asshole has little respect for her time. "What I know is that he cuts in on your personal time a fucking lot." Jesus, my chest is tight with knots thinking about this guy.

"It's the job. And I don't mind. I was already doing some work when he called. Oh, and I forgot to tell you that I spent a couple of hours doing some research for Harper's wedding. I have so many ideas for her now!"

I have to hold my tongue. I'm not a fan of Harper's. She takes advantage of Olivia and the guilt she feels over Harper's sister's death. Olivia is oblivious to this and the few times I've mentioned it, we've gotten into a disagreement. Right now, she just needs my support, so that's what I give her.

"That's great. When will you get a chance to talk with her about them?"

We settle into a conversation about the wedding planning, which leads into us talking about the next wedding we're attending. It's not for two weeks, which means no wedding next weekend. By the time we get to that, it's almost midnight.

"You should go to bed," I say. "It's late."

"Yeah." She's saying yes but I hear her conflict over ending our call.

"I don't want to stop talking either, Liv, but we both need sleep."

"Before you go...I was thinking about your crisis today."

"The crisis I wasn't having."

"Yeah," she says softly. "That one."

"What were you thinking about it?"

"I was thinking...all those times you were acting weirdly with me, was that because you couldn't stop thinking about me?"

I can't see the blush I know is heating her cheeks but I can hear it. And I wish she was standing in front of me right now. I want all her blushes and I want them in person. "Yeah. And Liv?"

"Yes?" I would swear she just bit her lip.

"You can ask me anything."

"I know I can."

"No. We're in a new place now and I don't want you to feel weird while we figure everything out, okay? Whatever you want to know, bring it to me."

She takes a moment. "Okay. I will."

"And one other thing. That black bra you were wearing that time I walked in on you at Rhodes's place?"

"Yes?" She's so fucking breathy.

"I want you to wear it on our first date."

18

OLIVIA

Do you think you'll be home tonight?

Like, do we think I should cancel my meditation class?

Shit, I am definitely not being needy here. If you come home tonight, you absolutely don't have to see me.

Although, I just want you to know I am all for sex tonight if you come home.

I'm just going to throw my phone away. Right now. Pretend you don't even know me.

CALLAN

I won't be coming home tonight but if I was, you would absolutely be sitting on my face once I got there.

OLIVIA

Good to know.

OLIVIA

I might still throw my phone away.

CALLAN

Liv.

CALLAN

There is not one thing you could say that would make me not want you.

OLIVIA

Okay, I won't throw my phone away.

OLIVIA

Also, I won't be wearing that black bra on our first date.

CALLAN

Because you're thinking of not wearing anything?

OLIVIA

Because I have another bra I think you'll like better.

CALLAN

Describe it to me.

OLIVIA

sends a photo

CALLAN

Fuck me.

OLIVIA

I thought so.

CALLAN

I need a photo of you wearing this bra.

OLIVIA

I thought so too.

OLIVIA

sends photo

OLIVIA

I have to run now, but here's a photo of me wearing the matching panties too. I'm looking forward to wearing them for you before sitting on your face.

OLIVIA

sends photo

19

OLIVIA

"You look like you're in heat," Blair says when we catch up over lunch on Tuesday. "You should not have been let outside today."

I steal one of her fries. "I do not."

"You really do. Have you humped anything today?" When I just roll my eyes at her, she says, "What time is Callan getting home today?"

"I don't know. He was aiming for around four p.m., but he's been delayed."

"Let's hope for your sake that he's not delayed until tomorrow. You really might start mounting guys on the street."

Thankfully, Sasha joins us at this very moment, saving me from more humping and mounting talk.

She slides onto the seat next to Blair across from me and says, "Okay, I want all the details from the weekend and if you leave anything out, I will not be happy. Rhodes has injured his dick and is out of action at the moment, so I'm—"

"You're in heat too," Blair says.

Sasha looks at her very seriously and nods. "Exactly. I need to live vicariously through Liv."

"Dare I ask what happened to Rhodes's dick?" Blair asks.

"I'm wondering that too," I say. "It's unlike Rhodes to let anything get in the way of sex, so it must be bad."

"He jerked himself off a little too hard to a photo I sent him. The doctor thought he'd fractured it at first," Sasha says.

I blink. "That's possible? From jerking off?"

"Apparently so," Sasha says.

"Holy shit," I say.

"Okay," Sasha says, "Enough about Rhodes's dick. Tell me all about sex with Callan."

Discussing our sex lives is something the three of us have always done. I've never kept details from them but I'm suddenly feeling very protective of Callan and the sex we had.

I glance between the two of them. "It was the best sex of my life."

Sasha leans forward. "And?"

Blair reads me perfectly. "And she doesn't want to share the details." Her voice softens. "And you shouldn't, Liv. Not if you don't want to."

I smile gratefully at her. "I don't think I want to. Not yet anyway."

"Ugh," Sasha says, but her expression says she understands. "I may actually have to resort to watching porn."

I laugh.

Blair looks stunned. "You don't watch porn?"

"I don't need porn," Sasha says. "Rhodes never leaves me alone."

I nod. "That is true."

My phone sounds with a text and I check it, hoping it's from Callan.

"Was that lover boy?" Blair asks.

I look up from my cell. "No, it was from Mom."

"Where are they now?" Sasha asks. My parents have just left on a two-month trip visiting Australia and New Zealand.

"Auckland." I frown as I read another text from her. "She just saw the news about some stocks she knows I have."

"What news?" Blair asks.

My stomach drops. "Funite's stock price fell overnight, which is on top of last week's decline." I'm looking at a loss of a couple hundred grand on those stocks now.

"Oh, Liv," Sasha says, "I'm sorry."

My mind drifts during the rest of our lunch and I find myself unable to keep up with the conversation. I've got money. Actually, quite a lot thanks to an inheritance from my grandmother. So, I'm not going to be destitute anytime soon. However, I'm careful with it and I find losing money on the share market stressful.

By the time I hear from Callan at five p.m., I'm ready for this day to be over. That's thanks in part to the stocks news as well as the fact I've got a mountain of work still to get through before I can even think about sleep tonight.

CALLAN

I've been delayed again. It'll be late by the time I get home, so I'll just go to my place.

I'm disappointed reading his text but it makes sense.

OLIVIA

Okay, makes sense.

CALLAN

Everything okay?

OLIVIA

Yeah, I'm just swamped with work. And I'm tired and grumpy, so it's probably a good thing that you won't have to put up with me tonight.

CALLAN

Shit, I have to go. Sorry. I'll text you later.

I stare at my phone for a long time after we text.

I hate this day. Hate it. And I really wish he wasn't so far away.

I work all night, finally closing my laptop just before midnight. I still didn't finish everything I should have, but I can barely keep my eyes open.

After I take a quick shower and brush my teeth, I put on one of Callan's tees that I may have borrowed from his suitcase during the weekend. It's an old navy T-shirt that I've always loved. I would say he won't miss it, but I know it to be a favorite of his, so he probably will. I could be persuaded to return it, but I really doubt that. I think this will be a long-term loan.

I crawl into bed and switch my lamp on. Some nights, I need it on to fall asleep and tonight is one of those. I'm almost asleep when a text lights up my phone. I debate checking it for a minute at which point it rings. My heart is instantly in my throat. It can only ever be bad news when a person receives a phone call after midnight.

I sit up and quickly answer it after seeing Callan's name on the screen. "Oh my god, Callan, are you okay? What's happened?"

"Ace." His voice is soothing in his attempt to calm me. "Everything's okay. I'm here."

"Here where?" My heart is still thudding against my ribcage. He's telling me he's okay, but it's taking a little time for that information to kick in.

"Here at your place. I didn't want to let myself in in case I scared you. But I'm coming in now."

I drop my phone on the bed and run to my front door. Callan is just coming through it when I arrive.

"I thought you were going to your place tonight."

He closes the door and looks at me, and goodness, *he's missed me*. "Why are you all the way over there?" His question is a rough growl, a demand, and it meets my core fast.

We crash into each other.

Our bodies.

Our mouths.

Our hearts.

"Fuck, I've missed you," he says after he tears his mouth from mine. His arms are around me tightly and it doesn't seem like he's in any hurry to change that.

I smile up at him. "I missed you too, but if you don't loosen your grip on me, you may choke me to death."

He still doesn't let me go. "I'll give you mouth-to-mouth if you start choking."

My smile grows.

He's home.

"Why are you here?"

"You seemed off, so I called Blair to ask her if you were okay."

I frown. I haven't spoken to Blair since lunch. She has no idea how downhill my day went after I saw her. "What did she say?"

"She told me you're in heat. That was before she told me that she's surrounded by women in heat due to me being away and Rhodes breaking his dick, and that she'd be eternally grateful if I returned as soon as possible so that you didn't start humping random men."

I laugh, feeling the first release of tension in my body since he left on Sunday. "That convinced you to come here?"

He shakes his head. "No. Although, the idea of you humping another man caused me some hell."

That confession settles low in my stomach in the very best way.

He loosens his arms but keeps them around me. "I think I'd already decided before I called her. When she texted me after our call to tell me your stocks had taken a dive, that cemented my decision." His eyes search mine. "Are you doing okay?"

"You came here because of my stocks?"

"Yes."

Tears threaten at the back of my eyes. "You're

exhausted and you've got a massive day of meetings tomorrow. You should not have come here because of my stocks. You should have gone home and gotten some good sleep."

"Liv," he says in the way that means I should listen to him.

I grip his arms. "I'm serious."

"So am I. Let me be here for you."

"You're already exhausted, Callan."

"Let me worry about that." His voice drifts off as his gaze drops to the shirt I'm wearing. A curse falls from his lips right before he lifts me over his shoulder and strides into my bedroom.

"Callan!" I laugh, loving every second of this.

He drops me onto the bed and prowls over me as I scoot up the mattress. "You stole my shirt."

"I prefer to think of it as borrowed."

He lifts a brow. "You intend on giving it back?"

"Probably not. But I did bring your vest, jacket, and bow tie back from the wedding, so we could call it a swap."

His mouth lands on mine and with one kiss he clears all the thoughts from my brain. "It looks fucking good on you." He slides it up my body, leaving it bunched at my throat. When I bring my hands up to remove it, he stops me. "No, leave it. I like seeing it on you."

I make a mental note to steal as many of Callan's shirts from him as I can.

He dips his face and sucks one of my nipples into his mouth while one of his hands cups my breast and the other reaches inside my panties. When his fingers slide through my wetness, he sucks my nipple harder and adds some teeth before lifting his face to mine. "You are so fucking wet for me."

"You kept me waiting." I pull his shirt over his head before reaching down to undo his belt. "Why must you be wearing so many clothes?" I grumble as I make my way through his belt and his trousers and his boxer briefs to get to his cock.

He pushes two fingers inside me. "Someone's greedy today."

My back arches when he finds my G-spot and I forget what I was doing. "Oh, *fuck*...do that again."

He rubs the spot again while also rubbing my clit with this thumb.

I rock with him while he fucks me with his fingers, moaning as I get closer to my orgasm.

It teases.

And teases.

And *teases*.

I clench my pussy.

"Fuck, Liv."

It keeps fucking teasing.

So. Close.

I take over rubbing my clit while bringing one leg up so I can rest my foot on the bed and get a different angle for his fingers inside me.

Callan's lips crash down onto mine and he growls some filthy words into my mouth before kissing me like he wants to ruin me.

I come while he's kissing me. Bright lights shatter behind my eyes as the orgasm consumes me. My entire body is blazing with pleasure that I want to go on and on and *on*.

Callan leaves the bed to get a condom and when he returns, he's already got it on and has a look in his eyes that says this really is going to be fast this time.

He moves over me and I wrap my legs around him as I say, "Don't take your time."

"Wasn't planning on it," he growls before thrusting hard inside me.

Holy god, I don't think I will ever want him to fuck me any other way.

He pulls out and drives inside again.

He then fucks me harder than I've ever been fucked.

His deep grunts with every thrust are noises I want to inspire in him regularly.

We come almost at the same time.

It's the fastest I've ever orgasmed in my life.

"Jesus," he says when he rolls off me onto the bed. "That was fucking intense." He exhales a long breath as he reaches his arm out to rest his hand on my stomach.

I glance down at his hand. He's not just resting it there; he's got it palm down like he's holding my stomach. I don't know if it's just my sex-haze brain, but it feels possessive. I like it a lot and before I can stop myself, I say, "I like your hand."

"That's a relief." His amusement is clear in his voice and it draws my gaze to his.

My cheeks heat. Honestly, I should tape my mouth closed at times.

But this is Callan. The man I've known since he was a boy. The guy who has helped me through some period disasters; the guy who has witnessed so many of my mortifying moments in life and only ever shown me compassion afterward; the guy who has gotten up on so many karaoke stages with me and not once made fun of the fact I can't really sing.

I put my hand over his on my stomach. "I like your hand here. Like this."

"I like it there too."

Two people can share so many big moments and build a life together, but it's in these tiny moments of vulnerability and honesty that a relationship is truly forged.

We lie in silence for a few minutes simply watching each other before I say, "You should get me a drink."

"Should I?"

I adore his playfulness.

"Yes. And you should make a note to always get me a drink after we have sex."

"I think we should be more equal in this and split the responsibility of getting drinks."

"No." I give a quick shake of my head and wrinkle my nose. "That doesn't work for me."

He chuckles. "Because?"

"Because it's not really the drink I want."

"What is it you really want?"

"I want to see your naked ass."

His eyes flare with heat. "Liv, in case I haven't been clear enough about things, my naked ass is always available to you. Even if it's fully clothed, you just say the word and I'll rectify that."

Five minutes later, after Callan's given me my fill of his ass, gotten rid of the condom, and brought me a glass of water, I settle his T-shirt I'm wearing back in place so I can sleep in it.

He turns off the lamp and pulls me close. "Talk to me. Tell me how you're feeling about your stocks."

I snuggle against his chest, thinking about how long I've wanted this with him and how it feels even better than I imagined. "The price will come back up."

"Liv."

I look up at him, making out his face in the dark. His features are very serious. Almost stern. "You're very bossy these days."

He takes hold of my arm that's across his chest. "I'm a whole lot of things these days, Ace, and fuck if I can control any of it. I need to know you're okay, so please tell me how you really are."

My heart squeezes with all my feelings for this man.

He came here to check on me. In the middle of the night.

He's being vulnerable with me. In a way I never imagined.

And he's desperate to know I'm okay.

I give him what he needs and open my heart up to share my fears and feelings with him. He listens carefully and doesn't tell me how to fix the situation like so many of the men that I've been with would have. He asks questions and only offers his thoughts when I ask for them.

This is a new side to Callan. As my best friend, he's tried to fix things for me at times. But there's something different about him now, and it's something I really like.

"Thank you," I say softly after we finish talking about my stocks.

"What? For listening?"

I find his eyes. "Yes. But mostly for coming here. For knowing I needed you."

"I won't always get shit right, Liv, but I'll always try."

"I know."

We lie in silence, drifting off to sleep until I murmur, "You know that time you walked in on me in that black bra?"

"Yeah."

"I was looking at your dick on my phone."

"What?"

I laugh. "I found it on a website, www.inmybigdicker-a.com. Did you know it was on there?"

"No. I've never heard of that website. How do you know it was mine?"

I glance up at him. "Well, I didn't before, but I'm pretty sure it was yours now." I wiggle up the bed a little so I can bring my face closer to his. "But don't worry, I got it removed."

His lips twitch and he smooths my hair. "I can always count on you to defend my honor."

"Always."

"Why the hell were you surfing that website in the first place? Is this a kink of yours I should know about?"

"It was for work. I had to have a client's dick taken down."

"And so, you just randomly searched for my dick while you were there?"

"Yes. And then you came in and I dropped my phone and you tried to catch it—"

"And that's why you screamed at me not to touch it. This is all making sense now."

"It was hectic. My boobs were everywhere."

"Don't I fucking know it."

"That's the dress I'm wearing to Sasha and Rhodes's wedding."

"Like hell it is."

I smile and then slowly bring my mouth to his. Before I kiss him, I say, "I love your possessiveness."

He kisses me. "Good because I don't think it's going anywhere."

"I hope not."

He settles me back against him. "Go to sleep. You've got an early start in the morning."

"No, I don't."

"Yeah, you do. Your mouth's going to get a workout at five a.m. before I get up to go for a run."

20

OLIVIA

WAKING up next to Callan is officially on my *Favorite Things* list. I've done it three times now and I don't need a fourth to verify my feelings.

"I've gotta go," he says just after seven a.m. on Thursday morning before hooking his arm around my waist and pulling me in for a kiss. His lips linger on mine after he kisses me. "You taste like strawberries and vanilla."

I put my hand to his back and hold him close. "It's a new lip cream I'm trying."

He kisses me again. "I hope it works out."

When I refuse to let him go, he gives me a sexy smile. "You've had my body for two hours, Ace. It needs time to recover."

I pout. "And here I was thinking you were pretty much an endurance athlete."

"At the rate I'm going, I'm not going to be any kind of athlete."

He's referring to the fact he didn't get any exercise in

the last two mornings before work. "I don't know, I think sex helps." I let him go and step away from him. "But I'll be sure to leave you alone every morning just in case."

"Don't you dare." He checks the time on his watch and curses. "I'll pick you up at seven tonight. Don't forget to wear that indecent bra for me."

Callan's taking me on our first date tonight. I have no idea where because he refuses to tell me. All I know is that he's taking me to dinner. And that I should wear that bra.

It's a long day. Work is causing me no end of headaches this week. The client who expressed concern over my work last week is still not happy to be working with me. After days of trying to placate him, I tell Hayden this morning to assign another lawyer to him. Unfortunately, he's not the only client spooked by the things written about me on social media. Two other clients have made it clear they're paying close attention to my work. It's stressful and I'm angry with Penelope for putting me in this situation.

Callan calls me at our usual eleven a.m. time. His day is also hectic and I can tell he needs to not be distracted even though it's clear he very much wants to be distracted. I only give him five minutes when what I really want is to give him five years all at once. Neither of us are happy to end the call.

Blair and Sasha text with me an hour later, improving my mood immensely.

> BLAIR
>
> Has Callan told you where he's taking you tonight?

OLIVIA

No. All I know is dinner.

SASHA

All that matters is the sex though, right?

BLAIR

I see Rhodes's dick is still out of action.

SASHA

Ugh.

OLIVIA

I've already had sex twice today.

SASHA

SHUT UP.

OLIVIA

Four orgasms!

SASHA

You are dead to me.

OLIVIA

I've never had four orgasms in one day.

BLAIR

Sasha needs that website with the big dicks. What's the name of it again?

SASHA

No, I just need a certain big dick to not be broken.

A text from Kristen comes through.

KRISTEN

I got your text with the schedule for our weekend away and am about to begin coordinating the guys but I just wanted to let you know that Bradford and I may not get there until late on the Friday. I'm sorry this couldn't be avoided.

OLIVIA

www.inmybigdickera.com

OLIVIA

Oh god, sorry! I meant to send that to someone else.

KRISTEN

OH MY.

OLIVIA

You clicked it, didn't you?

KRISTEN

Of course.

KRISTEN

And now I may not get any more work done today.

KRISTEN

HOLY SHIT THESE GUYS ARE HUGE.

OLIVIA

LOL. Yes.

OLIVIA

And no worries about getting in late on the Friday night.

KRISTEN

There's something very wrong with me. I just searched this website to see if my own husband's dick is on there.

OLIVIA

Trust me. Nothing wrong with you.

KRISTEN

I'm relieved not to find him.

OLIVIA

I would have had it removed for you if you had.

KRISTEN

I like having lawyers in the family.

Blair texts me.

BLAIR

Liv?

OLIVIA

www.inmybigdickera.com and now I'm done with that website. Don't make me look at it again.

SASHA

Oh.

SASHA

OH. Okay this might work for me. I just found the videos.

BLAIR

See. We've got you.

OLIVIA

What videos?

Seven p.m. comes far too slowly.

I leave work early and arrive home around five. I then spend two hours fussing over myself trying to make a final decision on what to wear and how to fix my hair.

I bought a new dress to wear tonight. The second I found it, I imagined Callan's eyes on me when he first saw me in it. It's one of the sexiest dresses I've ever owned, and the only reason I bought it was to have Callan strip it from my body. But now I'm unsure because I have two other great options.

I try on the other dresses. And I try my hair three different ways. It's ridiculous and not something I've ever done for any date. When Callan texts me at 6:50 p.m. to say he's running late, I'm relieved because I still haven't settled on a dress.

He arrives at 7:25 p.m. and the minute he sees me, I decide this red dress I bought yesterday was the perfect choice for tonight. It hugs all my curves and plunges between my breasts, and since I've worked out that Callan's a breast man, I'd hoped he'd love it. I couldn't have imagined just how much he does love it.

"Fuck, Liv." He can't keep his eyes off my body. "You look beautiful."

I move into him as I run my gaze over his black suit. "You're wearing a vest for me." Callan always looks good, but I can tell he's spent extra time on himself tonight. He's wearing a three-piece suit and I'm not sure we'll make it through the date before I try to take it off him.

He slides his arm around my waist before bending his head to kiss the skin below my ear. "I know how much you love a vest." He gently nuzzles my neck, scenting me in the most erotic way. It's slow. And deliberate. And so damn sexy.

One of his hands slides down over my ass while he does this. He cups my butt when he reaches the curve of my cheek and presses me into him. And holy *god*, he makes the filthiest sound when I rub against his erection.

I pull his mouth to mine so I can claim the kiss I'm desperate for. My tongue tangles with his while I show him what he does to me. Our kiss is raw and rough, and I almost lose my mind during it.

"Jesus, Ace," he says when he ends the kiss and looks at me, his eyes wild with desire. "What are you doing to me? I can't stop fucking thinking about you and I want to bend you over your dining table so I can see how wet you are for me."

I grip his suit jacket. "I'm soaked."

"Don't tell me that when I can't do anything with it." He actually appears to be in physical pain.

I give him a sexy smile. "Well, you could if you wanted to."

He toys with that idea for a long moment before finally letting me go and shaking his head. "No, I'm taking you on a date. Are you ready?"

"Almost."

I apply some lipstick, quickly fix my makeup, and put my shoes on.

Ten minutes later, we're in Callan's Aston Martin when he curses and gives me an apologetic glance. "We have to make a detour."

"Where to?"

"My place." He brakes before making a right turn. "I forgot something."

When he pulls into his parking garage, he cuts the engine and says, "I won't be long."

While he's gone, a text sounds from my cell. As I'm reaching into my purse to retrieve my phone, I cut my finger on a piece of paper in there.

I curse at the pain. And at the amount of blood. I'm going to need a Band-Aid.

Thank goodness Callan left his key fob here. I lock his car and head up to his condo.

When I step out of the elevator into his foyer, he's walking my way. His brows pull together. "I thought you were waiting in the car?"

I step out. "I was, but I just got a paper cut. I need a Band-Aid." Knowing that he keeps them in his bathroom, I make my way in there.

"Here," he says after following me in. "Let me help."

I clean the cut with soap and rinse it while he gets the Band-Aid. He then wraps a washcloth around my finger and applies pressure to stop the blood.

I watch him while he does this, taking in the serious expression on his face. "Anyone would think I actually wounded myself with how attentive you're being."

"You did."

I laugh. "Not really."

"This could get infected and turn nasty."

He's right; it could. But I've never had that happen. Still, I can't deny how much I adore the way he's caring for me.

"If you ever decide you want a change in careers, you

could try medicine. You've got a real doctor vibe going on here."

"Is this another kink of yours?"

There's a sexy edge to his voice now and I'm suddenly very aware of his proximity, his scent, his touch, his *everything*.

"I wouldn't be opposed to you dressing up as a doctor," I say as he secures the Band-Aid in place.

His eyes meet mine and I can't stop myself from reaching for his suit jacket. "You know, I bought this dress yesterday because all I could think about was you taking it off me. But here I am, the one who can't keep her hands to herself."

"Liv." His voice is rough. His eyes are flashing a warning.

I think he's saying *don't*, but since I can't hear that word, I keep going.

I slide his jacket over his shoulders and take it off.

He lets me.

But those blues of his are still flashing that warning.

"There." I let my eyes run all over his vest. Fuck, I love a vest on him. "But this needs to go." I undo his tie and place it with his jacket on the vanity. I then undo the top few buttons of his shirt and position the collar in the way I prefer it: sitting a little up and out. He looks reckless like this and it turns me on a *lot*.

I glance up at him again and holy hell, I feel his gaze low in my stomach. "You should wear your suit like this every day."

"We're not making it to our date, are we?"

Now, I feel him even lower.

I bite my lip. "We might be a bit late."

"If you take any more of my clothes off, we're not leaving this condo for the rest of the night."

"Promises, promises," I murmur.

Callan crowds me against the vanity, placing his hands on it either side of me. He brings his mouth to my ear. "Here's what's going to happen. Instead of me taking that dress off, you're going to give me a show and take it off for me. Then, I'm going to spend some time with that bra I hope you wore. After I do that, you're going to sit on my face."

I grasp the nape of his neck. "I want you to take my dress off."

"No. You're going to give me a show."

For the first time with him, I feel shy. I've never stripped for a man before. I think I'd be too self-conscious to pull it off.

My skin warms as I think about this and my pulse races.

It *would* be sexy.

But I really don't think I have it in me to be *that* sexy for Callan.

He watches me for a few moments, waiting. Then, he grinds his dick against me while kissing me and making the filthiest sounds that force all my shy feelings away.

His hands are *on me*.

They're telling me so many things.

How turned on he is by me.

How much he wants me to do this.

How far over the edge I drive him.

And then he sends *me* over the edge.

He drags his mouth from mine, takes hold of my neck, and growls against my ear, "Be bad for me, Liv."

21

CALLAN

Fuck.

I have never been as turned on as I am right now.

I knew the second I laid eyes on Olivia tonight that the date I'd planned for her wasn't likely to go ahead. I tried though. *I fucking tried.* However, when Liv wants something, I'm helpless but to give it to her.

This dress she bought for me is sinful.

It's the lace. I'm fucking sure of it.

I've seen her in dresses this length.

Dresses that show off her breasts.

Dresses this same shade of red.

I've survived all of them.

What I've never seen her wear is lace.

And fuck if I only ever want her in lace for the rest of our lives.

I need to watch her take it off. The blush that stained her cheeks after I told her I wanted her to give me a show let me know she's never done this for anyone. And that sealed it for me. I fucking love knowing I can have something of hers that she's never given any other man.

I wrap my hand around her neck and growl against her ear, "Be bad for me, Liv."

She moans and her eyes find mine right before she reaches for my hand and leads me out of the bathroom into my bedroom.

My eyes are glued to that red lace that's covering her ass so damn sexily. However, when she pulls me to her, places her hands on my hips, spins me, and forces me to sit in the armchair in the corner of my room, the only thing I'm looking at is her face.

This woman owns all of my attention.

Every fucking ounce of it.

She stands confidently in front of me, her eyes making all sorts of promises. When she brings a hand up to cup her breast, I wonder if I'll even make it as far as her removing the dress. My dick is so damn hard I may take over long before then and beg her to wrap her lips around it.

"I'm going to need to see some skin," she says. I hear her but I'm so lost in watching her caress herself that I'm slow to respond.

"Callan."

I find her eyes. "No."

She gives me a look that says she's not accepting that answer. Closing the distance between us, she slides herself onto my lap and eyes the buttons on my vest. "I need to see your hands on these buttons. Now."

Fuck.

"Bossy looks good on you, Ace."

She strokes my dick through my trousers and brings

her mouth to my ear. "Your cum will look good on me but you won't get to see that tonight if you don't start removing clothes."

Christ, I'm not going to last if she keeps this up.

I grip her neck. Licking a line from her throat up her neck, I say, "Keep talking dirty to me, baby. Tell me where I'm going to come."

She takes hold of my free hand and places it on her breast. "I want to watch your face while you come all over my tits."

"Fuck, Liv." I'm barely keeping my shit together. "I need this dress off."

"I need this vest off."

I don't take my time. My vest hits the floor in seconds, right after the buttons go flying. I don't wait for her to boss me into removing my shirt. It meets the floor soon after my vest does.

The sound Olivia makes when my chest is bare reaches deep in my gut. When she kisses a trail down from my chest to my stomach and slides off my lap to kneel on the floor between my legs, I groan and lean back against the chair.

I grab a handful of her hair and close my eyes when she puts her mouth on my cock through my trousers. She keeps her mouth on me while also stroking me with her hand.

I pull her hair and thrust myself against her mouth.

"Undo your belt."

Having Olivia boss me is fucking hot. It only takes me a second to comply.

She presses her mouth harder against my cock while

she looks up at me through long, sexy lashes. "I want your dick in your hand."

I groan. "I want it in your hand."

She smiles against my cock as she caresses my balls through my trousers. "Do it."

Her eyes are glued to my hand while I do as she says.

"I like your eyes on me." I take hold of my dick and stroke it. I massage the head and watch as her lips part. It's one of the sexiest things I've seen.

"*I* like my eyes on you." She slides my trousers down and strips me of them and my boxer briefs while I watch every second of it and continue giving myself a slow tug.

I anticipate her hands or mouth on my dick next but she does neither. Instead, she stands and proceeds to give me the show I requested.

"Don't stop what you're doing," she bosses. I fucking love the confidence in her voice.

I do as ordered, watching as she curves her hands over her breasts, tweaks her nipples, and sways her hips. I'm held completely captive by her.

She comes closer and puts her foot up on the chair between my legs. "I'll take my dress off but I want you to take my shoes off."

I'd do any-fucking-thing she demanded right now just to get that dress off her. I undo the thin red strap around her ankle and take hold of her foot while I slowly slide the shoe off. Then, keeping hold of her foot, I wrap my other hand around her shin. I lift my gaze to hers. "If that dress isn't on the floor after I do this, you're going to learn what happens when you don't give me what I want."

"Maybe I want to learn that."

"Liv." I'm only just holding on here.

When I've got both her shoes off, I take charge. I'm done with waiting. "Show me what's under that dress. Now."

She finally reaches for the zipper at the back of the dress and lowers it. I sit through the most excruciatingly arousing seconds of my life while I watch as she slowly lets the dress fall to the floor. And *fuck me*. Olivia came here with the intent of killing me tonight.

I'm out of the chair before she sees it coming.

The lingerie she's wearing is filthy.

"This isn't the bra I told you to wear," I growl as I cup her breasts and bury my face in them.

She digs her fingers into my hair. "You're complaining?"

I suck her nipple into my mouth. "Fuck, Ace. How much lingerie do you own like this?"

"A lot. And you're going to buy me a lot more."

She's fucking right about that.

I'm planning on buying an entire fucking factory and directing them to design her the filthiest lingerie year-round.

I let her go. "Turn around and show me your ass."

She gives me a sexy smile before killing me some more.

This red lingerie is all lace and sheer fabric and straps. And not very much of any of that.

I run my finger down one of the suspender straps over her ass while enjoying the hell out of the thong she's wearing.

"The thong can come off tonight but the suspenders are staying. And you can put your heels back on before I fuck you."

She turns to face me. "First, I want you in my mouth." She sinks to her knees, and a second later, she's got my dick in her mouth and is running her tongue the length of my shaft.

This is the third blowjob Olivia has given me. Each time she fucks me with her mouth, I forget everything but the pleasure she's giving. I could fucking lose myself in her mouth.

She feels so fucking good and the urge to throat-fuck her is strong.

Fuck.

I grab a handful of her hair and watch her head bob while she sucks me off. My gaze drops lower to the bra she's wearing and then lower. When I get to those suspenders, I'm unable to stop myself from thrusting deeper into her mouth.

I groan as she takes me in and makes a moaning sound that vibrates over my cock.

My muscles tense and I pull her hair.

"Fuck, Liv. I'm going to come."

She takes me to the back of her throat and gives me one last suck before taking me out of her mouth. "I want you to come on my tits."

That request almost makes me shoot my load.

When she holds her tits up for me, I take hold of my dick and finish myself off on her chest.

Seeing my cum on her breasts affects me in a way I've never been affected by this act. I feel a level of possession where Olivia's concerned that I've never felt, and this only heightens that.

I reach for her face at the same time she moves off her knees. By the time she's standing, her body is pressed to mine, her arms are around me, and we're kissing each other like it could be the very last kiss we ever share.

When she ends the kiss, she looks down at the cum on my chest. "Sorry." She smiles up at me. "But you were looking at me all caveman-like and it couldn't be helped."

I trace a finger over her lips. "All caveman-like?"

Her smile grows. "Yeah, it's that look you get in your eyes sometimes that says, 'you, mine.'"

"God help us if I start speaking like that."

"I don't know, I think I might find it hot. Especially if you say it all growly."

There's something teasing at the edge of my thoughts while I take in the flush of her skin, the sexy smile on her lips, and the happiness in her eyes.

Something that's been sitting at the edge of my mind for days.

"Okay," she says, "I'm getting in your shower and you should join me. And then you need to gather your energy so you can keep rocking my big-dick era."

As the words leave her mouth, it slams into me.

I realize I'm all hers and always have been.

I want Olivia more than I want anything in this world.

I never want her big-dick era to end.

Fuck.

How have I been so blind to this?

"Callan. Did you hear what I said?"

I nod. "Yeah, and I might even feed you while we recover."

"Well, I mean, since this is a date, I should hope there will be food involved."

"You skipped the date, Ace. Remember?"

"I did no such thing. I just made it so we're a little bit late to it."

I lift my chin at her. "Get your ass in my shower so we can get to the food part."

She doesn't move. "What food are you thinking?"

"Your favorite food."

"But I have so many favorites. How will we choose?"

"I'm not letting you choose. We'll be here all night."

She pouts. "That was mean."

I brush my lips over hers. "It was the truth." I tap her ass. "Go. Get in the shower. I'll be there soon."

"Make sure you order me two desserts."

"I wouldn't dream of anything less." Olivia always orders two desserts for dinner. She refuses to narrow her choices down to one. And I'm the one called upon to eat half of each because, "*My hips do not need two desserts tonight, Callan.*"

I always beg to differ.

Her hips are one of my favorite things about her.

I watch her make a quick detour on the way to my bathroom so she can swipe one of my T-shirts from my closet.

Fuck, I want so much more of this in my life.

22

OLIVIA

CALLAN SOMEHOW MANAGED to have a dinner picnic set up on his terrace while we were in the shower. A dinner filled with all my favorites.

His condo is dark when we exit his bedroom, lit only by a trail of candles out to the terrace where we find cushions, throws, twinkle lights, more candles, and the picnic.

I look at him and find him watching me. "Was this the date all along?" Putting together all my favorite food at the last minute seems unlikely, even for a top chef.

He shakes his head. "No. I'd planned for dinner on a private yacht. However, I suspected we might not get as far as the yacht, so I had a back-up plan."

I adore his back-up plan. Knowing that he put great thought into tonight makes me feel special.

We eat dinner and talk about our days. He knows mine was difficult but I omit the part Penelope played in it. He told me last weekend that he won't stand back and watch it happen if she fucks with me again. I don't want to drag him into this, so I keep that to myself.

Callan tells me the investor he went to see in Florida has decided not to invest in his company.

"I'm sorry," I say as I reach for one of the truffle-infused deviled eggs. "What will you do now?"

"I'm reworking the proposal to present to other investors."

"Oh my god." I pick up another deviled egg and pass it to Callan. "You need to try this. It's divine."

He takes the egg and eats it. I can tell by the expression on his face that he agrees with me.

I eye the two remaining on the platter. "You can't have either of those."

He chuckles. "I wasn't planning on it."

I point at the lobster tail. "You can eat those."

"You didn't like the lobster?"

"Oh, I loved it, but it's your favorite of all the things here, so you should have it." I pick up another deviled egg. "So, what will your new proposal cover?"

He details it for me and when he's finished, he adds, "Dad seems to think this will have a better shot."

And there it is. The real reason Callan's changing his plan. His father.

I love Callan's dad like a second father, but I didn't have to grow up with him or live under his roof, and I wouldn't have liked to. Edmund Black is a hard-nosed man who is extremely driven to see his family succeed in the political arena. He craves power more than anything and will do whatever it takes to have that power.

His sons learned very early in life to strive for his love and affection. In Edmund's world, love is earned. He will love you very well so long as you prove yourself worthy of that love.

Bradford, the eldest son, didn't have to try as hard as the younger boys. I adore Bradford, but he was born perfect. I swear it. His father saw great potential in him from a young age, and so Bradford always had his love.

Unfortunately, for the rest of the boys, their parents' marriage had problems by the time their second son, Hayden, came along. Problems that spilled over to their children. Callan wasn't planned and neither was Ethan, the youngest son. These two were born into a lot of turmoil and Callan had to work hard to gain his parents' attention, let alone their love and approval.

I've watched Callan pursue his business goals relentlessly. He pushes himself hard and I think some of that is for his father's attention and approval. I've never said this to him, but I wish he could look at the outstanding things he's achieved in life and feel the pride in them that he should rather than feeling like it's still not enough.

A text comes through for me as he mentions his father. I quickly glance at my phone in case it's an urgent work matter. When I see the text, I laugh.

SASHA

I've issued Rhodes with an ultimatum. No more jerking off without me or else I'll ration him to sex once every few days.

I hold my phone up to show Callan. "How long do you bet this will last?"

He grins. "Two days max."

"Come on, I think she'll last at least a week."

"Care to put money on that?"

"God no. I've seen how whiny you get when you lose a bet."

"When have I been whiny?"

"That bet you made with my client that I'm never allowed to tell anyone about. The one where you lost your pride because you had to wear a tutu and a tiara to a football game."

"I wasn't whiny. I was pissed off because your asshole client cheated. There's a difference."

I roll my eyes. "He didn't cheat." Callan has always had an issue with the sports stars I work with. This particular client was a pro football player who Callan ended up disliking almost as much as he dislikes Slade. He actually didn't care that he had to wear a tutu to the game; he cared more that he lost the bet.

"We're gonna have to agree to disagree, Ace. But just let the record show that he did in fact cheat."

I laugh. I enjoy it when he gets all cocky like this. "I'm gonna win the bet about Sasha and Rhodes."

"I thought we weren't betting."

"I'm quietly betting and I will quietly win." I shrug. "So there."

He chuckles before turning more serious. "I can't see Rhodes standing for an ultimatum."

"Well, I doubt Sasha is going to hold him to it. I imagine it's just a bit of fun."

"I've seen ultimatums get out of control fast. They're poison."

Callan's being super serious now and I slow myself down so I can pay close attention. "With people you know?"

His eyes bore into mine. "With Ethan and Samantha."

This is news to me. "What happened?"

"When they first started dating, she gave him the ultimatum that he either spend more time with her or he spend no time with her. That was why he began spending less time with our family, and it was also why she continued issuing him ultimatums throughout their relationship. She knew he'd always do what she wanted. She manipulated the hell out of him and he was oblivious to all of it."

"Oh, wow."

"Yeah." He appears lost in his thoughts. And in his anger.

I reach for his hand. "I'm sorry she came between the two of you."

"Yeah, me too."

He's silent for a few moments before pulling me onto his lap and kissing my neck. "I don't want to spend our first date dwelling on this. Tell me about your remodel. Tell me why you're hellbent on not giving yourself what you really want."

I pull my face back so I can look into his eyes. "What do you mean?"

"Come on, Liv, we both know what you really want is a fancy bath that overlooks the city, a walk-in closet that's larger than my bedroom for all those red shoes of yours, and a library for your books and planners. And yet, your remodel doesn't allow for any of those things. Why not?"

"Those things are expensive."

He doesn't say anything; he simply waits for me to elaborate.

"They are! I'm remodeling to a budget."

His arms tighten around me. "Why? And don't tell me you don't have the cash. You do."

"Well, I don't now since I just lost a stack of it."

"Bullshit." His eyes search mine. "Give yourself what you want, Ace. You deserve it. And from what I've seen so far, barely any work has been done so far. I'm sure they could rework the plans."

Callan's right. I can afford a more expensive remodel. However, I can't bring myself to spend that kind of money. I mean, losing money on my stocks only reinforced this belief.

"Do you know what I deserve?" I lean into him. "I deserve at least two more orgasms tonight and I want you to be the man to give them to me."

His eyes flash with that possessive fire I've come to adore. "I better be the only man on your list for that job."

I smile into his neck as I press a kiss there. "Do you think you have it in you?"

"I know you're deflecting and I'll allow it because I want my mouth on your pussy, but just know this conversation isn't finished."

I don't doubt it. Callan has always been intent on ensuring I have everything I want. I imagine he'll double down on that now that he's made me his. And now that he's become all bossy.

I smile to myself as I think about the fact I won't allow him to boss me into everything. I see a lot of him feeling frustrated ahead. And goodness if that won't mean a lot of hot sex ahead too.

I think I might just live for defying this man.

23

OLIVIA

"Do we have to leave this bed?" I snuggle back against Callan early Friday morning. "I'm too tired for work today."

He kisses my shoulder while he spoons me, tightening his arms around me. "You want me to call Hayden and tell him you're taking the day off so you can suck my dick?"

"I just told you I'm too tired for any work. Sucking your dick takes a lot of energy."

"I'll settle for a handjob."

I roll to face him as the alarm on my phone alerts me to the fact I have to get up. "Shit." I put my hands to his chest. "I forgot I've got Slade this morning." Thank goodness I set the alarm last night or I may have completely missed my early appointment this morning.

A moment later, I'm out of bed and walking into the bathroom.

Callan's arm hooks around my waist just as I enter the bathroom. Pulling me close, he growls against my ear, "I never want to hear another man's name from your mouth while you're in my bed."

Oh my.

He lets me go and strides into his other bathroom without another word.

Holy heck.

Okay.

He has feelings.

Feelings that I really, really like.

I take a quick shower and put my red dress on because I didn't bring any clothes with me last night. When I find Callan, he's in the kitchen making coffee.

Moving next to him, I place my hand on his hip. "Understood."

His eyes find mine. He knows exactly what I'm referring to. "I lose my fucking mind when I think of you with another guy."

"You know it's just work between me and Slade, right?"

"I know, but it doesn't matter."

"Okay. But you need to know I've wanted you for a long time and now that I have you, other guys don't even exist for me."

He turns his body to mine, his arm coming around me so he can pull me close. The intense expression on his face doesn't look close to easing. "I'm trying hard not to be a jealous asshole, Ace. I need you to know that."

I pull his face down to mine. "I know." And then our lips are joined and we're pouring all our feelings into a kiss that makes me want to cancel everything on my schedule today.

"You need to bring some clothes here."

My heart speeds up. This feels almost as big a step as having sex with him was. And while I'd have thought I'd be racing to bring clothes here, I'm feeling hesitant.

Callan watches me process this before brushing his lips over mine again and saying, "It'd save you time in the mornings."

He's right.

"Okay, I will."

He passes me a travel mug filled with coffee and we walk to the elevator where he kisses me and places a small jewelry box in my hand. "This is what I came back to the condo for last night. You distracted me so much I forgot to give it to you."

I glance at the white box. "You got me a gift?" I adore gifts.

"It's just something small."

He may be telling me it's just something small, but the look on his face lets me know this is something important to him.

Lifting up onto my toes, I kiss him. "Thank you."

"You don't know what you're thanking me for yet. You may not like it."

I reach my hand around his neck. "I like it simply because you gave it to me."

Callan takes my coffee while I untie the pink ribbon around the jewelry box and open his gift. My breathing slows when I see what he's given me. I look up and find him watching me intently with so much emotion in his eyes. This gift is not just something small.

I stare at the gold charm lying on the tiny silk pillow and my entire soul sighs. I stare at it for a long time before finding his eyes again. "I love it, Callan."

He reaches for my wrist, for the gold bangle I always wear. Undoing the clasp, he slides the bangle off and replaces the one charm it holds with the one he just gave me. He then secures the bangle around my wrist again.

I watch him in silence while he does this, committing every second to memory. This is a moment I never want to forget.

After he places my old charm in the jewelry box, he puts the box in my hand, kisses me, and says, "That's our first."

As the elevator doors close between us, I try to calm my madly beating heart.

I collect charms to remember all my firsts. The special moments in my life. I buy them for myself and wear the newest one until I experience another first that must be celebrated. They're never a gift from anyone else. Not even Callan has bought me one before. He knows I put great thought into the charms when I buy them; they each have their own special meaning that only I know.

The charm he selected for me is a star and I can't stop swooning over it.

Callan has listened to me ramble about stars for years. About my interpretation of their meaning. Giving me this charm is significant on so many levels.

That's our first.

I think he intends on starting a new charm collection with me for *our* firsts.

I think this charm represents our first date.

And I think he's telling me he feels hope for us because he knows that stars represent hope for me.

❧

My day starts well. I meet with Slade and find out that his team are happy with the work we're doing to fix his public image. After my meeting with him, I work on some contracts Hayden asked me to go over. And then I have a call with Mace who catches me up on the fact he and his wife are working toward a reconciliation. I stare at my phone for a while after I get off that call wondering if I could ever forgive a husband who cheated on me. I don't know that I could. Hopefully, I'll never have to find out.

Callan calls at eleven a.m.

"Tell me," I say as I wedge my phone between my ear and my shoulder so I can continue typing an email while we talk. "Yes or no to a dramatic ceiling for a wedding?"

"A what?"

"You know, a dramatic ceiling installation for a wedding reception. Yes? No? Tell me all your thoughts."

"If I knew what an installation was, I might be able to give you my thoughts."

"We clearly need to get you out more."

"We do not. We need to never go out ever again."

"Picture extravagant lighting, or fabric draping, or flowers hanging from the ceiling. Big balls. Stars. That kind of thing. That's a dramatic ceiling."

"Fuck no."

"Why not?"

"Because if this is for Harper's wedding, you don't need the stress of worrying that any of that will fall on someone and hurt them."

This man knows me so well. "You're absolutely right. I'm taking a dramatic ceiling off my list." I finish typing my email. "How's your day going?"

"Abigail has only threatened to serve me poison twice. I'd say it's a good day."

I laugh and lean back in my chair. "Did you tell me last night that you're going out for drinks with Gage tonight? Or did I imagine that because I was in a sex coma?"

"You were in a sex coma but you didn't imagine it. We're checking out a club he's looking at investing in."

Callan's not the only one in this relationship who feels possessive. I suddenly have a whole lot of possessiveness coursing through me. I don't love the idea of Callan visiting the kind of club Gage invests in. And while I try to keep these feelings to myself, I fail. "I'm sending a blindfold over for you to wear. It's either that or I lock you up."

"I'm concerned I don't know myself at all. I like the idea of you locking me up." I hear Abigail's voice as she says something to him, and then he says to me, "I have to go. I'll call you tonight and see where you are when I'm finished with Gage."

After our call, I seriously contemplate sending that blindfold.

It's mid-afternoon when my day becomes a day I wish I didn't have to live through.

Blair calls me at three p.m.

"Are you okay?" she asks.

"Yes. Why?"

A text comes through from her with a link to an Instagram post.

@thetea_gasp

. . .

Gather round, friends. Do we have some tea for you! @macehawkins looks set to leave the hockey team he said he'd finish out his career with. Word is that tensions have been high within the team and management has said #byefelicia because they no longer want the kind of trouble between teammates his wife has caused. This is gonna break the bank for them. The hockey world is shook and so are we. Mace, we told you to ditch @olivialancaster. Girl would rather attend a rager than do her job. See Exhibit 1, 2 and 3 for snapshots of her partying hard on the weekend with @callanblack. We heard whispers that clients are ghosting her here, there, and everywhere atm. Seriously, Mace, she's GTG. And Callan? Zaddy, what are you thinking? Our hands are up if you're still searching for your forever bae. Olivia is not your girl. Come TDTM.

"Liv? Did you read it?" Blair asks while I read the post a second time.

"Yes." I'm speaking calmly but I'm furious on the inside, something Blair would know. It takes a lot for me to fully show my emotions.

Fucking Penelope Rush.

"I will represent you and I will make her pay."

"You cost too much. I can't afford you."

"I won't charge you. It will be my absolute pleasure to do this for free."

I laugh while releasing some tension. "God, these

gossip accounts have some fucking nerve. I spoke with Mace this morning and he was fine."

"It has to be bullshit, Liv. Bullshit that Penelope caused."

"Shit. I need to go and see Hayden about this."

"I'm here if you need me."

When I get to Hayden's office, his assistant lets me know he's on the phone. I wait outside his office, scrolling the social media accounts I check daily for my clients. Instead of finding stories about them, I find more about me.

Variations of the story about me sleeping on the job and clients leaving the firm are everywhere and all I can do is scroll in stunned and horrified silence.

By the time Hayden's booming voice filters into my awareness, my heart is beating hard and my mind is racing with questions as to why anyone cares enough to post lies about me.

My head jerks up when I hear Hayden bellow, "You won't like the consequences of that, Ryan. I will come after you with everything I have if you drag Olivia any further into this bullshit."

What?

I walk into his office without waiting for his assistant to usher me in. His eyes meet mine with regret, and as I listen to him end the call with more threats, I wonder what the hell has happened. Hayden is not a man who issues idle threats.

"Fuck." He shoves his fingers through his hair as he studies me with concern. "Are you okay? I was going to come and check on you after that call."

"What's going on, Hayden? I've just seen all the social

media posts and now you're threatening clients. What is it?"

He paces the large floor-to-ceiling window in his office. "Ryan has left the firm. He told his new firm we fucked up his contract. That information has been spread around and other clients have left today. Fuck knows how the lies made it to social media, but I intend on finding out."

Ryan's contract is the one I worked on last weekend, and I'm pissed off that he said I fucked it up. "My work on that contract was perfect," I say fiercely. There's no way I'm accepting this.

"I know."

I push my shoulders back as my chest rises and falls with determination. "I fucking mean it, Hayden. I've worked hard to get where I am. I won't have gossip ruin that, ruin me, or ruin you!" I have never been this angry in my entire life. Every inch of my skin is crawling with fury. If Penelope Rush was standing in front of me, I think I'd actually punch her.

"Liv." He comes to me and places his hands on my shoulders. "I know your work was perfect. I checked over it myself."

"What? Why would you do that?" That contract was complicated and lengthy. It would have taken him hours to go through it.

"It wasn't to check up on you. I suspected Ryan might pull something like this."

I release the air filling my lungs. Hayden was protecting me. I should have known he would be. He and his brothers have been protecting me for decades and I have all the feels about that. "Thank you. And god, I'm sorry that my personal life has affected the firm in this way."

He shakes his head. "This has nothing to do with your personal life."

I arch my brows. "Did you see those photos of Callan and me posted?"

"Trust me, this may look like it's about you, but the entire situation is because of me." He exhales a long breath. "Ryan and I go back. There's bad blood there that I thought had been resolved. It's reared its ugly head again and you were caught in the crossfire."

"Okay, but you should know that Penelope Rush may have caused some of this too, so some of this may be on me."

He looks at me questioningly. "How does Penelope figure in this?"

"It's a long story that involves many people, but the crux of it is that she wants me out of Callan's life. She's also tied up in the whole Mace Hawkins saga and wasn't pleased when I stepped in the middle of all that. It's a mess and she's using social media to come after me."

"Jesus. We need to pay you more."

I laugh, grateful for the release of some tension from my body. "So, yeah, it may not all be on Ryan."

Hayden's expression turns somber. "The bad blood between us involves his wife. I think it's safe to say he's gunning for me."

I blink.

In no scenario, would I have expected Hayden to utter those words.

"I won't allow him to get away with what he's doing to you," he says while I'm still staring at him in shock.

I just can't imagine Hayden being tied up in a situation like he just described. But then, he also rarely gets worked up like he is. And issuing threats isn't the norm for him either. It makes me wonder what's hiding under that indomitable, steadfast face he shows the world.

His cell phone rings and after he checks caller ID, he answers the call on speaker. "Callan."

Callan's angry voice fills the office. "Your fucking clients aren't going to know what's hit them, Hayden. Not once I'm finished with them. This bullshit they're throwing at Olivia needs to end."

"I agree. I'm—"

"I'm not messing around here. I watched her waste her time last weekend for that asshole and I know how hard this week has been for her while dealing with other clients who've jerked her around. She's the fucking best at what she does and I won't have anyone damage her career."

"Callan—"

Callan cuts him off again. "Where do these guys—"

"Callan," I say.

Silence fills the office for a moment before he says, "Liv." He's wound tight. "Are you okay?"

I'm only kind of okay but I don't want to worry him. "I'm okay."

"You're not. I can hear it in your voice."

I love that he knows the intricacies of my voice. "I will be, though. And you don't have to burn down the world for me. Hayden has this under control." It can't be stated enough, though, just how much I *love* his desire to torch the world for me. I will show him tonight just how much I love that.

"We'll see." He's never been good at backing down when he's on a mission for me.

I smile at Hayden who thankfully isn't taking any of this personally. I'm glad it's not Gage who I work for. Gage wouldn't have handled Callan so calmly. I've always appreciated Hayden's ability to hold his shit together in the face of a storm. In the entire time I've known the Black brothers, I've only seen Hayden lose his mind once. And holy hell, when he loses his mind, he *loses* it. So, it's a great thing he's calm now. I don't need a Black brother fight on my conscience as well as this social media slander that's hurting the firm.

"I'll talk to you later," I say to Callan before Hayden assures him he's handling this.

After the call ends, Hayden says, "I'm sorry my problems are hurting you, Liv."

"Holy shit," I say as a whole lot of thoughts tumble into place in my head. "That time you drank yourself through Europe years ago…that was because of Ryan's wife, wasn't it?"

Hayden is like me in that it takes a lot for him to show his emotions. At the mention of that time in his life, his face remains clean of his feelings. His eyes, however, they reveal so much. He gives me only word in answer to my question, but I see old pain resurface in his blue eyes. "Yes."

I want to ask him so many more questions.

What's happened now?

Is he still in love with her?

Has he kept in touch with her all this time?

Why the heck did her husband hire Hayden as his lawyer?

Has he had an affair?

It's when I get to that last question that I stop. There is no way Hayden slept with another man's wife.

"Liv," he says while he watches me chase all these thoughts. "If you want to know something, ask me. There are no secrets between us."

He's right. In his family, Callan's the one who held my heart, Ethan's the one who tried to lead me astray, Bradford's the one who always watched over me from afar but who I knew was always there making sure no harm came to me, and Gage is the one who went out of his way to protect me and the one who called me on my bullshit. Hayden's the one who saw through the stories I told myself about the hard things I had to deal with and who took the time to learn the real truths about me in a gentle way that was very different to Gage's way. And in exchange, he shared his truths with me when I asked for them. The only reason I don't know about this woman is because I'd just fallen in love for the first time when he spent six boozy months overseas. I was too self-absorbed to pay a lot of attention.

"I'm sorry I wasn't there for you back then," I say softly.

"I wouldn't have let you be there for me back then," he says gruffly.

"Are you still in love with her?"

"No." He doesn't even hesitate.

I give him a small smile. "But that doesn't stop the hurt that lingers, does it?"

This time, he takes a moment to contemplate that. "No, it doesn't."

We share a silent moment, each a little lost in our

thoughts before I place my hand on his arm. "I'm here if you want to talk. I hope you'll let me be here for you this time if you need that."

"I appreciate that." He silences his cell when it starts ringing. "Am I correct in assuming something's happened between you and Callan?"

I smile. "Yes. And you should probably prepare yourself for hardcore-protective Callan to show his face a lot more."

He laughs. "I look forward to seeing that. Fuck knows it's been coming for long enough."

"You say that like everyone but us knew this would happen."

"Everyone but you two *did* know. I was hoping it wouldn't take you guys until you were on your deathbeds to figure it out." When his cell starts ringing again, he glances at it and says, "I have to take this."

"Okay. And thank you for looking out for me."

He nods. "Leave everything with me. I'll handle it all."

As I'm leaving, he says, "And Liv." I turn back to him. "Mom's going to be ecstatic. You should prepare yourself for *that*."

$\sim$

KRISTEN

Okay, update time! All our men are coordinated for our weekend away! And whew, that was a job. How have you managed that as well as all the planning on your own for so long? Honestly, Gage was one step away from being disowned from the family as far as I was concerned.

OLIVIA

Gage is ALWAYS the disobedient one! But wait until Ethan comes home.

KRISTEN

He's worse than Gage?

OLIVIA

No. He's the bad boy of the family and will have you twisted around his little finger. I can't tell you the number of times I've changed plans on everyone simply because Ethan convinced me to.

KRISTEN

When he comes home, he's all yours.

OLIVIA

Lol!

KRISTEN

I wanted to say too that I saw the gossip post about you on Instagram today and I'm sorry you're dealing with this. I DM'd them and gave them all my thoughts on the lies they're posting.

OLIVIA

Thank you, Kristen. I appreciate that.

KRISTEN

Let's hope for Bradford's sake that they don't screenshot my message. His enemies would have a field day with that.

OLIVIA

You've got lawyers in the family, remember?

KRISTEN

Thank goodness. And speaking of one of my favorite lawyers, what's she doing tonight? I'm having some friends over for drinks and would love you to join us. I imagine a drink is called for after your day today.

OLIVIA

You have no idea. I don't have any plans. I'd love to come over.

KRISTEN

This is great news because I think Gage is dropping by later, and I may need you to step in if he tells me one more time that he doesn't want to play board games on the Saturday night while we're away.

OLIVIA

Leave him to me. He's going to love the board game I've selected this time.

KRISTEN

Trust me. That man is all yours. I'm all Gage'd out.

I laugh.

Gage is a lot of man to handle. That is for sure. But underneath all that, he's a pussycat. He just has to be managed. And since managing the Black brothers is what I've been doing for years, I have zero doubt Gage will take part in our board game night. He grumbles about it every single time we go away, but he always ends up playing. And he always ends up enjoying himself. *Men.*

I arrive at Kristen's and Bradford's condo at seven p.m. and am struck again by the opulence of their home. I'm not sure I could live in such luxury. I don't think I'd want to touch anything. One of my favorite things about Callan is that while he could afford a home like this, complete with full-time staff, he chooses to live more lowkey.

"Olivia!" Kristen says. "I'm so glad you came." She welcomes me in and leads me into the grand salon where Bradford is sitting on a sofa talking with Beckett Pearce and his wife, Jenna.

"You know my sister, don't you?" Kristen asks as Jenna greets me with a smile.

"Yes, we met at your wedding." I look at Jenna. "It's good to see you again."

Bradford eyes me as I sit on the sofa across from him. "I heard today was hell. You okay?"

"I'm angry over the entire situation, but I'm okay."

He rests his arm across the back of the sofa as Kristen slides in next to him. "Well, between Hayden and my wife, I imagine things will turn around soon."

He clearly hasn't heard about Callan's outburst over the phone this afternoon to know he should have added Callan's name to that list.

Kristen rests her hand on his thigh as she says to me,

"I heard back from that Instagram account after my message. She's removed that post, thanks to Hayden, I'm guessing."

"Good." I haven't bothered checking again this afternoon. I was too worked up over it all.

"I've never known her to post content that wasn't true," Kristen continues. "So it surprised me to see the post about you. I asked her where she got her info, and while she didn't share that with me, I think she's aware now that whoever it was can't be trusted."

"I messaged her too." Poppy Morgan joins us. "And I'm on a mission to find out who is spreading those lies about you."

I've met Poppy once. At Bradford's wedding. We talked for a total of five minutes, so I barely know her. I've heard she's fierce and I don't doubt it based on the look in her eye right now. "Thank you. I appreciate you girls taking my back."

I don't share what I know about the situation with them. I've spent a lot of time this afternoon thinking about it all and have concluded it must have been a perfect storm of Ryan trying to bring Hayden down and Penelope still spreading lies about me. I really don't want to wade any further into the drama of Penelope Rush and have decided to let Hayden handle this now. However, I also spent time this afternoon starting a file on Penelope. I'm not sure yet what I would use it for, but having a file of every little thing I can discover about her life will surely come in handy one day.

Poppy comes to sit next to me. "You took Kristen's back when she needed help. We've got you."

"Is Charlize coming tonight?" Jenna asks Poppy.

"No. She's currently sitting in a dentist's chair. Probably being lectured on the importance of flossing," Poppy says.

I give her a questioning look when Jenna and Kristen laugh.

Her expression is super serious. "Tell me you floss."

"I do. Why?"

She releases a breath like I just told her I do something that will save my life. Before she can answer my question, Adeline Spencer walks into the room and drops her clutch onto the sofa next to Jenna. Looking at me, she says, "Boundaries around flossing are very important to Poppy. In her relationship, no flossing equals no blowjobs."

A laugh bubbles out of me. "Seriously?"

"Yes," Poppy says like it's a boundary she believes everyone should have.

Bradford glances at Adeline. "I thought Jameson was coming."

"Don't get me started on that man," Adeline says as she sits. "He'll be lucky to sleep soundly tonight."

"Oh, god." Jenna laughs. "What did he do now?"

The way she says *now* makes me think Adeline's husband is always in trouble with her.

"I shared with him last week that one of my cosmetics suppliers has been giving me hell and not fulfilling orders on time. So, what did he do with that information?" Her eyes go wide. "He bought the company and ordered them to stop supplying every other business they've been supplying for years and only supply me. You can imagine how much those businesses hate me now."

Jameson Fox has a reputation for being ruthless. His

wife has a reputation for being the opposite. I imagine the sparks fly a lot in their relationship, but from everything I've heard, Adeline is his life and he'll go to the ends of the earth for her. It seems that's true.

Bradford's lips twitch with amusement. "I take it he's not coming then."

"No," Adeline says. "I told him I don't want to see him for the rest of the day." She glances at Kristen. "I'm more than certain it's time for cocktails."

Kristen laughs. "You're right." She pats her husband's chest. "Bradford's making them tonight. I taught him how to make our favorite."

I adore seeing Bradford's happiness with Kristen. Having known him since we were kids, I've watched him date a lot of women and not find happiness with any of them. The closest he came was with a lawyer he was engaged to for a long time, but I knew she wasn't the one for him because happiness never lingered in his eyes while he was with her. He confirmed that one night when we got a little drunk together. He told me he'd been in love with another woman for a long while but that it would never work out with her. I now know that woman to be Kristen.

Bradford makes cocktails and I tell him that if the Senator gig doesn't work out for him, he could take up the mixologist life.

Kristen introduces me to everyone properly while Bradford makes the drinks.

Then, after the guys leave to talk business in Bradford's office, the girls and I drink our cocktails while having a long conversation that weaves its way through our plans for the weekend; our love of being given flowers; our current favorite lipsticks; the book we each plan to read next; and whether Adeline should be mad with Jameson for trying to help her. We actually can't decide on that. Not one of us. I think maybe we've had too many cocktails by the time we get to the Jameson discussion.

The hours fly by, and I enjoy every second of them, which I wouldn't have thought possible this afternoon when I was in the middle of a shitty day.

Just after eleven p.m., Poppy begins educating us on the importance of having an agreed-upon method with your partner for who gets to eat the last slice of pizza.

"Ooh," Jenna says tipsily as Beckett and Bradford wander back into the room. "Like rock-paper-scissors? Or putting each other's name in a bowl and choosing that way? Or blind, naked wrestling? Or who can make the other come first?"

Beckett gives his wife an amused look. "I think someone is ready to go home."

I laugh, feeling light. "I like the way your brain works, Jenna."

"What's your method?" Kristen asks Poppy while snuggling into Bradford's side.

"The last piece is always mine. That's a given," Poppy says. "But I could get on board with Jenna's last idea."

"I like the idea of blind, naked wrestling," I say.

"Me too." Callan's voice sounds behind me and I turn faster than I've ever turned to look at him.

His eyes are firmly on mine. As are Gage's, who is standing next to him.

"I imagine you like the idea of blind, naked wrestling with Callan," Gage says.

I grin while my happily-tipsy brain thinks about that. "I imagine you may be right, Gage."

Poppy stands and reaches for her purse. "On that note, I must leave. It's time to stop my husband from working too late and let him think he can boss me into doing filthy things to him."

It takes her less than a minute to say goodbye and leave. I stare after her. "Wow, she means business."

"She really does," Adeline agrees. "And nothing gets between Poppy and sex."

"So," Kristen says, glancing between Callan and me as he sits next to me, "you two are together? I didn't want to presume or ask earlier because it's one thing to have your private news spilled all over social media without permission and another to share it when you're ready."

Callan extends his arm across the back of the sofa, resting his hand on my shoulder. "Yes, we're together."

"I'm so happy for you both," Kristen says and I feel the genuine affection from her.

Adeline's phone rings and she excuses herself to take the call from Jameson. When I laugh at the stern expression on her face, Callan leans in close and asks, "What's funny?"

I turn to him, my hand resting against his hip as I catch him up on the Jameson fiasco. When I ask his thoughts on whether Adeline should be mad with her husband he says, "Fuck no."

I smile and lean in to brush my lips over his. How I've managed to keep my hands and my mouth to myself since he arrived is beyond me. "You would say that. You men stick together."

I feel his smile in our kiss. "You women don't?"

"Well, we are right, so there is that."

He grins and kisses me again. "How much have you had to drink, Ace? Like, are we looking at me having to put you to bed or are we looking at you showing me your ass?"

"That depends on how fast you get me home."

He takes hold of my hand and stands, pulling me up with him.

Kristen looks up at him. "Are you guys leaving?"

"Yeah," Callan says.

"They've got years to make up for," Gage drawls.

Because I'm feeling frisky, I say, "We really do, and it's going to take weeks, so if I hear one word about you grumbling over our board game night that's coming up, there will be hell to pay for the interruption you caused us."

Gage's lips twitch.

I don't get to hear his response because Callan's already directing me to the elevator. Once we're safely inside it, he pulls my face to his and strips my ability to think with a kiss that consumes me, body and soul.

He forces me back against the wall of the elevator as he lets my lips go so he can kiss his way down to my throat and then to my breasts. His hands are everywhere and when he curves one over my ass before reaching for the hem of my skirt, I'm a little concerned he's forgotten where we are.

"Callan." I grip his hair. "I'm not fucking you in Bradford's elevator."

He growls something filthy against my breasts before lifting his face to mine. "I want you every second of every day." He presses his erection against me, groaning as he does. "I'm finding it fucking hard to control myself."

I bring my hands down to his face. "I feel the same way."

He kisses me again before letting me go. The elevator reaches the parking garage and a few minutes later, Callan asks, "Do you want to sleep at my place or yours tonight?" as he pulls out into traffic.

I reach for his thigh and rest my hand there, feeling all the feels over him assuming I want to stay with him tonight. Over him wanting to stay with me. "Let's go to yours. My contractor sent me an update this afternoon and he's finally started on my bedroom."

"Fucking finally," Callan says. He's less than impressed with the contractor I chose. He thinks the guy is useless.

I squeeze his thigh. "How did you and Gage go tonight? Is he planning on buying the club?"

He brakes as he shifts down gears to turn left. Callan may not splash his cash on his home but he doesn't spare a cent when it comes to his cars. I listened to him grumble for a week straight when Aston Martin recently transitioned to only automatic transmissions. He paid them a fortune for a manual transmission six months ago when he bought this car.

"I don't think he will." He looks at me. "I should have skipped the club. It was shit."

"Why?" I can't imagine Gage looking at buying a club that isn't up to his high standard. His preference isn't to have to put a lot of work into his investments.

"The music was too loud."

I almost burst out laughing. Not only at what he says but also at the grumble in his tone.

Callan has frequented clubs for years. I'm under no illusions about his sex life. I know he's slept with a lot of women and indulged in all kinds of kinks as well as threesomes. Gage's clubs were a common destination for him. Loud music has never bothered him once in his life.

I angle my body to his and reach up to run my fingers through his hair. I let my hand linger at the nape of his neck while I say, "Was it, baby?"

This is the first time I've called him that and it's clear in his eyes that he likes it a lot.

He doesn't answer my question. Instead, he turns back to focus on the drive. We sit in silence for a minute while my thoughts all converge around what he was really saying.

The music wasn't too loud; he just didn't want to be there.

He wanted to be where I was.

I trace my finger over his skin. "What are your plans for tomorrow?"

The look he gives me tells me the only plans he has for tomorrow involve me.

I smile as that look makes its way through my veins. "I thought I might put my hair up in a sexy librarian bun and put my glasses on for you tomorrow afternoon when I get home from the farmers market."

"Fuck, Liv." The car jerks forward when he presses a little hard on the gas. Callan is a little obsessed with my glasses. I don't wear them often and have decided I should.

"Also, you're not coming with me to the market."

"Why not?"

"Because you will try to hurry me along and I don't like being hurried while I buy fruit and vegetables."

"I don't hurry you. You take fucking forever to choose between tomatoes."

"There's an exact science to selecting tomatoes."

"Which is?"

"I'm not telling you. It's not information you will ever use."

He chuckles before looking over at me and turning serious. "How are you after today?"

I drop my hand from his neck and rest it between us. "I'm okay and I mean that this time. I think everything will work out."

His features darken. "It will. I'm making sure of it."

I frown. "What?"

"My lawyers are all over this. I'm not standing back any longer, Ace. Once I'm finished with all these social media accounts, you won't ever have to worry about this kind of shit again."

I take in his hard expression and determination and know he's definitely not standing back any longer. When Callan Black decides on a course of action, no one and nothing can stop him. The fact that this course of action is all for me has me eyeing his lap, wondering if he could still drive with me sitting in it. He makes me want to be reckless like I have never been.

"Can you drive faster?"

He looks at me, confused. "Why?"

His confusion is warranted. I'm the girl who tells him to slow down, not speed up. Safety first.

"Because I want to put your dick in my mouth and I

want to do that soon. And I really don't think it would be safe to do that while you're driving."

He curses and says some filthy things to me about what he wants to do to me after I suck him off.

He then puts his foot down and it has to be said that for the first time in my life, I find his preference for speed sexy as hell.

24

CALLAN

I STEP into the elevator that will take me up to Penny's condo and grit my teeth. She was surprised when I called earlier to let her know I wanted to see her. And she tried to talk some dirty shit to me that I was quick to put a stop to. I don't want to be here, but I have some things to say to her that she needs to hear.

"Callan." She's waiting for me in her foyer. I hear the hesitation in her voice and see it in her eyes. Penny's not a dumb woman. She knows why I'm here. However, she's clearly still trying to weasel her way out of having to acknowledge the trouble she's caused.

"I think you know why I'm here, so let's just cut straight to it." I'm having difficulty even looking at her. How I spent so much time with her is beyond me because all I see now is a toxic woman.

Her features wobble. "Why are you here? I mean, it's a lovely, unexpected surprise, but I've been wondering why you called out of the blue."

"I can spell it out for you if you need me to, but I'd

rather you not waste my time. I'm here to make it clear I won't tolerate you fucking with Olivia anymore."

She takes only a few seconds to figure out which path to go down with me. Then, she removes the pleasant mask from her face and says, "She's manipulating you. You know that, right?"

"I suspect the only woman who's been manipulating me is the one I'm currently looking at. Olivia doesn't have one bone in her body that would allow her to manipulate anyone."

She folds her arms across her chest. "I have never tried to manipulate you."

"Regardless, I'm not here to talk about me. I'm here about Olivia."

"So, what, all the time we spent together meant nothing to you?"

"We were friends, Penny. I never led you to believe anything else."

Her face twists. "You men are all the fucking same. You use women to suit yourself and when you no longer need us, you throw us away without a care for how we feel."

"I never used you."

"You used me for sex."

"You knew it wouldn't go any further. And let's remember correctly. You were the one wanting it to begin with."

She presses her lips together before spewing her ugly thoughts all over the place. "Olivia won't make you happy like I could. You'll wake up in twenty years and wonder why you chose a woman who became frumpy and fat when you could have had a woman who took care of herself."

I clench my jaw. "What the fuck did you just say to me?"

"You heard me. And you know it's all true."

I take a step toward her. "That's the last thing you will ever say about Olivia. To me. To the gossip accounts. To the fucking world. And if you ever do say something about her and I find out, you will fucking regret it."

When she doesn't respond, I add, "My lawyers will take everything from you if you so much as look in Olivia's direction. Keep that in mind before you go running to the fucking gossip accounts."

With that, I stalk out of her condo and out of her life.

I spend a couple of hours in my gym after seeing Penny. I need all those hours to work my anger from my body. I'm stepping out of the shower when Olivia returns from the farmers market.

She wanders into my bathroom as I secure a towel around my waist. "You'll be pleased to know I found the perfect tomatoes."

I reach for her. "So, what, we've got two tomatoes to last us the entire week?"

Her body presses to mine as she rolls her eyes. "Smartass."

I cup her ass and dip my mouth to her collarbone. "Fuck, you smell good. Is this perfume new?" I've only just memorized her favorite perfume.

"Yes. I'm trialing it."

"No need for a trial. Give me the name of it and I'll make sure you never run out."

She laughs. "Have you had a good morning?"

"It's better now that you're home."

"That was eye-roll worthy. Don't go soft on me now, Callan Black."

I lift my head and grin at her. "What's a man gotta do to convince you to get your clothes off? That's what would make my morning better."

She puts her hands to my shoulders and gently pushes me away. "Still soft. Do better. And after you get dressed, come and help me in the kitchen."

"With what?"

"With the two tomatoes I bought. We've got visitors coming tonight who we have to cook for."

"Who?" This is news to me.

"Rhodes, Sasha, and Blair are coming over for drinks. I decided we'd also cook dinner for them."

"Right, so you have a few sleepovers with me and you take that to mean you can host dinner parties here?"

She grins. "That's better." She turns to leave, calling over her shoulder, "Wear that new black T-shirt of yours for me. You'll probably have more luck convincing me to take my clothes off if you do."

I put my new black shirt on and spend the afternoon in my kitchen cooking with Olivia. It takes us all afternoon to prepare dinner because I fuck her three times. Once in the kitchen. Once in the living room. And once under the chandelier above my formal dining table, while I tell her she can plan as many dinner parties here as she wants, so long as she's aware I get to eat at the table first.

"I want you to take me to the beach tomorrow," she says while we're in my bathroom getting ready for dinner.

"I think they're forecasting rain for tomorrow." I watch as she pulls her hair up into a ponytail. The filthy thoughts that fill my mind as I look at that ponytail are some of the dirtiest I've ever had. It seems the more sex I have with Olivia, the more I crave.

She shrugs. "I still wanna go."

I move behind her and circle my arms around her waist, resting my hands on her stomach. I fucking love her softness. Dropping a kiss to her shoulder, I say, "The beach it is." I run my eyes over her breasts. "You can do filthy things to me in the rain."

A text comes through on her phone which is sitting on the vanity in front of her. After she checks it, she says, "Blair's here."

I let her go. "I'll get her a drink. Do you want something?"

She reaches for me with a smile, her hand briefly touching my arm as I turn to leave. "I'd love some wine."

My gut tightens at her touch. At that smile. At fucking everything in this room right now.

The simplicity of being with her.

The ease.

I never imagined the day I'd be happy to cook for an entire afternoon and enjoy every minute of it.

I think about my parents' marriage and what I've witnessed between them during my life. Struggle, anger, disappointment. But also, friendship, respect, commitment.

Gage's advice from weeks ago comes back to me. *Take*

another look at their marriage and you'll see what's possible when two people work at a relationship.

He's right. And I've been blind to it for a long time because all I could ever see was the pain and hurt and confusion of my childhood. My parents did work at their relationship. I don't know when or how because I was shut down to it by my teen years, but they're now in love and care deeply for each other.

Happiness *is* possible within a marriage.

The thing about happiness that I've learned in my own life is that it takes careful cultivation and an awareness that it doesn't look like what the world leads us to believe. The marketing machines of the world share photos showing perfect moments, supposedly happy moments. They tell us to simply choose happiness, to smile and be happy, but that's a crock of shit.

Some days don't feel good. They're hard to get through and feel soul-destroying. And just telling ourselves to be happy doesn't change our feelings about how shitty that day is. And yet, as I look at Olivia and think about all the days we've helped get each other through, I remember how she never failed to make me smile at least once on those days. She made me happy even while I felt unhappy because we've put the work in and know how to be there for each other.

I never wanted a relationship with anyone because I feared what I thought marriage does to people. I had it all wrong and the very relationship I used to base my thoughts on proves that.

Happiness is possible within a marriage if you choose *to work for it.*

> **OLIVIA**
> I'm moving to the beach.

CALLAN
No, you're not.

> **OLIVIA**
> You're not the boss of me.

CALLAN
I'd fucking like to be.

> **OLIVIA**
> You say the sweetest things to me,
> Callan Black.

I'M SWELTERING my way through July. New York is having record temps and I'm alternating between begging Callan to take me to the beach as often as he can (everyone should get a boyfriend with a helicopter); driving him wild by walking around his condo naked as often as I can (I highly recommend this to every woman out there; men say yes to so many things while under the influence of naked asses); and wishing more brides chose indoor weddings. Callan and I have attended four weddings this month and I've vowed never to have an outdoor summer wedding.

I also spend the month alternating between wanting to fire my contractor (he keeps ghosting me for days at a time because of his divorce nightmare that's apparently interfering with his ability to work...buddy, we've all got problems and the rest of us keep showing up to work); having dinner at Callan's parents' home (Hayden was right: their mom is ecstatic that Callan and I are together, and she has begun hosting way more Black family dinners); praying that the current stock market rally continues because I'm seeing my stocks slowly go back up in price; and texting back and forth with Harper trying to get her to settle on wedding plans.

I can't decide which is more stressful this month: the heat wave, dealing with my contractor, or dealing with Harper. By the time the Black family weekend away arrives at the end of the month, I'm a hot mess.

"Oh my god!" I cry on the morning of the Friday that we're leaving for the Catskills. "I didn't bring my hat!"

Callan reaches for my hands to stop me from madly pulling my packed suitcase apart. "Babe. Stop. We can get your hat on the way out this afternoon."

I know he's just trying to help, and I know he's right, but my entire body is filled with some kind of weird turbulent energy this morning that I can't get a handle on. This causes me to snap, "We're already going to be pushed for time. I don't want to have to stop on our way out. And stop telling me to stop. It annoys me. And don't call me babe. I don't like it."

He arches a brow and gives me a look that says *I see it's going to be one of those days*. Then, he says, "There's no rule that says we have to arrive at a specific time. We're getting your hat."

This only irritates me more. "Stop trying to boss me, Callan. I'm really not a fan."

"Don't I know it." He draws a long breath. "I'll buy you a new hat. You can wear it or not." With that, he walks out of the bedroom, leaving me to stew over all my feelings about what he just said.

I've been staying at Callan's for the last five weeks since my contractor started work at my condo. I've loved this time with him and I know he has too. However, over the last few days, I've been in a mood. I don't know why, but I'm feeling prickly about everything and have been difficult.

Callan has remained calm throughout every little outburst while I've started wondering why I'm so lucky to have a guy who is so calm when he has every right to argue back.

I know I'm being difficult and yet I can't stop myself. I'm glad for a weekend away; I'm hoping to find time to think about the cause. The last thing I want is to fight with Callan over dumb things.

I finish packing and meet Callan in his kitchen for breakfast. We move past my outburst and discuss the logistics of getting away this afternoon. We both have a busy work schedule this morning. Our goal is to leave just after lunch, which is really pushing it for me. I don't mention that, though. I am the one after all who just argued with him over having to leave at a certain time.

He drives me to work like he has for most of this month. This started because I told him I didn't want to walk in the heat. After the last few days of my moods, I'm pretty sure he'd drive me next door just so he didn't have to listen to me complain about the weather.

By the time we arrive at my work, I feel awful about snapping at him earlier. After he stops the car for me to get out, I place my hand on his thigh and lean across to kiss him. Letting my mouth linger near his, I say, "I'm sorry I've been so difficult this week."

He curves his hand around the nape of my neck and pulls me back for another kiss. "I've made a mental note to move us to the Arctic before next summer."

I smile as I search his eyes. All I see there is affection. No irritation. "You know I'd just switch my whining to how cold I am, right?"

"This does present a whole other problem. You should create me a spreadsheet of all the possible locations around the world with weather that's acceptable to you."

"You know you should never ask for a spreadsheet unless you really want one."

"Oh, I want one, Ace. I want to watch you put your glasses on and get all nerdy creating it."

I grip his shirt and steal one last kiss. "Don't buy me a hat. We'll stop by my condo and collect mine."

I stand on the sidewalk and watch as he pulls back out into traffic. I ignore the heat for a few minutes while I watch his car and think about him.

I think this man would do almost anything for me

and that thought has me pressing my hand to my stomach to settle all the feelings I have over that. I can't even begin to pick my way through those feelings, but there's a *lot*. Happiness, excitement, joy, anxiety, uncertainty. I need to plan for some thinking time because my mind is beginning to feel a little full and overwhelmed thanks to all those feelings.

My morning is chaotic. After the shambles of last month when the firm lost clients thanks to Ryan and Penelope, we've brought in a lot of new clients this month. I finished working with Mace Hawkins when he walked away from his team to rebuild his marriage. I also finished working with Slade Sullivan when the team told him they were happy with the work he's done on himself and his career. He texts me often and keeps me updated on his relationship with Christa. The last text let me know they've been dating for weeks and getting to know each other properly after their original whirlwind period of getting to know each other. My new clients aren't athletes, but they're keeping me just as busy. Today, particularly so.

I text Callan just before our regular eleven a.m. call.

OLIVIA

> I'm too busy for our call today. But the great news is you get me for an entire afternoon drive and then a whole weekend. How lucky are you?

CALLAN

> If I was the boss of you, I'd order you to call me regardless.

OLIVIA

> I'm so glad I decided a long time ago to never get a boss.

CALLAN

> You owe me, Ace.

OLIVIA

> Like, what are we talking here? A handjob? Blowjob? I'm not doing either of those while you're driving this afternoon if that's where your brain has gone.

CALLAN

> Fuck, you're filthy. I was thinking I could steal you away for a few hours tomorrow morning for time alone to talk, but I like your ideas better.

OLIVIA

> It's settled then. I'm the boss of us.

CALLAN

> You always have been, baby.

Lunch comes and goes without me stopping to eat. And then, just after lunchtime, everything starts to go wrong.

Callan calls and I hear his stress straight away.

"I'm not going to be able to get away until later today." His voice holds both his stress and his apology.

"What's happened?"

"My CFO has just hit me with some reports that show I've got a problem in Canada. I need to go over everything today." He blows out a long breath. "I'm sorry, Ace, but I can't put this off."

"It's okay. And honestly, I've got a lot of work that I should do today, so this works for me."

"You don't have to wait for me. You could drive with Gage and Luna."

"No, I want to go with you. I don't mind waiting."

We agree that he'll keep me updated and let me know what time we'll likely leave. I then get to work trying to complete everything I have to. It'd be great not to have to do any work over the weekend.

Callan texts around five p.m. and lets me know he should be ready to leave in an hour. I call it a day and decide to go to my place and find my hat. I'm on my way there when Slade texts me.

SLADE

Where are you? I need to see you.

OLIVIA

Why?

SLADE

I need you to help me choose an engagement ring.

OLIVIA

What? Why are you choosing an engagement ring? Have you learned nothing, Slade? Jesus. Stop with the engagement rings after a few dates! And don't you have a sister or a mother or a friend who can help you with this?

SLADE

Nope. This is why I need you, Olivia. You give me shit straight. Tell me where you are now. I'm coming to you.

OLIVIA

Do I really have to help you?

SLADE

Your current location?

OLIVIA

Ugh.

I send him the address of my condo and tell him he's only got half an hour before I won't be there any longer. I then send him another text and tell him not to put his safety at risk in order to get there on time.

When I arrive at my condo, I find the disaster of disasters in my bedroom and I'm in the middle of a hot-mess moment when Slade arrives.

He takes one look at me when I let him in and says, "Fuck, who died?"

I fling my arm in the direction of my bedroom. "It's in there." I don't manage to get any other words out. I think I'm all worded out. Callan was right about my contractor. I should have just hired his guy.

Slade heads into my bedroom. I hear his, "Fucking hell," from my living room. Then, I hear, "What the fuck happened, Olivia?"

"I can't come back in there," I call out. "I'm just going to curl up on my couch and close my eyes and pretend everything is okay."

Half a minute later, he's standing in front of me. "I can fix that for you."

I blink. "Huh?"

He jerks his chin toward my bedroom. "I can fix your bedroom."

"Slade. There's a massive hole in the wall between my bedroom and bathroom. The bathroom is destroyed and cannot be salvaged. I'm not sure anyone can fix it."

"Well, I sure as fuck wouldn't let the guy who did it back in to fix it, but it's absolutely fixable. And since I grew up helping my dad build shit and then worked for him for a while, I can help."

"What have you built?" It was probably a dog kennel.

He pulls out his phone and scrolls his photos until he finds what he's looking for. Showing me, he says, "I helped Dad remodel his place this year. We did his bathrooms, kitchen, and laundry."

"Wow." I'm unable to hide my surprise as I look at the photos. "You did all that?" The work is top quality and the ideas they brought to life are impressive.

He looks at me proudly. "Yeah. And actually, I did most of it because Dad's arthritis is pretty bad these days." He turns serious when he says, "I've got you, Olivia. I promise you I can fix this."

I'm beginning to think he really can.

"You're so busy. When would you find time?"

"I'd make time for you after everything you've helped me with."

"Thank you. I'd appreciate that." I can only blame the shock I'm in for my agreement. Usually, I'd dedicate a great deal of time before making this kind of decision. But then, it didn't work out so great for me with the guy who demolished my bedroom and bathroom.

His smile fills his entire face. "I'll get started this weekend. Send me the plans you've got and I'll send you my suggestions."

I agree to that and then say, "Okay, show me these rings and tell me why you're proposing again so soon."

He scrolls to some other photos and holds his phone out. "I'm not proposing yet. I just like to be prepared."

I look at the rings. "These are both beautiful, but I don't think you should choose either of them."

He frowns. "Why not?"

I hand him back his phone. "Because you can't decide between them." I smile gently. "I believe when the time comes, and you find the exact right ring, you will know deep in your soul that it's the one. You won't even contemplate asking me if I think it's the one." Then, I use my best stern voice on him. "And if you even consider getting engaged within the next few months, I will hunt you down and slap some sense into you. Spend some time getting to know her and letting her get to know you, Slade. If this is the woman who you'll spend the rest of your life with, there's no need to rush this. You'll have forever after all."

"The man you end up marrying will be a lucky fucker. But I pray for his balls." He grins. "I want you to meet Christa soon. I think she'll like you."

After Slade leaves, I gather the courage to go back into my bedroom and assess the damage my contractor has done. It looks like he took a wrecking ball to the room. I can't begin to imagine how he managed this damage.

He'll be hearing from me, but not until tomorrow. Tonight, I just need to breathe.

When I step out onto the sidewalk, I send Callan a text.

OLIVIA

I have my hat.

CALLAN

You have eleven hats.

OLIVIA

Huh?

CALLAN

I sent Abigail out today. She selected ten hats for you in case you couldn't find yours.

OLIVIA

You are too much.

CALLAN

I wasn't taking any chances.

OLIVIA

I'm very fussy with my hats. I might not like any of them.

CALLAN

I'm aware.

OLIVIA

You feel very bossy tonight. It's actually kind of hot.

CALLAN

Good to know.

OLIVIA

Don't settle into it too much. You know my moods are all over the place right now.

CALLAN

Your moods don't scare me, Ace. I have a knee and I'm more than happy to put you over it.

Holy hell.

I have never wanted to get up close and personal to a knee so much.

OLIVIA

I think I'm feeling a mood coming on right now.

26

OLIVIA

By the time we arrive at the Catskills, it's after 11 p.m. We're both tired and ready to fall into bed, but Callan's family are still awake and want to spend some time talking.

Callan's mom insists I sit next to her. Callan smiles at me as he takes the seat across from me next to Bradford. His smile says *I've got you, Ace. I'll get you out of here soon.*

I talk with Ingrid for twenty minutes and answer all the questions she has for me. We also talk about my parents' trip and the fact they're currently in Perth, which is in a country Ingrid desperately wants to visit one day.

After Callan draws his mother's attention, I turn to Gage, who's sitting on the other side of me. "Did Luna get to sleep okay?" His daughter has trouble sleeping in new places.

A dark look crosses his face. "She didn't come."

"Why not?"

His jaw clenches. "Shayla put a stop to it."

This surprises me. Gage and his ex have been in a

good place for the last year. "What's happened? I thought you two were good now."

"We were. Until the asshole she's with cut in on that."

"Shit. I'm sorry. Is there anything I can help with?"

"No. I'm handling it."

The way he says this tells me he's not treading lightly like he did for so long after they broke up. Gage is one of the best fathers I know and his daughter comes first above everything else in his life. He let Shayla get away with a lot of shit after they broke up. He did that for Luna's sake. But now, I think any treading lightly is off the table. I think Shayla's in for a rude awakening. The man she had wrapped around her finger for so long is gone and in his place is this new Gage.

I lean toward him. "Good. I'm glad." When he looks at me with surprise, I say, "She took you for a ride. I'm glad you're not allowing that anymore. You have rights as Luna's father and Shayla needs to remember that."

"Liv." Callan draws my attention and I find him standing. "It's time we put your moody ass to bed."

His mother looks horrified. "Callan," she chastises.

I laugh and touch her arm. "No, he's right, Ingrid. I have been moody. And I really do need sleep."

We say goodnight to everyone and Callan leads me to our bedroom.

"I don't have the energy for sex tonight," I say as I search for my pajamas.

"You can just sit on my face. I'll do all the work."

I roll my eyes. "Do you know how many core muscles that takes. Besides, we both know where you eating me out leads and it's not to sleep."

His arm is around my waist and his chest is pressed to

my back faster than I can move away from him. "Next time you tell me we're not having sex, don't use words like *eating me out*," he growls against my ear.

And just like that, I'm suddenly awake. Smacking at his hands, I turn and reach into his shorts. "You need to get me off fast." I stroke his dick, loving the hiss that falls from his lips. "And if you try to fuck me while I'm sleeping, there will be another mood for you, and it won't be one that I'll want to be put over your knee for."

He strips me. "When the fuck have I tried to fuck you while you were sleeping?"

"Pretty much every morning." I grip his hair while he buries his face in my tits.

He chuckles and lifts his face to mine while taking hold of my hips and pulling my body against his. "You're fucking cute." He kisses me. "You're the one who wakes me up with your pussy to my dick, and then you turn that into me trying to fuck you while you're sleeping?" He kisses me again, this time a lot rougher. "Keep it up, Ace, and see how fast I put you across my knee."

"Just shut up and fuck me already."

He shuts up and fucks me.

After, he pulls me close and murmurs, "We need to get away more often."

I snuggle into his chest. "We need to get through a million weddings first."

"We're almost done. And then you're all mine."

We wake to rain. It's light and soothing to my soul. And while I was looking forward to getting out for a hike, I'm happy to sit outside under cover with a tea and the mountain views.

The guys spend the morning fly fishing while Ingrid, Kristen, and I stay at the house we've rented. It's a lovely few hours with the girls and by the time Callan returns with his dad and brothers, I'm feeling a lot lighter than I have all week.

Kristen and Bradford are on lunch duty and make us the yummiest burgers. I ask Kristen for the recipe while the guys discuss our plans for this afternoon. Thanks to the rain, our planned hike has to be canceled.

I glance around the table. "I thought we could play board games this afternoon instead of tonight."

When Gage groans, Kristen looks at me, her lips twitching.

"Stop your groaning, Gage," I say. "We all know you secretly love board games."

Callan puts his arm across the back of my chair and chuckles. "What games are we playing?"

"Game," Gage says, correcting him.

"I don't know," Hayden says, amusement in his eyes, "it looks like this rain has settled in. I think we could fit a few games in."

I stand and begin gathering plates as I look at Gage. "I think you're going to love the game I've selected."

"I'm going to fucking love it once it's finished."

Bradford eyes him. "I'm making a note to buy Luna board games for Christmas."

"Oh, I like your style," I say. "I'm doing the same."

Gage doesn't say a word. He just shoots us both daggers.

Callan helps me clear the table and load the dishwasher. I then grab the board game I bought and Kristen and I set it up at the table.

"Right," I say once everyone is settled and ready to begin. "This is like R-rated Pictionary."

Gage leans forward, interested like I knew he would be, but still making out like he isn't. "You know none of us can draw, Liv."

"That's the fun of it, Gage. Now, pair up and get excited."

It only takes the guys ten minutes to really get into the game. I think it's the meat curtains that Gage has to draw for Hayden that does it. Or maybe it's the queef that Bradford has to draw for Kristen. Either way, we're all soon laughing and madly drawing naughty pictures for each other while the guys' competitive streaks kick in. I love a good competition myself, but I've honestly never come across four men more competitive than these Black brothers.

"What the fuck is that?" Hayden asks Gage halfway through the game, looking at the scribbles on the paper in front of the two of them as the timer ends.

Gage looks at his brother like he's an idiot. "Blue balls. How the fuck did you not get that?"

I laugh as I eye the naked stick figure with large hanging balls set against the sky. It looks like the stick figure is floating amongst clouds. Gage has drawn arrows between the balls and the sky, and I see his meaning now, but I'm not sure I would have guessed blue balls from the drawing.

My phone buzzes with a text while we're all laughing over Gage's blue balls.

I check it and find a message from Slade.

SLADE

> Do you like these ideas?

I tap the file he's sent me and scroll through it, finding new plans for my remodel, along with photo examples of his ideas.

"What's that?" Callan asks.

I hold out my phone to him. "I haven't told you yet, because…well, because I really didn't want to think about it, but my contractor has ruined my remodel. Slade was there when I discovered this yesterday and he's offered to help fix it."

His brows pull together. "Slade was at your place?"

"Yes. Long story, but he wanted to show me some engagement rings he's looking at." I put my phone in his hands, wanting him to focus on the remodel more than the fact Slade was at my condo. "Look at the photos of what my bedroom looks like at the moment."

"Fuck," he says as he scrolls through the photos.

"What is it, Liv?" Bradford asks.

Callan looks up. "Her contractor has fucked her remodel."

They pass my phone around the table and all take a look. None are impressed.

When the phone comes back to me, I hand it back to Callan. "Check out Slade's ideas. I mean, he's gone over-board, but I like some of what he's suggesting."

"I'm not following. Why is Slade making suggestions?"

"His father is a contractor and Slade worked for him when he was younger. He showed me the remodel he did for his father earlier this year and it was impressive."

He looks through the file Slade sent me and surprises the heck out of me when he says, "There are some great ideas in here."

I stare at him. I thought for sure he'd have something to say about me considering Slade for this job.

Before I know what he's doing, he's tapping out a reply to Slade. The two of them then engage in a few minutes of texting. I just watch with shock.

When he's finished, he gives me the phone. "I made some more suggestions. He thinks they're great ideas too. He's going to rework the plans tonight and get back to you tomorrow."

I arch my brows. "So, what, you two are just taking over now?"

He grins. "I have to take the opportunities when they arise, Ace."

"What opportunities?" I tap my phone to read through his texts with Slade, stopping when I get to the word *library*. "Oh my god, you did not!"

He just gives me one last grin before turning back to the table and asking if anyone wants a drink.

I go back to my texts and reply to Slade.

OLIVIA

> Ignore all of Callan's suggestions. I just want what I already had planned.

SLADE

> Really? His ideas were great and I can easily make them happen.

OLIVIA

> I don't want to spend that kind of money.

SLADE

I've got contacts in the industry. We'll get the cost down.

SLADE

Let me price it up for you.

OLIVIA

Okay.

OLIVIA

And thank you.

Callan comes back to the table with drinks, and after we engage in pointed looks that convey our positions on my remodel, we get back to the game.

Bradford and Kristen win the game.

Gage accuses them of cheating.

Hayden decides Gage is right.

Callan declares his brother is a filthy fucker who likes to draw dirty shit.

I state my belief that Kristen won the game in fact. "She's smart enough to read her husband's mind and decipher his drawings, and she's smart enough to know how to draw what Bradford would understand. Next time we play, I'm on Kristen's team."

Callan's father laughs and asks, "When are we planning on going away again?"

"I can get away in October," Hayden says.

"That would work for us," Bradford says.

Callan pulls out his phone to check his calendar. "I can't do the first week in October."

"Are you heading to Utah?" Gage asks.

Callan nods. "Yeah."

"Have you found someone to do the Alps with you?"

Gage asks.

I knew Callan was heading to Utah for highlining in October but I'd forgotten. Or more likely, intentionally pushed it from my mind.

"Not yet, but I'm going to talk to the guys while we're in Utah. I think some of them may be interested," Callan says.

"How about you, Liv?" Bradford asks.

My brain is all caught up in thinking about Callan risking his life up on a rope. I've always hated that he does this, but it suddenly seems even worse to me.

"Liv?" Gage says. "How does October look for you?"

I drag myself from all my thoughts over Callan highlining. "I'm good for October."

As the conversation drifts to Bradford's work and I turn inward with all my feelings and fears, Callan looks at me questioningly. "You okay, Ace?"

I nod even though I'm not sure I am. "I'm good."

His eyes narrow at me. "Are you sure?"

"I'm sure." I smile. "But I'm thirsty. I'm going to get a drink. Would you like something?"

He watches me for a long moment like he's not quite convinced. Then, he says, "No, I'm good."

I'm unable to push my thoughts over Callan's highlining from my mind for the rest of the day. I don't bring it up with him because I know they're my fears that I have to learn to deal with. And highlining is something he loves to do. I would never ask my partner to give up a hobby he loves. However, none of that changes the fact I feel an intense fear deep in my gut every time I think about him stepping out onto that rope, and I'm not sure if I'll ever be able to manage this fear.

27

OLIVIA

THE RAIN EASES by Sunday morning and Callan and I head out for a hike just after breakfast. We talk about our week ahead and he shares with me that he's having dinner with a guy tomorrow night who may invest in his German expansion.

I learned last night while listening to him and his father talk, that his dad is the one who has encouraged him to find an investor for this expansion. All the pieces of the puzzle fell into place for me at that point.

Callan loves risk, so I've wondered why he's not just backing himself with the business growth he's chasing. He hasn't built a company the size of his by not backing himself in the past. Now, I know this change in his behavior is because his father has put this idea in his head.

We make some plans for the week ahead and he tries to convince me again to run with Slade's ideas for my remodel. He also expresses frustration with Harper over the fact she's told me she doesn't love my suggestions for her wedding but won't put the time in herself to figure out what she does want. I agree with him, which I know surprises him. I've never said a bad word about my cousin, but lately, I'm feeling used. And I'm wishing I hadn't said yes to helping her with the wedding.

After a long, lazy lunch with everyone, we drive home while listening to the playlist I made with some of our favorite songs.

When the country song starts playing that Callan turned up once during one of our other drives home, he looks at me with a shake of his head.

I grin. "I know how much you love your country."

We get back to his condo around five p.m. after stopping a couple of times along the way. Callan heads into his gym after we unpack while I prep my lunches for the week and do some life admin.

Neither of us are too hungry, so we decide to skip dinner in favor of something light to eat on the couch while we watch a movie.

After five minutes of searching for something to watch, Callan eyes me. "It's all shit."

I laugh at his grumbly tone. He hates looking for shows or movies to watch and can never find anything of interest. "Pass me the remote. I'll find something."

I scroll for a few minutes and when I land on a documentary about alpine climbers racing to set new records, Callan says, "That looks good."

It's one of the last shows I would ever choose to watch, but since he appears super interested in it, I let it play.

As I watch the truly terrifying things these guys do,

like climbing solo without equipment, I say, "I don't understand why they would do all this."

Callan looks at me. "There's a lot of reasons. Pushing limits, conquering fears, learning things about yourself."

"Surely there are other ways to do those things."

"We've all got our preferences for how we accomplish things."

"I get that, but...I don't know. What about their families? Do they think about their partners and children before deciding to climb a mountain and chance death?"

"I can't answer for them, but I would."

"And you'd still climb the mountain?"

"The majority of climbs are done safely."

I gesture at the television where the documentary is still playing in the background. "Some aren't. That guy fell to his death."

"That guy took greater risks than is usual."

"And I think that's the thing. I think the more he risked and survived, the more he risked again. Where does it end?"

Callan turns quiet for a moment. "Are we still talking about these guys or are we talking about me now?"

My heart beats faster. "Where does it end for you? Will you just keep searching for higher highlines? Longer highlines? Will you want to do it more often?"

"I can't answer that, Liv. I don't know."

"If we look at where you started, I think the answer is yes to all of those questions. And then what? Do you move onto other extreme sports?"

He looks at me carefully. "Where are you going with this?"

"I don't know." My heart moves into my throat. "All I

know is that I can't stop thinking about you falling to your death."

His voice is gentle when he replies, "I'm not going to die, Ace."

"You don't know that. Accidents happen all the time." *And people die when they shouldn't.*

"I know, but I'm not going to stop living because I could die."

"And that brings me back to wanting to know where this all ends." I push up off the couch feeling an intense need to be standing. I feel like there's a whole lot of air trapped in my lungs right now and sitting is only making the suffocating feeling worse.

Callan frowns. "Where are you going?"

"Nowhere." I start pacing. "I just need to stand."

He stands too. "Why?"

"Because I feel like I can't breathe. You won't answer my question and I feel like I can't breathe!"

"I can't answer your question because I don't know where this all ends."

"So, I just have to keep wondering if you'll suddenly come home one day and tell me you're going to do something extreme like climb a mountain without oxygen?"

"No, that's not what I'm saying."

"Well, what are you saying?"

He exhales a breath. "Not everyone dies, Liv. You have to let that go."

It pisses me off when people tell me to let the death of my cousin go. They have no idea of the burden I carry over that. Saying "let it go" diminishes everything I've been through. It always makes me feel dismissed, like I'm an idiot for still feeling the way I do. When Callan says it, it's worse. He knows how I feel about this, so it feels like he's just torn a jagged cut through my heart.

I step back from him, my body turning rigid. "I don't have to let anything go."

"Fuck." He looks regretful but I barely acknowledge that. I'm too far down in my feelings now. "I don't want to fight with you over this. I just want you to consider that your cousin's death affects your rational thinking when it comes to me highlining. Especially considering I take every safety precaution I can."

"Accidents happen, Callen. I don't know how many times you need to hear that."

"And risk can be managed. That's what you're choosing to ignore here."

My eyes go wide. "I'm not ignoring anything." I take another step back. "I think I'm going to go."

"No, you're not," he says, quickly reaching for my wrist to stop me. "We're going to keep talking about this."

I snatch my wrist out of his grip. "I don't think there's much else to say."

As those words leave my mouth, an unsteady feeling sinks to my stomach. I think by the look on Callan's face, he feels the same.

That feeling terrifies me.

What am I doing?

And yet, I can't stop my feet from moving.

"Olivia," Callan says as I walk away from him. "You are not fucking running from me."

With my heart doing its best to break my ribs, I keep walking toward his bedroom.

I need to gather my things.

"Olivia!" Callan comes after me. "Don't do this."

I grab my suitcase. "I need some space to think."

"I'll sleep in another room tonight. Stay here and think."

"No."

"You're not thinking properly."

My head jerks up and I look at him. "You have no idea what I'm thinking. No one I know does because none of you know what it's like to be responsible for a death. I remember that moment clearly like it was yesterday, and the last thing I will ever be okay with is someone I love carelessly putting their life at risk so they can feel good for a moment."

"That's not fair, Ace. I'm never careless when I step out onto that rope. And I don't do it just to feel good for a moment. There's so much more to it than that."

"I can't do this, Callan."

His body stills. "You can't do this right now, or you can't be in this relationship?"

My breaths come fast as all my thoughts collide. "I don't know."

28

CALLAN

CALLAN

I don't know if Liv told you or not, but we started dating six weeks ago.

CALLAN

Apparently everyone but me knew I was in love with her.

CALLAN

I think I've been in love with her for a long time.

CALLAN

Fuck, I'm all fucked up.

CALLAN

She left tonight and I don't think she's coming back.

CALLAN

Jesus, Ethan, I know I said some shit that I shouldn't have, but you need to fucking get past that.

> I fucking need you tonight. More than I've ever fucking needed you.

I DRAIN my glass of whiskey and pour another. I've almost drained it too when my phone rings.

"Fuck me," I mutter when I see my brother's name flash across the screen. I stab at it and answer the call. "I didn't think you'd bother replying."

"You're making me regret this already."

I shove my fingers through my hair and work like fuck to hold my shit together. "Don't hang up."

We're both silent to the point where I wonder if we'll even manage a short conversation. Then, Ethan says, "Why'd she leave?"

"She's running."

"Yeah, but what was her reason?"

"She wants me to quit highlining."

"Fuck."

"Yeah."

"The one thing you'll never quit." He pauses before adding, "And you fucking hate ultimatums."

"Yeah."

"Would you consider it for her?"

"I'd rather she considered learning about the safety precautions I take."

"Right, but I think we both know there's no way she's going to do that."

I throw some more whiskey down my throat. "It's fucked up and I don't know what to do to get her to listen to me."

He's silent for a beat. "I'll call her."

"I don't think she'll listen."

"All I can do is try. And Callan?"

"What?"

"You need to think about what you really want here. I know what highlining gives you, but will you be happy with that decision when you're old and staring at your grave after a life of not having Liv in it?"

Long after we end the call, I'm still thinking about his question. I fall asleep just after three a.m. and still don't have an answer. The only thing I know is that for the first time in my life, I can't see the future. There is no future I've ever contemplated that didn't have Olivia in it.

I wake early Monday after very little sleep. I shower and head over to Olivia's condo without eating breakfast. She didn't answer any of my calls or texts last night and I'm going out of my fucking mind.

Larry, her doorman, lets me know she's not home. He hasn't seen her since Friday.

I step out onto the sidewalk and call her. This time she answers.

"Hi," she says tentatively.

Fuck, she sounds so distant.

"Where are you, Liv? I'm coming to you and we're going to figure this out."

I'm met with silence.

"Liv." Every muscle in my body is tense. I can't fucking lose her.

"Callan." Her voice cracks. "I don't think we can figure this out."

Fuck.

"Don't say that, Ace. Tell me where you are."

"Can you give me some more time?" She pauses. "Please?"

Time and space are the very last things I want to give her, but I know that pushing her won't get me anywhere. "How long do you need?"

"Give me the day."

This is going to be the longest day of my life. "Okay. Where will you be tomorrow morning? I'll come to you then."

"I'll call you tomorrow."

Olivia isn't just running from me.

She's shutting down on me and I have no fucking clue how to reach her.

I make it through the day. Fuck knows how, but at seven p.m., I find myself sitting across from Damon, the guy I'm hoping will invest in my company. The fact he reached out to me after hearing about my plans leads me to believe I've got a shot here. However, fifteen minutes into the dinner, I'm not sure I can work with the guy.

He's a cocky asshole and while I can generally handle cocky, tonight, all I can hear is Olivia's voice in my head. *Come on, Callan, you could never work long term with an arrogant ass like him.*

Yet, I find myself pushing through because I also hear

my father's voice telling me not to get ahead of myself. *Be smart, Callan. You need a backer for this.*

"So," Damon says after I've listened to him for an hour and a half. "What are your thoughts on my ideas?"

I start to speak but we're interrupted by a woman's voice from behind me. "Callan. What a lovely surprise!"

Jesus.

I glance up to find Penny coming to stand in front of me. "Penny." My tone leaves no room for misunderstanding: I'm not fucking interested.

She smiles at me like she didn't just hear the way I spoke to her before turning her attention to Damon and gushing over him. "Hello there. It's always good to meet a friend of Callan's. I'm Penny."

Damon immediately sits forward with interest and introduces himself before insisting, "You must join us for a drink."

"No." I meet her gaze. "We've got a lot still to talk about. You two can have a drink another day."

She brushes me off and takes a seat. "I'll just stay for one drink. It would be rude not to, wouldn't it, Damon?"

I have no idea what game she's playing at here, but I intend on putting a stop to it.

Standing, I give her a look that says I'm not taking no for an answer. "Come with me to the bar."

She's up and out of her chair fast. As we walk to the bar, she hooks her arm in mine and leans in close. "I know you didn't really mean what you said the last time we saw each other. And there's no need for an apology."

"I meant every word I said, Penny." When we reach the bar, I move in close so she can hear every word I utter. "You're going to walk the fuck away from me, leave this restaurant, and never come near me again. Because, in case I haven't been clear enough, I'm not fucking interested in you."

She places her palm to my cheek and brings her face near mine. "You know what, Callan? I'm not fucking interested in you either. And yeah, I'm going to walk away, but I'm not leaving the restaurant because I was actually here before you. And just because you're a rich asshole, doesn't mean you can order people around. Fuck you, and I hope you get what's coming to you."

I watch her walk away, wondering what the hell just happened. I've never known a woman who blows so hot and cold.

I'm in the middle of wondering that when a text comes through on my phone. I'm surprised to see Olivia's name on the screen. I haven't heard from her since our call this morning and while I'm fucking happy to hear from her now, I wasn't expecting it.

OLIVIA

> I know you're having dinner with the investor tonight, and I know you think you need him, but I wanted to remind you of all the things you've achieved in business on your own. Callan, you don't need anyone backing you but yourself. No matter what your father tells you.

Fuck. Me.

I want to tell her I love her, but I don't want the first time I tell her that to be by text. Or by phone. I need her in my arms when I tell her that. So, I slip my phone in my trousers and make my way back to Damon to tell him I no longer need an investor.

Olivia's right.

And the realization that I've been an idiot slams into me. Nobody loves me like Olivia does. Nobody sees me like she does. And I'd be a fool not to do everything in my power to make her mine forever.

29

OLIVIA

I'M ALMOST asleep Monday night when Ethan calls. He tried to call me this morning but I was working and unable to take his call. We texted back and forth a few times and agreed he'd call me tonight.

"I didn't realize you meant midnight when you said you'd call tonight," I say sleepily.

"I'm in Paris, Liv. It's fucking six a.m. here. I got up early for you."

I smile. God, I miss him. "So, let me guess, Callan called you."

"Smart woman."

My heart cracks a little bit more at his confirmation. Callan isn't the kind of man to ask for help or to talk about the things hurting him. His father taught him to stand strong by himself and that's what he strives to do. For him to call Ethan, especially when they haven't spoken for so long, reveals his pain over what I've done.

"Is he okay?" I hold my breath and wait for his answer.

"No."

I close my eyes while my heart squeezes.

I hate that I've hurt him.

"Don't run," he says.

I open my eyes. "I'm not running."

"You are. It's what you do."

"What does that mean?"

"You either run from people or you pull them in close and manage the risk of loving them." His voice softens. "You're afraid of losing the people you love, and I get it, but you miss out on so much because of this."

I grip my phone harder. "I don't think I can be with him, Ethan," I whisper, hating every word I've just said. "I wouldn't survive losing him."

"So, you'll walk away and lose him anyway? That makes no fucking sense."

Tears slide down my face as I imagine a life without Callan.

No more eleven a.m. calls.

No more bantering with him.

I glance down at my charm bracelet.

No more firsts with him.

No more of anything with him.

Ethan's right. I'm being an idiot. And I *am* running, but it's so ingrained in me that I don't know any other way to be in this world and keep my heart safe.

"I don't know how to stop running, Ethan."

"Yeah, I get that too. Fuck, do I get that." He releases a breath. "I think we've just gotta make the choice to stop running and hold on for our fucking lives."

~

I don't sleep well and drag myself out of bed with little time to get ready for work. I'm rushing all morning, and I'm more than aware that I promised to call Callan this morning, but I have clients in back-to-back meetings from eight a.m., so instead of calling, I send him a text just before my first client.

OLIVIA

> I'm sorry I'm texting rather than calling. I'm running late for work and have meetings all morning. I promise I'll call at lunch xx

I switch my phone to silent so I can focus for all my meetings.

My morning is a blur. New clients. Old clients. Clients I don't particularly care for. And all the while, Callan is front and center.

I've replayed my conversation with Ethan hundreds of times since last night. *I think we've just gotta make the choice to stop running and hold on for our fucking lives.* I've asked myself just as many times *how do you hold on for your fucking life?* I still have no good answer.

My last meeting finishes at 11:45 a.m. at which time, I check my phone and find it's blown up with texts.

BLAIR

> Okay, so this Insta tea bitch is going down. I'm seriously done with her.

BLAIR

> Are you okay?

BLAIR

> Where are you?

KRISTEN

Olivia, just checking to make sure you're okay.

BLAIR

Why are you ignoring me?

SASHA

Holy fuck. I have no words. I don't understand what's happening rn.

KRISTEN

Adeline just texted me. She said Jameson's solution to the whole ordeal is to, and I quote, "just buy the fucking Instagram account and shut the fucking thing down." I'm seriously thinking that's a great idea. I'm here if you need me xx

I stare at my phone, wondering what the hell has happened. Clearly something on the Instagram account. A moment later, my heart crashes into my chest as I read the post.

@thetea_gasp

Well, this is an interesting turn of events, friends. Just last month @callanblack was getting raunchy with his bestie @olivialancaster. It seems that friendship might be over now because look at him getting cozy with @therealpeneloperush last night. You may recall he was all over Penelope weeks before he was all over his ex-bestie. Oof. This is so a hard launch, but then that's what we thought after we saw those pics of him with

ex-bestie too. It seems this Black brother just isn't up for a forever bae. We feel sorry for Olivia in all this. Girl just can't catch a break.

The photos of Callan with Penelope at a restaurant last night are hard to look at. They're extremely close in all three photos. He's saying something against her ear in one of them. She's got her hand resting on his cheek in another. And they're walking arm-in-arm in another.

I take a seat and switch my phone back to silent.

I need a minute.

Scratch that, I need many minutes.

I'm with Sasha. I don't understand what's happening right now.

"Okay," I pep talk myself. "Think about this. Think about everything that's happened. And fucking think about the fact Callan's your best friend and has been since you were eight."

I take a deep breath.

I switch my lawyer brain on.

And I think this through rationally.

I don't reply to any of the texts from my friends. There's no time. Instead, I tell Hayden I'm taking the rest of the day off, I make some calls to contacts I have, and I go find Penelope fucking Rush.

Thanks to her Instagram stories, I find her at a hair salon. She spots me the moment I walk in and watches me with a self-satisfied expression.

"Look what the cat dragged in," she snarls when I'm standing in front of her.

"I won't take up a lot of your time."

She lounges back and crosses her legs. "Oh, go ahead. Take as much as you need. I imagine you're feeling like a fool today and need to get some of that off your chest."

"Actually, no, I'm not feeling like that at all."

"Oh, really? I would be if I was in your shoes. Callan really played you, didn't he?"

"You'd like me to believe that, wouldn't you?"

She shrugs. "I don't care what you believe, Olivia."

"That's not true, though, is it? I mean, you set that entire scenario up last night for my benefit. That says a lot about how much you care. But here's where you and I differ, Penelope. I ask myself what the greatest assumption is that I can make about a person before I assume the worst. You're always looking for the worst in people and giving the worst right alongside that."

"That was a lot of words for having said not much."

"I called around the photographers I know through work. The guys that assholes pay to snap photos of my clients to screw them over. One of them confirmed he took the photos of you and Callan last night. At your request. You saw Callan at the same restaurant you were dining in and you found a photographer to come and take photos of a lie."

That slows her all the way down. And causes her to glare at me.

"I hope it was worth it," I say. "Because the only thing you managed to do was remind me how much I love Callan and how much I want to grow old with him." I smile. "Thanks for that. It actually came at the exact right moment. I guess the Universe really does work in mysterious ways."

I hold my head high and leave Penelope Rush far behind. It doesn't even matter what shit she tries to pull in the future; none of it will ever touch me again because I won't let it.

I've just stepped out into the sunshine when Callan calls.

"Liv, tell me you haven't seen the fucking Instagram post, and if you have seen it, tell me you don't fucking believe it. Fuck, I swear it's not what it looks like. She—"

"Callan. I don't believe it."

He exhales a long, relieved breath. "Thank Christ." Then, he says, "Where are you? We need to talk and we need to do that now. I'm done waiting. I'll come to wherever you are."

Callan might not wear his heart on his sleeve for most people but he wears it all over his body for me.

"Can you give me one more hour?"

"No."

I smile even though this is not a smiling matter. But then, that's how Callan and I always get through hard times. We stick together and we find ways to smile.

"Baby, please."

"You're going to stop running?"

"Yes."

I hear the reprieve I've given him in his rough tone when he says, "Okay. One hour. If I'm not looking at you then, I'm coming to find you."

All I can think after we end the call is thank goodness for Ethan and Instagram.

Ethan told me to hold on for my fucking life.

Instagram and all its bullshit helped me see how to do that.

Over the last two months, I've had the people closest to me, and some I've only just met, help get me through the awful gossip posted about me. They showed me that they've got me.

I think the way to hold on for my fucking life is to hold onto the people who care about me because life really is about the people.

The second I step foot inside Callan's office, he's up and around his desk. And he's got his hands on me, his arms around me, his mouth on mine. As it should be.

His kiss is intense as is his hold on me. This is him saying *I'm never fucking letting you go.* When we come up for air, we're both breathless.

"I'm sorry," I say as I grip his arms.

"I'm sorry, too."

"No, you've got nothing to be sorry for."

"I said some things I should have thought through first."

"I shouldn't have shut you out like that. I wish I could promise you that I won't ever do that again, but I think finding our way through life together is going to be filled with moments like this. And all I can promise to do is learn from them and try not to make the same mistakes again."

"When you say 'finding our way through life together', do you mean what I hope you mean?"

I smile up at him. "I want to grow old with you, Callan."

His chest rises as he inhales a long breath and it falls as he exhales it. "Thank fuck, Ace, because I was already moving on to figuring out ways to kidnap you."

And just like he always does, he makes me laugh. Then I say, "I'm going to get more therapy."

"No, I'll stop highlining and just go back to basic slacklining."

I shake my head while my heart explodes with love for this man. "I never want you to stop doing the things you love. The problem isn't highlining. The problem is my trauma. I don't think I've been ready to let it go before. Somehow, it was my brain's safe place. It was easier staying stuck in a groove I already knew how to work with and how to manage. Stepping outside that feels hard, but I know I have to do that if I want to experience all that life has to offer me." I take a breath. "We can't stop living because we could die."

Callan takes my face in his hands. His eyes are wild with emotion. "I love you and I am going to love you until the day I fucking die." He doesn't waste one more second before kissing me and showing me just how deeply he feels every word he just said.

I've got his face in my hands by the time our kiss ends and my body pressed so hard to his that it's hard to know where we each end and begin. That has always been Callan and me; inseparable. "I love you more than you will ever know, Callan Black."

He kisses me again. He kisses me for a long time, and somehow, we make it to the couch in his office. By the time we've had enough of each other, I'm sitting on his lap with his face where I think he will always prefer it, in between my breasts. Our clothes are still on but only just. I'm pretty sure Callan's already making plans to get me naked. I mean, the man lives for my naked ass, so it's a logical assumption.

"I bought you something." I leave the couch to grab my purse off his desk. When I come back to him, he doesn't allow me to sit anywhere but back on his lap. "Well, I bought both of us something."

He watches while I retrieve two jewelry boxes from my purse.

"For our first fight," I say as I hand him his box.

He arches a brow. "You want to remember this?"

"Yes. I want to remember that we got through it. That we found a way to put our love first and remembered how important we are to each other."

He listens intently to what I say before murmuring, "We're going to work at this."

I nod and brush my lips over his. "Yeah, baby, we're never going to stop working at this. I love you too much not to." I lift my chin at his box. "Now, open your gift."

"And there's my bossy girl."

We open our boxes together and I know by the expression on Callan's face that he feels my gift in his soul.

"Here," I say, "Let me put them on you."

I take the cufflinks from the box and replace the ones he's wearing with these. They're silver and have a phoenix engraved on them.

Once they're on him, I hold out the matching phoenix charm to him and he puts it on my bangle.

"Don't take my other charm off. I want to see all our firsts every day."

After he spends another half hour with his hands and mouth all over me, he says, "I'm going to need you to sit your ass on my desk."

I give him a sexy smile. "And here I was thinking you'd prefer to bend me over your desk."

"Trust me, you'll be bent over it by the time I'm finished. But I want to start with my mouth on your pussy." He smacks my ass when I don't move immediately. "Liv. Don't make me wait. I'm fucking done waiting."

I stop making my man wait.

I sit my ass on his desk.

And for once, I let him be the boss of me.

30

OLIVIA

Three Weeks Later

"You're the lawyer representing that asshole?" Callan says over the rim of his glass as he eyes Blair's date at Rhodes's and Sasha's wedding.

Hunt shrugs. "Everyone deserves a defense."

I put my hand on Callan's thigh. I know how deeply he feels about the man who fucked with Bradford's and Kristen's happiness, keeping them apart for almost two years. "He's right," I say gently. "Even if I agree with you that Phillip is an asshole." I also don't believe that Hunt will be able to stop Phillip from getting what's coming to him, which looks to be three years in jail and a likely $2M fine for insider trading.

Blair picks up on the rising tension between Callan and Hunt and whispers something in Hunt's ear that causes him to stand and follow her out of the wedding reception.

Sasha watches them leave. "I have feelings about Hunt but I can't figure out what they are."

I laugh. "Me too."

Callan scowls. "I can figure mine out and not one of them is a good feeling."

Rhodes reaches for his drink. "Let's hope to fuck that Blair doesn't suddenly start liking the guy."

Blair still dislikes Hunt intensely. However, she's getting some of the best sex of her life out of him at the moment, which is the reason why he's her plus-one.

A text comes through for Callan and after he reads it, he passes me his phone so I can read it. "Slade's almost finished. Look how fucking good your library looks."

These two have been sending texts back and forth all day and Callan has been showing me the updates that Slade's been sending though to him. He switched to updating Callan rather than me about a week ago. And I haven't failed to notice all the other random messages they've sent each other too about sports, sports, and more sports. In amongst plans they're making for Callan to start teaching Slade slacklining.

My boyfriend is in the middle of a bromance with Slade Sullivan.

And the two of them took over my remodel.

And have given me the most perfect luxury bath that overlooks the city, a walk-in closet that gives me so much more space for so many more shoes, and a library for my books and planners.

"It's perfect." I lean in and kiss him. "Thank you. And you'll be pleased to know that Blair updated me this morning on the contractor saga. She's getting my money back for me." I hired Blair to sort out the mess with the contractor. She was desperate to sink her teeth into something on my behalf. I think she would have preferred I send her after the Instagram tea bitch (her term of endearment for that account, not mine), but I've let all that Instagram stuff go.

"So," Rhodes says, looking at me. "I'm laying down some ground rules for this reception. There is to be no whiskey consumed by you or my wife. You'll have me to answer to if this occurs. And not even your boy will be able to save you."

I smile as I glance between him and Sasha. "I'm so happy for you guys. And I promise, not a drop of whiskey will be consumed."

"Besides, you need a clear head for tomorrow," Sasha says, referring to the fact I was supposed to be Zooming with Harper tomorrow to force her into finalizing her wedding plans I've been pulling my hair out over.

"No. We had an argument over that last night and I told her I'm done."

"As in you're not planning her wedding now?"

I nod. "I was feeling used and my therapist is helping me understand how Harper has been using my guilt our entire lives to manipulate me into doing what she wants. I feel such a weight off my shoulders since I told her no."

Sasha smiles. "I'm glad. I was worried about the stress it was causing you."

This reception is one of my favourites of the season. We spend the night with our friends dancing and laughing, and just after midnight, Callan leans in close and says, "It's time for you to show me your ass."

It's been a long day and he's absolutely right.

"Do you know what I've been thinking?" I say as we walk to the elevator to go up to our suite.

"What?" His hand settles on my ass.

"You still haven't met Ricardo."

"I'd fucking love to meet Ricardo."

I lean into him. "I brought him with me this weekend."

"I hope you wore that lingerie I bought you."

"I hope that out of all the lingerie you had delivered yesterday, that there wasn't one particular set you wanted to see first. I mean, I did contemplate trying to wear it all at once for you, but I decided that actually wouldn't be sexy."

He looks down at me with a shake of his head and a look that says he thinks I'm cute.

"You went a little overboard," I carry on. "Did you buy an entire store?"

"I came fucking close."

This man.

He's taken every moment he could over the last few weeks to show me how important I am to him. He even came home from work three nights ago and told me he'll go to therapy with me if I want him to. I was speechless, because I hadn't asked that of him and also because Callan has always insisted that nothing would convince him to go to therapy. When I asked him what brought this on, he told me he's been doing a lot of thinking about couples making a choice to work for happiness.

We make it to our suite and when I walk into the bedroom, I find a laptop with a big red bow tied around it sitting on the bed.

"Is this a gift?" I ask him, confused because I don't need a new laptop.

"Yes."

"Ah, thank you, but you know I just bought a new laptop a couple of months ago." He spent a day pointing out all the reasons I needed to upgrade my old laptop, so I'm unsure why he's forgotten this.

"I know, but I want you to put on your glasses and get all nerdy with me while we look at what's on that computer."

I try not to laugh. "Is this a new kink of yours?" My eyes go wide. "Oh my god, is this a porn computer?"

"What the fuck is a porn computer?"

"I don't know. I'm making stuff up as I go here, but it would not surprise me if you had a computer dedicated to filthy porn."

"I don't need a computer of porn, Ace. I've got you and your filthy mouth."

"I still wouldn't put it past you to—"

"Olivia."

I blink at what I hear in his voice.

He *really* wants me to put my glasses on and get all nerdy with him.

"Okay, okay, just let me take out my contacts."

Five minutes later, I've got my glasses on and am sitting on Callan's lap on the couch in the living room. "Are we planning a trip?" I say as I untie the bow and slide the ribbon from the computer. "Is that what's on here? Plans for a vacation together."

He kisses my neck as his hands settle on my stomach. "Not yet, but we should."

"Where would we go?" I open the laptop.

"I'd like to see Australia after hearing your parents talk about it."

I'm only vaguely listening to him now because I've found what he wants me to look at on this laptop and my heart is beating so loudly it's almost all I can hear.

"Callan," I whisper.

"Liv," he whispers back.

"Oh my god."

It's a spreadsheet titled *Olivia & Callan*.

A spreadsheet that he's made.

A spreadsheet with columns titled *Reasons To Get Married*, *Reasons To Stay Single*, and *All The Ways Your Husband Would Love You*.

He has meticulously filled out each column.

He's linked some cells from this sheet to other sheets he created, detailing his suggestions for where to get married, how to get married, when to get married, who to have in our bridal party, and who to invite. Then, there's a sheet of honeymoon destination ideas, and a sheet for suggestions of where we could live after we get married. I laugh as I read his highlighted note telling me *you still need to make me a spreadsheet of all the cities with acceptable weather*.

"And you let people think you have no organizational skills," I say while trying to calm my heart.

"I don't. Except when it comes to you."

I place the laptop on the low table in front of us and turn to face him, my legs either side of him on the couch. "You make some good points as to why we should stay single."

His lips twitch. "What? Less stuff to take with you if you decide to move?"

"It's a valid point. As is the fact that you don't have to buy twice as much when you buy something yummy."

He searches my eyes and I know by the intense look in his that he's impatient for my answer. "Ace, tell me you'll marry me. All the reasons to stay single are bullshit. I had to google to even come up with one of those reasons. I don't want to be single anymore. I want to be your husband and spend every day of the rest of my life showing you all those ways I would love you."

As I stare into the eyes of the man I've loved since he was a boy, I know I will do anything to have him love me forever. "Yes, Callan, I will marry you." I kiss him. "I will love you and cherish you forever, and if you're lucky, I will even let you be the boss of me sometimes."

EPILOGUE
CALLAN

One Month Later

"CALLAN! WHAT ARE YOU DOING?" Olivia says as I slip into the room of the church where she and the bridesmaids are getting ready for our wedding. "It's bad luck for you to see me before the wedding!"

Fuck.

I come to a complete stop as I take in her dress. "You're wearing red?"

She puts her hands to her stomach. "Yes. Do you like it?"

Olivia doesn't need my approval for fucking anything, but still, I know it makes her happy when I like something she chooses. "I fucking love it." I run my eyes down her body over the red fabric that hugs the fuck out of her curves until it reaches her legs where it turns into ruffles that trail down to the floor. When I find her eyes again, I say, "You look beautiful."

The room we're in is tiny. And noisy. Two makeup artists and two hairdressers are working on Blair, Sasha, and our mothers. Everyone is talking at once but my mother is the loudest. When she launches into a story about something dumb I did as a child, I shake my head and give all my attention back to my fiancée.

"Why are you here?" she asks.

"We've got a small problem."

The fact that no panic flares on her face is testament to how well her therapy is going. "What's happened?"

"Ethan's not here yet."

"He's coming. He promised both of us he'd be here."

"I know, and I believe he'll show, but we can't get married until he arrives...and well, we're ten minutes out and I'm not sure he'll be on time."

"Why can't we get married until he arrives? I mean, I know you really want him here, but if we don't get married in ten minutes, we can't get this church again for over a year." Her eyes cut to our mothers. "And we promised we'd get married in this church."

We did.

It's the only concession we made for our mothers who were both horrified when we told them we were getting married so soon after I proposed. They put forth all their reasons why we should take our time and plan a proper wedding. Fuck knows what the difference between the wedding we've planned and a proper wedding is, but to stop the headache they were causing us, we told them we'd get married in this church. The one they both got married in.

I don't care about the promise to our mothers. My problem with Ethan not being here yet has more to do with the rings.

"Ethan has the rings," I say.

Liv frowns. "What? How?"

Her confusion is warranted. Ethan is my best man, but since he wasn't flying in until this morning, Gage was in charge of the rings.

"Gage forgot to bring the rings with him. We asked Ethan to collect them after he got into New York, on his way here."

"Honestly, you Black brothers should never be in charge of wedding rings." She looks across at our mothers and the girls and says, "Blair."

Blair's head instantly turns to us. She frowns when she sees me. "Where did you come from? And why are you in here? Jesus, Callan, I will have to get the sage out now." Then to Olivia, she says, "What?"

"We need some rings. Can you go and find some?"

"Oh, yes, absolutely. I'll just go across the road to the jeweler, shall I?" She gives me a stern look. "How could you forget the rings? Seriously, you give a man one fucking job, and he can't even get that right."

"Callan," Mom says. "What happened? I thought Gage had the rings."

"It's okay," Olivia says. "We just need to borrow some."

The door to the room opens as she says this and Kristen joins us. Eyeing me, she says, "He's still not here."

Bradford follows her in. "I can't get through to him. I'll keep trying, but wanted to let you know."

When Gage and Hayden also stride in, Blair says,

"Yes, okay, let's bring the entire Black family in here. This room is so big we could invite cousins in too."

The room erupts into conversations between my brothers and our mothers with some grumbling from Blair and Sasha over how squished we all are now.

"I'm sorry, Ace." I pull Olivia into a corner.

She puts her arms around my neck. "We don't need rings to get married. It'd be nice though if Ethan was here for you."

It would, but not even his absence today could upset me. Not when I'm marrying the woman I love and making her mine forever.

As the conversations grow louder around us, I say, "I was thinking about kids today."

Her face lights up. Olivia has always wanted children. "And? Are you thinking what I'm thinking?"

"That depends if you're thinking you want five kids."

She blinks. "What? No. Jesus, Callan, who in their right mind would want five children? Well, I mean, besides your mother. God, if we had five boys, I would end up living in a corner of our house, rocking myself into oblivion."

I grin. "I'm fucking with you, Ace. I was thinking three kids."

As I say this, Ethan's voice filters across the room and I turn to find him standing in the doorway.

His eyes meet mine and a grin spreads out across his face. "I'm sorry I'm late, but it's been a fucking day."

I glance down. "Why are you holding a puppy?"

A blonde woman steps next to him and shoots me a smile. "Because we just saved it."

"Holy fuck," Sasha exclaims as she stares at the

woman. Then to Ethan she says, "Why is Madeline Montana standing in this room with you?"

"And why is she wearing a wedding dress?" Blair frowns.

Ethan looks at the woman standing next to him. "That's your name?"

Sasha is aghast that he didn't know her name. "How can you not know her name? Everyone knows her name."

Before anyone can clear up the confusion of my brother showing up to my wedding with a woman he doesn't even know and a puppy that looks like it's in need of a meal, my father joins us and looks at me. "Let's get you married, son."

Olivia's hand slips into mine and she squeezes it. Brushing her mouth against my ear, she says, "I love you, Callan Black, and I would love to have three kids with you. But first, we need to get married so we can win our karaoke competition tonight."

I grin at her. "You actually think any of my brothers aren't going to come out fighting tonight?"

"You forget who your partner is. I can sing anyone under the table."

I chuckle. "Yeah, baby, you absolutely can."

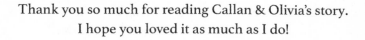

Thank you so much for reading Callan & Olivia's story.
I hope you loved it as much as I do!

Want more?
Download their Bonus Epilogue here:
https://geni.us/YABonusEpilogue

The next book is...

Recklessly, Wildly Yours

Ethan & Maddie's story
a runaway bride romance
COMING 2024

ACKNOWLEDGMENTS

Firstly, I want to thank all my readers for your patience after I delayed this book. I've had a lot going on this year between my perimenopause journey (gah, if you've been here, you know!), my dad's health journey, my daughter moving states while I was writing this book, and really, I think just trying to find myself in all of that. Or should I say, not lose myself in all of that. I've delayed every book of mine for a little while now and you guys are always so supportive, and for that I truly thank you.

Thank you for reading my books. I hope you loved this one!

Jodie, I say it every time, but I really could not finish writing a book without your unwavering support and encouragement. Thank you for being the absolute best friend a girl could ever have.

Letitia, this cover is everything. I love working with you because you make it so easy. Thank you for another spectacular cover!

Rose, thank you for being so amazing to work with! You polish my words beautifully. Thank you for your support over the years. I truly value you and the work you do on my books.

To all the bloggers, influencers, reviewers, and fellow authors who read and review for me, and who help me get the word out about my books: THANK YOU!!! I still get to write books ten years after starting to publish and you guys have played such a huge part in that. I am so grateful and thankful for all you do to help me.

This book was as much a labour of love as all my books have been, but I think because of the timing of when I was working on it (my hormone hell & my daughter moving away from me), it feels like even more of a labour of love. Having said that, it was a joy to write. I may have had to spend twelve plus hours every day for weeks straight to finally get this story out of my head, but I was excited every single day to be with this couple. And to say I'm excited to write the next book in this series is an understatement!! Gah! A runaway bride romance with a road trip and shenanigans... sign me up!!! I've set the release date for May on all the stores, but I'm aiming to release it before then. I just don't want to overcommit myself. I'm tired of having to delay books when life gets in the way, so I'm going to write the book and announce the release date as we get closer.

And lastly, I've just launched my online store!!! I have a new website: www.ninalevineromance.com and am building my little kingdom on the internet. Jodie and I have so many fun new things planned for this site so come and check us out!

ALSO BY NINA LEVINE

Escape With a Billionaire Series

Ashton Scott

Jack Kingsley

Beckett Pearce

Jameson Fox

Owen North

Only Yours Series

(The Black Brothers Billionaire Romance)

Accidentally, Scandalously Yours

Yours Actually

Storm MC Series

Storm (Storm MC #1)

Fierce (Storm MC #2)

Blaze (Storm MC #3)

Revive (Storm MC #4)

Slay (Storm MC #5)

Sassy Christmas (Storm MC #5.5)

Illusive (Storm MC #6)

Command (Storm MC #7)

Havoc (Storm MC #8)

Gunnar (Storm MC #9)

Wilder (Storm MC #10)

Colt (Storm MC #11)

Sydney Storm MC Series

Relent (#1)

Nitro's Torment (#2)

Devil's Vengeance (#3)

Hyde's Absolution (#4)

King's Wrath (#5)

King's Reign (#6)

King: The Epilogue (#7)

Storm MC Reloaded Series

Hurricane Hearts (#1)

War of Hearts (#2)

Christmas Hearts (#3)

Battle Hearts (#4)

The Hardy Family Series

Steal My Breath (single dad romance)

Crave Series

Be The One (rockstar romance)

PLAYLIST

"Dress" by Taylor Swift
"I Lived" by OneRepublic
"Yours In The Morning" by Patrick Droney
"...Ruined" by Patrick Droney
"Headphones" by Jon Bryant
"Can't Do Better" by Kim Petras
"Nobody Loves Me Like You Do" by Patrick Droney
"Limit" by Patrick Droney
"Pour Some Sugar on Me" by Def Leppard